Also by Kathleen Shoop

Historical Fiction:
The Letter Series:
The Last Letter—Book One
The Road Home—Book Two
The Kitchen Mistress—Book Three
The Thief's Heart—Book Four
The River Jewel—A prequel

The Donora Story Collection:
After the Fog—Book One
The Strongman and the Mermaid—Book Two
The Magician—Book Three

Romance:
Endless Love Series:
Home Again—Book One
Return to Love—Book Two
Tending Her Heart—Book Three

Women's Fiction:
Love and Other Subjects

Bridal Shop Series:
Puff of Silk—Book One

Holiday:
The Christmas Coat
The Tin Whistle

Cinder Bella

Bestselling Author

KATHLEEN SHOOP

kathleenshoop@gmail.com
kshoop.com
Twitter: @kathieshoop
Facebook: Kathleen Shoop

ISBN: 9798498619446

Quotes from *The Moonstone*, by Wilkie Collins (1868), used under public domain.

DEDICATION

To Cindy who loves her pets more than anything. Yes, the
chickens may be virtual, but still. Her big heart is always open to all.

CHAPTER 1
Bella Darling

1893
Shadyside, Pennsylvania

The week before Christmas…

Bella's breath caught. The coyotes' high-pitched yips and howls trailed from a distance. Living in a city, she hadn't thought they'd get so close to the Westminster property, but now her livelihood was threatened. She should have acted sooner. She kept on. The snow fell thick, brightening what would have been a dark night without the land blanketed in white to reflect the crescent moon's shine. She swallowed her rising fear as she stepped through the fresh fall, winding along the maple- and evergreen-lined path that led from the barn to the coop. Bella hated the thought of shooting any living thing, but she would do it if necessary.

The coyote calls came again. Closer. A chill spun up her spine. She stopped and juggled the shotgun under one arm, the tin bowls tucked under the other, and jars of vinegar clutched to her midsection. Her cat, Simon, accompanied her, stopping when she did. Bella turned her head to hear better. The coyote cries were coming from the east end of town. She clicked her tongue at Simon. He leapt onto her shoulder. His landing was gentle as could be, but still Bella's coat seams tore a little more as the cat nestled into her.

She forced her feet to move again and picked up speed. "Tomorrow we bring the hens inside. No more of this evening trek to lay new vinegar. Those pesky coyotes can hunt somewhere else."

Simon meowed and nuzzled her ear with the top of his head.

She reached the coop. Simon hopped down and made his rounds, circling the enclosure. He hopped through the high snow, crisp landings breaking the silence. The hens were snug and safe, but the idea of coyotes rustling around her prized hens was too much. She hadn't slept well for days.

Margaret, the Westminster's housemaid, had informed Bella that she'd heard stories that the four-legged hunters had been making their rounds in Shadyside and East Liberty, feasting on Christmas turkeys, chickens, even pets. The yipping drew closer and Bella poured vinegar into the bowls and circled the coop with them, hoping it would be enough to keep the predators away, that the fresh snow wouldn't dilute the sharp vinegar scent. With the bowls in place she sprinkled some cayenne pepper near the foundation of the coop as well.

Finished with that chore and Simon back on her shoulder, she held her breath listening for preying animals. Silence. Only Simon's purring and the shushing of fast falling snow filled her ears. Still, she wouldn't sleep well. She had to keep those hens alive and laying. Her very existence depended upon it. She and Simon trudged back to the barn and soon she was tucked into the bed she'd made in the loft.

It would be a long night, but she had her books, a view of the coop from her loft bed and she had Simon. She struggled to stay awake, tearing her gaze from her storybooks when any sound startled her. But at some point, sleep came. She awakened quick and shot to sitting. The coyotes? Nothing. Just her dreams. She fell back onto her pillow with a deep exhale, arm tossed over her forehead, the cat warming her feet. Bella scratched the quilt. "Come on, Simon."

She turned on her side as Simon crept up her body then plopped beside her and curled into her belly. Bella rubbed him behind the ears and looked through the window. Christmas was coming. The best time of the year. Stars twinkled between spindly winter maple tree branches and peeked over evergreen crowns.

The crescent moon glimmered and Mother Nature's great lights turned the snowy expanse beyond the barn into a jewel box waiting for a debutante to pluck a few stones. Pittsburgh's princesses were daughters of industry, bankers, politicians, and inventors. Their fancy holiday balls thrown by families who mimicked the wealthy habits of royalty were legendary and grew larger and more decadent each season. She imagined the Frick, O'Hara, Schenley, and Westminster daughters with snow laid diamonds strung through their hair, draped around necks, and ringing wrists and fingers. The women were known to sparkle like the winterscape itself. Their jewelry was that beautiful, magical.

Bella stretched and yawned. A New Year's ball. That's where Bella's latest fictional heroine was headed. Once upon a time… she spun a tale like she always did when she wakened to a fresh day. This tale involved a protagonist fending off evildoers—the four-legged, furry kind. The silly story made it clear—Bella would set the hens up inside the barn at night until the coyotes moved on.

She eyed the empty oil lantern, the candle burnt to a nub, and the borrowed books stacked on the orange crate beside her. It was her night reading that led to daydreams of someday writing her own stories. Not that she had the time. Opening a book and slipping into the pages of worlds others had created was plenty for her. It had to be.

The sun was waking, drawing a thin sapphire line across the horizon, the signal it was time to rise. Bella jumped out of bed, readied for the day with an extra set of stockings and her sweater with leather buttons. It had been knitted by Mrs. Lambert who said the eggs Bella sold her were magic. Just a week back, the woman appeared at the barn door with the sweater and a hen no longer interested in laying, asking if Bella would get her to produce, and save a few eggs out for her each week.

"Just a few's all I need and you can do what you will with the rest," Mrs. Lambert had said.

Charmed. Magic. The woman had said the words a dozen times, insisting that though Bella's eggs seemed ordinary on the outside— what they did once cracked open was inexplicable.

Though outlandish, the woman boldly claimed the eggs made the best cheese and potato casserole her husband ever ate, and that being the case, he turned sweet on her all over again. "A new man—the man I used to know—appeared with every bite he ate."

"Egg casserole did that?" Bella had doubted. Absurd.

"It might sound ridiculous to you, a young woman probably juggling dozens—well, at least a handful of suitors—but yes. I'm quite sure the eggs did it."

Bella didn't reveal that she had exactly zero suitors. She buttoned the sweater, remembering Mrs. Lambert's bright eyes. Magic. The idea was silly, but somehow felt true and so Bella had embraced the gifts.

Who was she to argue with what might turn a spent husband loving again? If all it took were eggs, perhaps she ought to fire up a scrambled egg table at the market and maybe even find a man for herself. Perhaps a nice Christmas advertisement in the *Pittsburgh Gazette* would bring the right caller.

Bella chuckled. She didn't have the funds for things like publicizing her desire for someone to share her life with. But she did have ideas. When Mrs. Lambert had left and was nearly gone from sight it occurred to Bella to ask a question. "How did you find me?"

But the winds were picking through evergreen stands and hid her voice from the woman who just kept on. Bella Darling wasn't someone people could just "find." She was a loner, a family of one, plus her hens and the cat, just grateful she'd lucked into the chance of living in the barn of one of the wealthy Ellsworth Avenue families in Shadyside, a neighborhood on the outskirts of Pittsburgh. And so Bella added another spent hen to her flock, loved on her, fed her the special oat mixture, and marveled when the newest addition began to lay alongside the two she'd been gifted from Mr. and Mrs. Westminster.

Bella would have thought it was magic, too, if she'd read it in a fairy tale. But, since it was her real life and she was no one extraordinary, she decided it was simply her kindness and devotion that brought on the laying.

Her kindness was what brought her the hens in the first place. She'd saved the life of Mr. Westminster and he'd rewarded her with the original pair of spent hens. When he saw that she got them to lay and his wife proclaimed that the three eggs added to the bread recipe made three times the amount of bread, they offered Bella the old barn to live in.

"She can only stay as long as the hens lay," Mr. Westminster had said.

"I can make syrup, too," Bella said. "Noticed you have quite the stand of maples."

Mr. Westminster studied her, scratching his belly. "Mr. Hansen will be by to tap the maples. I'm sure he could use a hand. If you help him collect the sap and make syrup you can stay."

Mrs. Westminster had leaned into her husband and whispered something.

"No. Barn'll do," he said. "Plenty of warmth with the fireplace added. I hear the loft is toasty as can be."

"For as long as she needs a home, then," Mrs. Westminster added.

Bella could tell Mrs. Westminster was irritated with her husband.

"If she's lucky," he said, "getting spent hens to lay and helping Mr. Hansen will continue for as long as she needs a home. We aren't running a poorhouse. So don't spread it around, Miss Darling. We'll have a line of hopeless souls down the drive and onto the avenue if you tell anyone where you live." Mr. Westminster tore a hunk of the bread from the loaf and shuffled out of the kitchen.

"Oh, that *is* good," his voice had carried from down the hall.

And so, since February 1893, Bella Darling had lived in the barn, tended the hens, nurtured the cat, made maple syrup, and lived contented in spare shelter and with borrowed books. The only time she felt dissatisfaction was when she turned to share an exciting bit of a story with someone else and no one but Simon was there. She didn't need the parties and balls and excursions that were described in the novels in order to be happy. Just someone to share her life with, her books with—that, she wanted more than anything.

Someone to love. If only magic could deliver her the man of her dreams. She arranged the holiday pine boughs and holly sprigs on the fireplace mantel then tugged on her boots to go collect the day's eggs and head to market. He, whoever he was, didn't have to be a man who loved stories like she did—but he needed to like them enough to listen as she reported what happened in them. Someone to gasp and hold her tight as she grew teary-eyed over the life and times of characters who weren't even alive. Then her contented world would be fully whole.

CHAPTER 2
Bartholomew Baines

Mrs. Tillman smacked Bartholomew Baines's back end with her spatula. Face hot with surging anger, he spun toward her but bit his tongue. He wouldn't fire her. He clamped his palm over his mouth. Fire her? What nonsense. He chuckled, wondering if he'd soon be committed to Mayview for lunacy. He was no longer in a position to fire anyone, least of all the woman who generously invited him into her boarding house when it was already full to bursting with a motley crew. He couldn't keep them or their lives and times and crimes straight. Something about an unemployed baker, a fiddler, a gardener who doubled as a candlestick maker, former wives of well-to-do men, and never-had-anythings, and criminals. Wait? Was that correct? Mrs. Tillman had said criminal, hadn't she? He couldn't recall all the details except, obviously, that they were lost souls of every variety.

She shook the spatula. His vision blurred and his hearing dissolved as she scolded him for swiping bacon before it was ready to be served. How had this happened, his slide into a stew of undesirability? Mrs. Tillman came like a locomotive. "Listen," she said through gritted teeth. She sighed then wrapped her arm around him, pulling him into her side as she flipped the remaining bacon.

"When I found you sleeping dead center of the crab apple, the maple, and the pear tree, I thought, *This sweet man's down on his luck. His coat's fine, his satchel and trunk and briefcase're top of the line. Clearly this is a leading citizen in need of a hand.* But I did not invite you into my home to take over like you're the next king of England."

He nodded, mouth watering, as the bacon aroma saturated him. If only he could live off the scent of food.

"We discussed the plan," she said.

He nodded, defeated. Part of the deal for letting him sleep on the settee in the front parlor was that he agreed to help her with errands since her kitchen girl ran off with a railroad conductor earlier in the week. When he wakened the first morning, he figured he could talk his way out of his promise, but the short, broad-shouldered, round-bellied woman blocked his exit then blocked his bacon larceny.

"Four dozen eggs." She elbowed him. "You listening?"

"I am."

"One dozen from the fancy egg lady whose selection is pink and blue and brown and every shade of white under the sun. She only allows the purchase of one dozen so to spread the magic among the citizenry."

He glowered. Magic eggs. Ludicrous. He was a Harvard-educated man reduced to collecting eggs just so he could eat and have a place to lay his head at night but he didn't have to surrender to believing in magic, of all things. That wasn't how the world worked.

"Wipe that obnoxious look off your face," Mrs. Tillman said. "Someone, meaning *I*, am giving you a place to stay in return for an errand. The least you can do is smile through that bitter taste of having lost everything. Don't blame the world for your stinkin' bad luck. Should be grateful you lived in luxury for the time you did. Most of us get a broken back the day we're born. Now you're just like the rest of us. You haven't actually lost a thing. You still have your breath. Some people lost their lives in this here crash and bank panic and depression."

Did he have his breath, though? Since the bank panic began to domino, one bank, one depositor, one homeowner, one business owner, one family at a time, his breath had gone icy solid in his chest as often as it was airy fresh. Mrs. Tillman's words hit him like a falling house. She'd seen his photo in the newspaper and told him so when she invited him into the boarding house. He knew she thought even though not a criminal by the law's definition, that he was guilty of being a terrible human being. But that was not true.

He couldn't take her holding that characterization one more second. "I lost a fortune but it's not what you think. I'm not like those other bankers who stole away in the night and hid their reserves claiming they couldn't pay out a dime to their depositors. I'm—" He shook his head. What did it matter at this point?

Ignoring his defense, Mrs. Tillman laid down her spatula, grabbed the last egg in the bowl and gently lifted and lowered her palm. "For the twelve special eggs, you have to feel every single one for weight and well… for feel."

"Feel of what?"

"You'll know when you sense it. Don't get distracted by the pretty colored shells. It's what's inside that counts."

They'd been over this several times. He knew there was no arguing with her and there was no way for Mrs. Tillman to change her mind or explain what she wanted any more than she had. The only consolation was that there was zero chance of running into anyone he knew standing in line at a market.

"I want as many double yolks as you can find. The girl who brings her eggs stacked in a big box is who you buy the special twelve from. Corner of Penn and Center, first table, with the chubby lady who makes the same bread in different shapes and charges extra for rectangle just because."

"I will. I promised I would. And I will deliver. I'm not a shirker or a sponge." He wasn't a delivery man either, but here he was performing just that duty. Maybe he was a shirker inside and he'd just dash away with the circus when he had the chance. Maybe he ought to.

Mrs. Tillman smiled. She pinched Bartholomew's cheek. "Underneath all your fancy clothes you're a good fella at heart. I know it."

Bartholomew forced a smile. He wished his generosity back in May and June, when it all went bad, had been enough for him to believe he was still a good fella. Maybe it was, but it hadn't resulted in anyone else thinking it mattered. Doing the right thing didn't mean he was able to piece his life back together. So it must not be so. For men like him didn't end up taking a room—not even a proper room, a settee in the front parlor—in a boarding house if they were good, decent people. So he knew for sure, he must not have been.

Standing in line at the special egg lady's table, he waited. Apparently she was late. The bread lady was there as Mrs. Tillman had described. She was performing a slick song and dance about the virtues of rectangle-shaped bread, reassuring customers the special eggs would soon arrive. "She'll be here in the blink of an eye."

The woman with a basket over each arm in front of Bartholomew growled. "Blinked a thousand times since I got in line. Not buying your bread until she gets here. And I want the round loaf. That one right there."

"Well, the next blink will bring the lass for sure," the bread lady said.

Bartholomew startled at their gruff tones, that they spoke up and to each other like they had. The women in his world spoke in soft, melodious voices, *suggesting* people do their bidding, never speaking in sarcastic, impatient words, but always getting results.

Frankly, when he admitted it, at that moment he understood the rough behavior of the women at the market just fine. This waiting, the exposure while performing such basic tasks, was humiliating.

Bartholomew felt the heaviness of his current position, his lost place in the world, and though he understood the irritation of the woman ahead of him in line, he wouldn't bicker with a bread lady of all people. Haggling over market goods like he used to negotiate contracts and loans and debate the value of silver, gold, and worthless bank notes, was miles beneath his station.

He pulled his pocket watch from his coat pocket and flipped it open. Eight-thirty. He should be in his office right then, feet up on his desk, draining his fifth cup of coffee, finishing the second newspaper of the day, confirming midday luncheon plans at the Duquesne Club, and dinner plans with Melinda—the woman he'd thought was his one true love. How wrong he'd been about her, about everything. His heart clenched. His opulent life grew dusty and faded, no longer sequined with daily promises of riches and grand dinners and balls. All the right things had been upended by a worldwide silver debacle, a horrible president, and one very short-sighted decision.

A group of men, women, and children trailed through the market singing Christmas carols, smiling and laughing, handing out peppermint pieces. He refused to look at them and absorb any bit of their cheer. He scanned the market noting two other vendors selling eggs that weren't this apparent special variety brought by the very enchanted egg girl he'd been tasked with finding and buying from.

What harm would there be in pretending to get the special ones but buying the fourth dozen from someone else? He tapped his toe.

Would Mrs. Tillman really be able to tell the difference? He looked into the sky, shut his eyes, and let the silver dollar-sized snowflakes crash down on his face. He imagined the flakes were actual coins, falling over him, stuffing his pockets full. With closed eyes, the scent of pine boughs and trees brought to market for Christmas, he could pretend that he and his father were simply out to cut trees for their foyer, parlors, and kitchen. Though his father could have paid Mr. Harrison, the property manager of their estate, to retrieve the trees, Bartholomew's father enjoyed the time with his son in the woods. He'd gone with his father as a boy and wouldn't give up the tradition. The warm memory made Bartholomew stick his tongue out and catch the snow as it tumbled down in fat flakes. For those moments he felt as though he were ten years old again, full of Christmas wonder and the warmth that came from feeling safe in his parents' home, the two doting on him, full of love for their son and neighbors.

So many should-have-beens. Bartholomew's father should still be alive, his mother, too. He should be engaged, even if not in love. He and his betrothed should be selecting finishes for their home, hiring household servants, dreaming of their honeymoon travels abroad. He sighed. None of what made him yearn for the ruined marriage plans had anything to do with the woman. And realizing that was something he saw as a positive from the failure of it all. At least he didn't have to live in a loveless marriage. He still had a chance to find what his parents had enjoyed until they died just days apart.

Bartholomew thought of the bankers and investors and inventors he'd befriended since coming back from Harvard. His bank was one of 500 that closed when railroad investments went into receivership, stocks crashed, and gold and silver went dangerously low. He'd heard discussions about JP Morgan, that he'd lent the U.S. government millions in gold as the only means of keeping the country running at all.

Bartholomew had the unappealing position of having been wealthy, as compared to many Americans, but not as rich as the Fricks, Mellons, Morgans, Carnegies, Thaws and those who were easily surviving the depression. His parents had left Bartholomew some money, but they saw his ambition, education, and friends who invested in his bank as evidence they could leave large amounts to poorhouses and foundations for Civil War veterans. Though they'd wanted Bartholomew to take over the family trapping business or build a company in iron, coal, or steel, they'd believed in him. And he'd failed them. Luckily they didn't know it.

When Bartholomew's depositors came for their silver and gold and cash, he explained that he didn't have it, that he was waiting for loan repayments from others and for investments to pay off. His father's words came back, warning Bartholomew that the day might come when people arrived at his bank with frightened big eyes, the size of the silver pieces they were hoping to withdraw. But Bartholomew had been having too much fun enjoying good cigars and whiskey and buying jewels for a woman who didn't return them as his bank was going under.

He had believed that the United States wouldn't suffer another panic and depression like he'd heard about. It had been twenty years since the last and he trusted another would never come. Until it did, showing up like a shadow falling over an already cloudy, smoky Pittsburgh day.

He wasn't alone, although that's how it felt. Twenty-five percent of Pittsburgh's workforce was unemployed, thousands of businesses had failed, and he'd tried to do the right thing. He kept telling himself that. But it didn't matter. The end result was he couldn't help anyone because he was penniless and shamed. For him, the fall was steeper, more violent as every seam of his clothing was ripped and torn with his cliffside tumble from economic wealth and prosperity to the pits of a boarding house full of… who were they again?

His losses changed his existence so completely he wasn't sure his friends would even recognize him if they ran into each other. And therefore he didn't think the losses of his boardinghouse compatriots compared in the least. Though he was bristly about staying at Mrs. Tillman's, at least he wasn't taking his meals at the soup kitchen. At least he wasn't bunking at the poorhouse. That was for people unwilling to work.

That wasn't the problem with him. He missed work deeply. But those who still had phones wouldn't take his calls. Now instead of the scent of polished mahogany, leather-bound books, and cash and coin in a grand bank building, he inhaled the scent of outdoor produce and raw goods.

He shifted his feet, standing in line like a peasant. He thought of the evolution of losing everything and how he'd seen the May 23rd crash at first. Back on that day, when his bank didn't crumble, he thought he might be all right. But little by little, he doled out and kept back funds until he couldn't do that anymore. Then the day came that changed his life for good. He pushed the memories away, the woman's face.

He thought he'd already lost everything, but then he played poker at the Tavern on Walnut Street and lost the very last bill in his money-clip. Daily he marveled at the difference between what he'd thought was *everything* in the past and what he'd come to know it as now. Left without means to even pay for a hotel room, he'd skimmed along, staying at his remaining friends' homes, bouncing out of one guest room and into another until every last one of them lost their homes or their patience with his presence. All he'd been left with was what he could wear or carry in a satchel, briefcase, and trunk. He was just like everyone else now—well, most of the world whom he'd not seen himself as a colleague to before. He was better than most. Or so he'd thought. But now? Could he argue he wasn't just like the masses who'd gone unnoticed to him unless they entered his bank bearing cash, coins, and goodies to hide away in his vault? Could he deny he was just like them?

CHAPTER 3
Bella

Bella's thin coat invited every breeze and shot of wind right inside, right into her bones. She shielded her eyes and looked down Ellsworth Avenue. Where was he? Her mitted hand blocked the sun, but the movement of reaching to her brow allowed three fingertips to jut through holes. She balled her fingers into her palm and put mending on her list of things to do later that night. Wagons rolled by. Grim faces of drivers and passengers peered out from their hats and scarves, faces creased from the heaviness that came with worry of not having what they needed for daily life, let alone the coming holiday.

"Hey, golden girl!"

Bella startled and squinted up at the man who'd stopped his wagon beside her. Mr. Hansen. She smiled at the fat snowflakes piling on the brim of his hat.

"You wanna ride, or you gonna haul that loada eggs all the way to market on the top of your noggin?"

He started to get out of the wagon but she stopped him. "I've got this."

She lowered the wagon hatch and hoisted the box into the back. With everything secure she hopped up beside the driver, relieved that this part of her day was underway. The sooner she was finished at the market, the sooner she could burrow back into her little barn home. She plopped a bundle of holly wrapped with red ribbon between them. "Sorry. I tore off some of your Christmas decorations when I relatched the back."

"It's all right. I'll tie it back on."

Bella squeezed his hand. "Take it easy with the speed this time. That hole in the road up near Hiland caused me to lose three eggs last week and that's too much when a girl's socking away her pennies for a rainy day." She couldn't believe that in a time when so many were eating stone soup for dinner, she was able to save a little for the first time in her life.

He nodded, shaking the snow drift off his hat brim. Chuckling, he wiped his cheeks and squeezed her hand back. "Hurricane." He shook the reigns and got the horses moving.

"Hurricane?"

"Been pouring buckets of rain since May—you're gonna need piles of gold and maybe even silver if its value ever comes back. But yeah, at least pennies for the hurricane coming next."

She smiled and shook her head. "Tornado, Mr. Hansen. Pittsburgh doesn't get hurricanes."

"Well, Shadyside seems to be getting all the weather these days."

She sighed. "If you're talking figuratively, you are correct. I may soon be at the poor farm with the rest of the ne'er-do-wells." She shrugged. "Don't know how much longer Mr. Sellers will keep bringing coal to Maple Grove Farm what with—"

"Stop. You stay with your hens, and James up at the big house will stay butlering and Miss Margaret will stay there maiding and when the bankers surface with the money owed to all of us, and the stock market climbs and the railroads start their chugging again, well the Westminsters will return and it'll be like they never left. You'll see."

"But I can't just keep staying on the Westminsters' property when I'm not even sure if they own it anymore—"

"You can. Westminsters must be paying something. Seen the sheriff?"

She shook her head.

"Then the bank hasn't moved in yet or you'd know. You have your loft in the barn with the best stone fireplace in the land. You've got your hens, your books borrowed from the man who's building the most magnificent library in the world. Hell, you could move into Maple Grove Cottage with Margaret if you wanted to be closer to people."

"I like my aloneness, thank you very much. And Margaret doesn't allow me past the foyer, Mr. Hansen. She's a high-brow maid and I'm just… well. Not that. Besides, I gotta keep watch over the girls at night. They're everything, my only thing, and the coyotes are sniffing around."

"You're a high-brow mama hen. You read more books than a schoolmarm—far more than Margaret ever has. We're lucky for your chicken skills, that's for sure. My dear Norma made three days of food from one day of your eggs. She's got enough cake and bread to share with the soup kitchen and neighbors. Someday you're gonna tell me your secret with those hens."

Bella giggled, always loving how he exaggerated to make her feel good. "Just luck. Lady Luck had me saving Mr. Westminster from the hog wagon just in time. The mistress of good fortune made sure he offered me two spent hens that hadn't laid in a year. And sweet Luck made sure Mr. Westminster noticed me selling their eggs the next day when they laid for me, luck that—"

"Now cut that out." Mr. Hansen's voice sheared the thick smoky air. "You've got skills with the spent hens, getting those biddies to lay pinks and blues and every shade of white eggs. You have a gift and I don't want to hear you discounting it like day old bread. Living in the barn is nice and all when you got nothing, but don't act like the Westminsters gave you access to the guest room on the second floor with the attached bathroom. You ain't takin' anything that you ain't due."

"But—"

"But nothin'. Now. We're here. You go an' drop your load while I drop mine and if you make good time I'll haul you back to Maple Grove Cottage. Otherwise, the missus'll see you later to select her eggs for the week."

Bella nodded and retrieved her box, heading for the market where she'd paid to set up. There was a line of folks waiting at Mrs. Taylor's table. Seeing so many waiting made her nervous. She was always hesitant to start conversations in large gatherings, and she was beginning to feel pressure in her belly every time someone asked her what was the secret to getting her hens to lay. She didn't have an answer, not really.

Mrs. Taylor, with her belly so round it required her to stitch extensions onto the ties monthly, stood with hands on hip, scowling. "Well, there's the queen of England. Did your morning tea and ministrations delay you? *No.*" Mrs. Taylor shook her finger. "It was the servants, wasn't it? They were late to break your fast. Oh, wait, no. It's bathing day. That's right. Perhaps your bath made you tardy?"

17

Bella swallowed her laugh and gently slid her crate onto the checked cloth that Mrs. Taylor had laid for the poultry treasure. "Sorry 'bout that. Got here as fast as my chariot would allow."

Mrs. Taylor brushed Bella's shoulder, the gentle pressure too much for the fraying garment and the shoulder seam split. Mrs. Taylor covered her mouth with her hand. "I'm sorry, Bella. I didn't mean to tear it. That coat won't hold up to the end of the day at the rate it's disintegrating."

Bella nodded. "It'll be fine." More mending. She picked up two eggs from the top of the pile, feeling the weight of each in her palm before replacing them. She hoped the returns on the purchases would yield far more than money this time.

Mrs. Taylor turned her back on the first person in line. "No one's gonna pay for my bread and canned fruit until they get your eggs so let's get this line moving. Maybe then you can get that coat replaced."

Bella agreed on getting the line moving.

Mrs. Taylor patted her back and shoved a dollar bill into Bella's hand. "I'm going to play Rockefeller as Santa Claus and give you this. Tuck it away until its value comes out of the gutter. Or go get a winter hat from Ada Pritt over there."

Bella stared at the dollar. She knew her eggs had infused Mrs. Taylor's table with sales she hadn't seen in years and so she didn't try to turn the money back. She put her clenched hand to her chest. "Thank you, Mrs. Taylor. Merry Christmas." And she hugged her tight.

Mrs. Taylor stiffened then pushed Bella away. "Go on before I change my mind. I'll sell your eggs until you're back. I don't give just anyone gifts, you know."

Bella's hands flew to her head. "Gift. I have something for you." She drew a slender bottle with a thin red ribbon tied around its neck from her coat pocket and presented it to Mrs. Tillman. The amber liquid inside clung to its clear glass.

Mrs. Taylor's eyes watered. "Maple syrup? Oh my. The missus let you tap her maples—yes, I remember you telling me that."

"Hope you like it. Oh, here." Bella pulled a second, smaller glass bottle from her other pocket. "Traded Mr. Tripp some eggs for a bit of bourbon. Add a few drops to your syrup on Christmas morning."

"Ohhh." She hugged the bottles to her breast. "Mr. Taylor will… well, let's say we may have some very good mornings with these wonderful treats at hand. Thank you, dear Bella. Your appearance in my life has certainly sweetened it with more than maple syrup. Thank you."

Bella couldn't stop grinning. How she wished for a man to hold close in daily life, to have someone to love like Mrs. Taylor had her mister.

Mrs. Taylor straightened, re-establishing her soldier-like demeanor, posture straight, hands at sides even, chin lifted. "Now move along, like I said…"

Bella backed away and noted the line of people had grown. Most were maids marketing for wealthy families who could still afford household staff. A few men were in line and that made her smile. The men reminded her that even with little to her name, she held rich hope deep in her heart. Yes. She had faith that one of those eggs—the special one—would bring her a friend, a lover, a husband, anyone who might see the world the way she did. Otherwise contented, she'd live in the barn forever, on the street if she had to, if she could find someone who'd sit alongside her, while she rested her dreams on the words created by the gifted authors of the world.

She scanned the male faces. Two of them came weekly—one for his bedridden mother, the other for his ready-to-give-birth wife who also worked as a maid at the Fricks'. She hid her belly to keep employment as long as she could and her sweet husband trekked to market when his few mill shifts a week finished.

The third man in line made Bella stop just as she was about to turn. Clad in a fine wool coat and fresh top hat, he bore all the signs of a man who weathered the panic and current economic depression without a loss to his name.

Perhaps he was one of the predators shoveling up foreclosed properties by the dozen? Perhaps his money had been stuffed between mattresses and behind false walls so that the stock market crashing and banks slamming their doors by the hundreds did not touch his fortunes. He stood with the ease and comfort of a man with everything, a man who'd never yearned for impossible things because every single dream had already materialized in his palms then been stowed away for safekeeping.

Broad shoulders, hands clasped behind his back, whistling, he looked skyward, like a man waiting for his floor maid to bring his scotch. At one point he stuck his tongue out and caught falling snowflakes, further intriguing Bella. She smiled at the childish act. This was a man who probably housed a library inside the walls of his home. So what was he doing in the egg line at a market, building a snow bank on his tongue? What was he doing waiting in line for anything at all?

CHAPTER 4
Bartholomew

He didn't know how long he'd been daydreaming before excited murmurs drew him back to the line he was standing in and his assigned errand. So distracted by his childhood memories, he hadn't even noticed the egg girl arriving and fitting her bin into the table space the bread lady had cleared. But he did watch as the bread lady hugged the egg lady and though he could see her only from behind, he could tell the egg girl was much younger. A scuffle in the line drew his attention to two women in front of him, one shouldering ahead of another for the "best selection of the special eggs."

The dustup died down when the bread lady huddled up to referee. The egg girl was prancing away looking like she had the world on a leash, like he used to feel every day. Imagine feeling like that in such dire times. He watched those ahead of him gently place eggs in their baskets, only permitted to select twelve at most. None of them picked up eggs and weighed them in their palm. Choosing in the hopes of winning a double yolk was apparently only the desire of Mrs. Tillman and as he inched closer to his turn he was growing more self-conscious about what he had been commissioned to do.

When it was his turn he followed his orders, picking up each egg, closing his eyes and feeling the weight or whatever in his palm before either placing the egg back in the box and selecting another or putting it into the basket.

When he'd gotten to egg number six the woman behind him pinched the back of his arm. Not that it hurt through layers of clothing, but it startled him. "What?"

"*What* is right, all right. Think I got all day and night to wait for you to court each egg like it's the princess you're taking to the Christmas ball?"

He flinched and stared at the woman. Sooty cheeks and raw hands gave her station in life away. And her treatment of him caused him to lose any chance of responding. How dare she?

"Cat got your tongue, fancy pants? Let's go or I'll butt right in front of you."

"Yeah, get the lead out," another voice came from farther down the line.

"Ain't got all day, sailor," a third heckler joined in.

He lifted his basket. "I've been issued specific instructions for—"

A snowball smacked into his back, shutting him up. He spun around and scanned the crowd for who'd thrown it.

"See, even people *not* in line with us are tired of your mouth. Move it." The woman behind him held his gaze.

He'd never felt so… he didn't even know how to describe how this treatment made him feel. He tried to stop himself from rattling off the specifics of his resume and instead went with the general query of, "Don't you know who I am?"

Another snowball thwapped his back.

"A regular jackass," someone said from down the line.

He turned again to see who'd hit him with the snowball and the woman behind him used the opening to slide in front. He turned back and stuck his hand into the box, blocking her out. "I'll hurry. Just let me get the other six."

She crossed her arms, the baskets resting in the crook of each bent elbow. "Six seconds for six eggs. Get on with it, moneybags."

"Thank you," he said. He reached for an egg and lifted it in his palm as he had the others.

The woman started counting one, two, three and the rest of the line joined in. They were serious about him moving quicker. Mrs. Tillman would just have to understand. He didn't doubt they'd toss him out of line if he didn't just pluck eggs from the box and move on. And so he did. The last thing he wanted was to break eggs and have to shovel coal or something to make up for it when he got back to Mrs. Tillman's.

"I have things to do, too, you know," Bartholomew said. "You folks aren't the only ones with obligations and—"

"Yeah, whada you have to do today, change into other pairs of fancy pants another three times before burrowing into a bed laid with golden goose feathers?" the woman who'd pinched him asked.

His tongue tied, but he didn't stop himself from responding. "Uh..."

"Uh? Smoke a pipe of the finest tobacco? Yeah, what else? Sit all day with the paper while someone shines your shoes?" another voice from down the line said.

He straightened, face burning hot, blindly plucking eggs from the pile and placing them into his sack. All of those things would have been fairly close to his daily life *before*. Before it all crashed around him. "No. Newspapers, yes, but for the market reports and..." Suddenly his studying the news of the day seemed like a luxury instead of the work it was when pronouncing the task to the particular crew waiting in line. Suddenly, he had no words at all. "Forget it." It was as though none of them knew he was a nice guy. It was as though they assumed he'd done something awful—that it was written across his forehead. He hesitated before moving to pay, considering whether to give them an education in all his achievements and good works. But the woman muscling past him sapped the last bit of energy he had that morning.

He paid and stalked away having been saturated with enough degradation to last the day, to last a century.

CHAPTER 5
Bella

Bella sang Christmas carols as she swept the lower level of the barn, stopping to pet her hens Matilda, Mississippi, and Mabel. She provided each of them and Simon with bowls of warm oats made in a small pan on the grate in the fireplace. She added raisins, sunflower seeds, walnut pieces, and her secret ingredient—maple syrup made by her very own hands. The bottled syrup was the only thing she owned when she arrived at Maple Grove Cottage.

Though still living in rags, except for the sumptuous knitted sweater she'd been gifted, her days were full. She hummed along with the care and feeding of her hens and cat, reading books, and helping out in the kitchen at the big house or in the bedrooms occasionally when the family had needed it. And the making of syrup. That was something she hadn't fathomed the family would have loved for her to do but they had. She marveled at her good luck as the rest of the world's had turned bad.

None of the Westminsters or Bella, or Margaret the maid, or James the butler, or Mr. Sellers the coal man, or Herb Watson the ice man, or Percival Hicks the milk man, or Mr. Hansen, foresaw the tumble the world would take beginning the past May 23rd. Apparently no one in the whole world knew it was coming. So the Westminsters found themselves overseas on vacation featuring time with Queen Victoria when the world began to fold in on itself in America.

Only a few letters were sent to Margaret and James, the last stating that they should stay the course until the family returned. They carried on with whatever maintenance they could provide the home and its property. After the first, the letters hadn't mentioned Bella specifically. They probably assumed the spent hens stopped laying and she'd left. But Bella stayed on, remembering their original conversation—that she could remain as long as they laid. And so Margaret, James and Bella simply hovered and haunted like apparitions who didn't understand they'd met their demise and should have moved on.

Though Bella lived without owning anything substantial or wielding any power, it was the undoing of the wealthy that seemed to unsettle the poorer classes more than their own undoing. Bella was accustomed to scraping by and stitching meaning into an otherwise insignificant life. Her books gave access to things she would never probably see with her own eyes and that was worth more than the thought of losing anything else material.

Still, she wouldn't have turned down the chance to build a small home with proper rooms and shelves for books that maybe someday she would buy.

Up in the barn loft where she slept, she dusted the books borrowed from the Westminsters' library, thrilled with the thought of pouring over the selected Christmas tales. She eyed the notebook and ink near her sleeping pallet. Ada Pritt had given her the two items as Christmas presents, saying that Bella ought to start writing her own tales. "I didn't have enough for an ink pen but I figure you could scrape one up at the Westminsters. They must have scores."

Little did Ada know that Bella was already writing lots of things, just not stories. Not yet. She didn't have a tale worth being shared. Not yet. But this precious paper, thick and creamy, and the ink—a blue so rich it was almost black—was like nothing she owned. She'd been writing on paper scraps gathered on her walks through Shadyside, using a pencil sharpened either in Mr. Westminster's den or in the kitchen, depending on which room was empty when she needed access.

If a pencil went dull late at night she simply used her knife. A home outfitted with multiple glittering pencil sharpeners and rooms stuffed with books were the luxuries she dreamed of. Not a mansion—but a snug abode lined with shelves, books, writing tools, and paper. With the writing she was doing, she felt she was sharing what she loved about books with the world even if her identity was secret. She'd found a way to share her literary love with others and that thrilled her as much as anything.

With her selling and buying at the market finished and her barn freshened up, she traipsed to Maple Grove Cottage—the main house on the Westminster property. She always chuckled at the label of *cottage* to describe the home. It was three stories tall and four wings deep and wide, made of brick and outfitted with the latest in plumbing and heating and lighting. But she knew it was just one of the homes the Westminsters owned and so to them, it was a spare, a place to get away from stresses and troubles. Their pond at the back end of the property served as summer entertainment central—that was what she'd been told anyway. Due to them being overseas that summer, the end of the season soiree had been canceled.

After finishing at the market, Mr. Hansen had dropped Bella and the supplies she'd purchased at the kitchen door of the big house so that she could easily get them inside when she was ready to do so. She'd put aside a dozen eggs for Margaret and James as well as the sugar, flour, cured meats, oats, and coffee she'd bought so Margaret could make the week's meals.

Bella had been included in one meal a day when the Westminsters had been there and Margaret continued to feed her, taking over the role of cook, preparing the most basic dishes.

Heading to the cottage from the barn, Bella followed the path through the gardens, now skeletal from having grown wild with the departure of the chief gardener and his troops. Then the snaking, wild branches grew spindly and tired from winter weathering that had begun its work in the weeks following Thanksgiving. Bella wound through the grounds, marveling at how quickly the prize-winning rosebushes and manicured beds had turned ordinary as if with a curse set by Mother Nature's evil third cousin.

When Bella came to the cobblestone courtyard that led to the kitchen, a gust of wind shoved her back. The icy burst made her wrap her arms around herself and when she did, the coat ripped right down the back seam. She sped up, as the wind picked past the stitches, plucking the threads apart like it had fingers. In seconds all that had held the flapping sections of coat together was gone.

Bella opened the kitchen door, scooped up the crate holding most of the purchases, and entered the servant's cloakroom with the final cotton sutures at the neck of the coat giving way, the pieces falling right off her back, sleeves collapsing down her arms, hanging by her wrists. Bella released a burst of laughter, envisioning an observer witnessing her coat split and flap in the wind like hobbled birds trying to take flight.

She entered the kitchen and stopped short at the sight of a woman sitting at the worktable, back to Bella. At first she didn't recognize her. At first she thought the Westminsters must have returned. The woman's sable cape—its rich brown coloring—was as inviting as the warmth it must have provided.

The woman turned.

Bella drew back, confused. "Margaret?"

Margaret stared, but didn't respond.

Bella set the crate on the bench near the door and straightened. Her worn wool coat fell completely from her arms in two pieces. "What are you doing with that cloak?"

Margaret's eyes went wide, but she stayed mute. Ribbons of hair had sprung from her normally tight bun and hung in loose coils near her cheeks. Her face was swollen and the stern, condescending mug that typically graced her face was soft, sorrowful, unrecognizable if Bella hadn't known for sure who the woman was. Margaret's hands shook as she folded a paper and shoved it into an envelope, ignoring Bella's question.

"Leave everything where it is. I'll start—"

Margaret seemed fragile and small right then. Bella stepped toward her and reached out.

Margaret flinched away as though Bella had shoved a lit torch at her. "I don't need anything."

"But, Margaret." Bella stepped closer still. "Why are you crying?" Although Bella had suffered her own losses alone and with as little drama as possible, she knew most people liked comfort from others when they were sad. She reached out again, taking Margaret's hand, wanting to be helpful.

Margaret wrenched her hand from Bella's and stood, putting her back to Bella again. The maid was normally cold and dismissive to her, as though her position placed her so far above everyone else. Bella didn't like her much, but leaving a person in distress seemed cruel. Margaret heaved as though having to force breath into her body. She looked over her shoulder at Bella, her face reddened to a shade of beet.

Bella approached like she'd come across a wounded bearcat. "Margaret, let me help."

Margaret shook her head. "You can't help."

"Sure I can."

Margaret slipped the cape off and turned with a sigh. In profile, the problem was obvious. Margaret was right. Bella could not help. Not in a way that would make it all go away.

Margaret buckled and grabbed her pregnant belly.

Bella sprang forward, catching her under the arms. "Sit." Bella pulled a chair out from the table with one foot.

Margaret doubled over and wretched. Bella grabbed the slop bucket and got it under Margaret's mouth just in time. When she finished emptying her stomach, her breath came in choppy inhalations.

"Come by the fire." Bella pulled Margaret to the settee in the keeping room area of the kitchen and helped her lie down. She ran cool water over a rag and draped the cloth across Margaret's forehead. Silent tears fell down the woman's cheeks. Bella sighed, understanding how devastating this pregnancy must be given Margaret was unmarried.

"The nausea won't stop. I thought I was done with it but it's worse now that I'm further along."

Bella nodded and strode to the cupboard where the tea was kept. "Ginger. That will settle your stomach." Bella moved from cabinet to cabinet, searching. She opened the set of three pear-shaped tea boxes but none of them contained ginger tea. She opened the caddy with a maple leaf and Maple Grove Cottage engraved on the top. She shook her head. "Nothing." It must have been months since money'd been sent to replenish the tea supply.

Bella crossed her arms. "You know. That woman—Mrs. Tillman who runs the boarding house on Walnut Street? I met one of her boarders last week. She said Mrs. Tillman had the most splendid teas. Went on and on about them. Said if I gave her a couple of my eggs then she would give me tea in return. I'll go get some from her."

Margaret groaned. "I don't even care if I live. I can't take one more minute of this."

Bella studied Margaret then moved toward her, pulling a knit blanket from a basket at the end of the settee. The maid had been transformed from a petty, but hard woman to a soft, sorrowful creature whom Bella wouldn't have thought she'd ever feel sympathy for until that moment.

She covered Margaret with the blanket deciding she better take some money just in case Mrs. Tillman didn't see the trade of eggs for tea as equal. "I'll head to Mrs. Tillman's. There's got to be some petty cash here somewhere. Just enough for ginger tea. Just in case the eggs aren't enough."

"It's all gone. Except what you have left over from egg sales after buying supplies. The Westminsters haven't sent money from London in two months. I've been scraping coins together by rooting through every tin and box in the pantry and… I have no idea what's happening with the Westminsters, but there's nothing here. It's like they knew the crash was coming and they escaped with all their money and left us to…"

"Well, I've got eggs and maple syrup."

Margaret turned on her side and bawled.

Bella knelt beside her. "Should I get a doctor?"

"No money."

"Midwife?"

"No money."

Bella sat back on her knees. "Well. I'm going to take some eggs and get you what you need. You've got to eat and… You can walk me through the week's baking and…" She stood. The list of things she might be able to do to help felt overwhelming compared to when she was nestled in her tiny barn. "One thing at a time. First," Bella lifted her arms. "I've got to borrow a coat or something. All I've got is my new hat from Ada Pritt and this thin dress."

Margaret spoke through more crying. "Hurry. Just wear the cloak. Mrs. Westminster's gone with the wind. Surely she won't care."

Bella bit on her thumbnail and studied the sable cape. She picked it up and brushed it against her cheek. She'd never even held such a sumptuous garment let alone worn one.

"Please." Margaret tried to sit up. "It hurts."

Bella nodded, got Margaret water, and slipped the cloak over her shoulders. The fur warmed her immediately. She brushed her hands over the garment, hugging herself. She did a little spin, unable not to. "This is unbelievable. I can see why you were wearing it."

As she accepted the idea of wearing the splendid cloak, James, the butler, wandered in. His gaze went directly to Margaret. He stopped short, his eyes falling to her belly.

He sighed and pushed a hand through his hair. "Cat's out of the bag, eh." He gave a sympathetic smile. Margaret started to cry hard again and James dashed to her and took her in his arms.

Bella was drawn to the ease between them. *James is the father?* It made sense with them knocking around the empty mansion alone together for months.

He gently shushed Margaret then shook his head as he made eye contact with Bella. "Wasn't me. I'm not—you know. I'm just… well, doing whatever I can to help."

Bella nodded, surprised at the tenderness. They actually made a handsome couple and seemed to enjoy a closeness even if they weren't a pair, even if he wasn't the father.

It wasn't her business what those two were engaged in. But she was compelled to help Margaret. She jammed her thumb over her shoulder in the direction of the back door. "I'm headed for ginger tea. Hopefully anyway. I'm going to try to trade eggs for tea, but not sure how much Mrs. Tillman'll give me if any at all… I don't know. We have the egg money from today. Should I use that if needed?"

James gently laid Margaret back and scratched his chin. "No. Margaret, you said that money's for the coal—right? Gas is off and we're lucky to have the old coal furnace to run."

She nodded and flung her hand over her forehead.

"Wait a minute," James said. He brushed Margaret's hair back, tucking it behind her ears. "Did you pay the window man and the roofer from the envelopes in the front hall?"

Margaret swallowed hard. It appeared that considering the question was painful. "What envelopes? I paid everyone out of the money their accountant dropped off monthly and the egg money until… well, until just this month."

James snapped his fingers. "Leave the eggs and follow me, Miss Bella Darling. You may have plenty of money for all the tea Margaret needs."

She followed him through the butler's pantry, jogging to keep up with his long strides, through the dining room and into the foyer.

"Mrs. Westminster used to keep envelopes in the desk by the front door, organized by errand—one for the milkman, one for the coal man, one for the ice man…"

"The cook or Mrs. Elliot didn't take care of that at the back of the house?"

He sighed and turned the desk key. "Mrs. Westminster liked to cushion her good fortune by doling out the money to the merchants and vendors who came to the house. Mrs. Elliot filled them, but handing them out allowed Mrs. Westminster to feel as though she was actually *doing something* in the household. Grew up poor as you and me, apparently, and she didn't like *feeling* as wealthy as she actually was."

Bella giggled. "So handing over the cash in envelopes solved that problem for her?"

He withdrew the key. "Apparently." He grasped the knob on the drop-down desk and paused. "Here's hoping Mrs. Elliot organized the envelopes before she was let go by the Westminsters."

He drew the door down into its desk position and the two leaned in. "Holy Christmas, take a look." He ran one finger along several envelopes that were slotted along the top of the opening.

Bella watched as he opened the first envelope. She could see the word blacksmith scrawled across the front. "Haven't seen him in four months."

"No need for horseshoes if the horses are gone to the countryside in Butler."

He shuffled through the contents and pulled out some coins. "Should be plenty for whatever you think Margaret needs."

Bella could see the concern in his eyes. He lifted a velvet ribbon with a dangling silver reindeer out of the desk and turned to her with it. "Oh my." He looked sad. "This ornament fell off the tree last year when we were removing the piney carcass." He held the ornament into the daylight spilling through the entryway sidelights. "Little reindeer never made it back into the attic with the rest of the ornaments. Mrs. Westminster had said, '*Next year it will be first to go on the tree.*' So casual and self-assured. None of us would have guessed that this Christmas would be marked by so much… *nothing.*"

He smiled at the glistening ornament. "Hundreds of people used to come between Thanksgiving and New Year's Day. And now." He shrugged. His eyes glistened with rising tears and Bella realized her late entrée into the Westminster family and its servant tribe meant she harbored no sad holiday memories related to the home.

He tucked the ornament back into the desk. "Kind of forgot it was Christmas season until seeing this guy," James said. "What without all the hustle and bustle of present buying and decorating and parties and…" He leaned back against the wall. "Suppose Christmas Eve will be quiet. New Years, too."

"They had Christmas *and* New Year's Eve parties?"

A big grin came to him. "Yes, parties all of December, but balls, too. Christmas Eve, New Year's Eve, New Year's Day gatherings. New Year's Day was always my favorite of the festivities. You should've seen all the callers who'd come to celebrate. Friends and loved ones. Men coming to see all the Westminster daughters from the eldest, Miss Simona Westminster, to the youngest daughter, Ludmilla. And cousin Phoebe from Raleigh who came yearly and was always a draw for callers. Even Auntie Helene from California who was thought to be much too old for courting would collect thirty calling cards of men hoping to get a chance at a quiet talk before the next man stumbled in to kiss the back of her hand."

Bella thought of her New Year's Day celebrations. "That day was one of the few I ever had off. I'd just tuck into my bed—I mean, I used to when I worked for the Browns as their laundress and I had a bed—and I would read and eat decadent chocolate. The Browns always gave me the day off with chocolate."

"Trees." He ran his hand through his hair, glancing back at the ornament in the desk, shutting it. "We should be scouting out trees near the well to cut for decorating."

"Yes. We should do it."

"Oh, I don't mean *we* should do it. I meant *they* used to do it. Three big trees downstairs and several small ones upstairs in the landings and bedrooms. Pine boughs with red and gold ribbon draped everywhere. Tiny gift tins with coins and dollar bills hidden in the pine boughs. Stockings filled early Christmas morning, presents stuffed under the trees. It was something to see. And when I did witness it, I nearly always thought to myself there was indeed a Santa Claus."

She could imagine. The Browns didn't have a mansion and farm property, but their stately city home had been elegant, decorated to the hilt, too.

"James!" Margaret's voice came muffled and weak from the kitchen.

Bella waved him away. "I'll return lickety split." She exited the home through the front door.

"Wait."

She turned back just before she reached the cobblestone drive.

James dashed outside. "Wear these. Your fingers will freeze off with this wind."

She pulled on the soft leather gloves that must have belonged to Mrs. Westminster and wrapped the cloak tight against her.

"And this." He swiped her knit hat off her head and plunked a velvet one, sprouting peacock feathers that were against the brown. "It's like you were made for being rich," he said with a bow before backing away.

She held her arms out and spun, *feeling* like a rich person might. She stumbled and looked at her feet. She lifted one into the air. "But my boots. Someone's going to think I looted an empty mansion if they measure my feet against the rest of my garb."

"Nonsense." James was shutting the door. "Only petty women notice shoes. Everyone else will be mesmerized by your beautiful blue eyes and glowing skin."

Her cheeks went hot and she was speechless.

"Oh—" He shoved the door back open and dashed to her. "Stop at the apothecary for eucalyptus liniment, too. Margaret had trouble breathing last night."

Bella was confused for a second.

"She told me," he said. "I didn't… I wasn't… She said so, I mean. Not that I knew firsthand or—"

Bella lifted her hand to stop his explanation. "I understand and I'll be quick as a rabbit."

James disappeared into the house and she held her hand in the air, admiring the leather gloves. How beautiful these fine materials were. She didn't even think a woman needed jewels when she had sable, velvet, peacock, and leather to whirl around in. And for that moment, Bella was every bit as wealthy in body as she was in her mind. She started down the winding driveway that would lead to Ellsworth Avenue then Aiken then Walnut Street.

She hummed "Hark! The Herald Angels Sing," using the tune to soothe her worries about Margaret's pregnancy. Though she couldn't imagine how Margaret was going to manage a fatherless child, Bella felt useful in that she was able to help run errands. In fact, Bella knew of one incredible woman who managed her single mother life from time to time just fine. Fanny Fern—the novelist and columnist who'd been dead now for years.

Fanny Fern had kept her expectations and her desires where they belonged—with the skills she had for carving a life out of troubled times—she had enjoyed two out of her three marriages. Though Bella would love to fall in love with one man. Just one she could marry and have children to share books and ideas with. She admired Fanny Fern. The first female columnist in America had three children and three husbands, but always knew who she was at her core, man or not. Bella loved to read Fanny's columns and read about her. And perhaps the lessons of Fanny Fern were all Margaret needed to learn herself.

CHAPTER 6

Bartholomew

Bartholomew returned to Mrs. Tillman's having avoided bumping through the midday crowd well enough that he didn't think any of the eggs had broken. Once in the kitchen he carefully set the box on the table, drank two glasses of water, and called for Mrs. Tillman. He could use a cup of tea while he took a breather in the front parlor and made a plan to right the life that had gone so wrong.

The errand to the market just solidified his need to figure out how to recreate the life he'd loved, to somehow right the missteps that had put him out of his social circle and landed him in a boarding house, sleeping on a parlor settee, of all things. He'd planned to dig through his trunk for his notebooks and list of contacts he'd curated during the four years at Harvard and five short years of his banking life. He'd also saved and packed the notebooks his father had cataloged over decades. Bartholomew had been ousted from the finance world he knew better than anything and was at a loss at how to get everything back again if his former colleagues and acquaintances wouldn't even accept his correspondence.

Losing his material wealth, the regard of colleagues, his fiancée, and longtime family friends felt like someone had made an accordion of his midsection, pumping and releasing air pockets, leaving him with too much or completely lost breath at least eleven times a day. He'd tried to be a decent man, but even in doing what he'd thought had been right when the bank panic started, he still ended up in the same place with people looking down on him and wishing him ill will. It was as though no one could see who he was as a man. They only saw what they thought was greedy failure, and at that moment, Bartholomew was feeling mighty put-upon by it all.

He was about to yell for Mrs. Tillman again, when voices coming from down the hall drew closer. The whole crew of fellow boarders crashed into the space, cackling and talking and guffawing like they were holiday gala partygoers instead of poverty-stricken sad sacks. Leonard Hill, a dying old man, shuffled in—the only one of them who didn't laugh like a mannerless lout. Miss Clemmie Towson, a dour middle-aged woman, slid in with her ironing board posture—also quiet, but so acid in mood that Bartholomew could practically taste her bitterness. Arnold Aries, a former gardener for the Reynolds family, waltzed in with his gift of gab filling the space. Nathaniel Hobbs, a musician who played every instrument under the sun, had been cut loose from the Monongahela House and he conducted an invisible orchestra while whistling "O Christmas Tree." Penelope, a baker laid off from the same hotel as Nathaniel, sang and danced according to Nathaniel's happy conducting hands. Bartholomew was equally mesmerized and repulsed by their delighted ease.

He didn't feel that way with anyone in the world. He supposed he deserved it. Not even his friends could forgive him for what they'd lost. They'd cast him off and he was alone except for this crew of fellows. Perhaps it was because these people didn't have anything to lose—yes, jobs, maybe, but they hadn't lost real things—a life's work, the society of people and places that defined them. Penelope still had her bowls and stirrers and recipes. Nathaniel still had his instruments. Arnold lost access to gardens but there was always another patch of land to grow on. Bartholomew had been told Leonard had been dying for years and had lived at the Tillman Boarding House for decades so he didn't seem to have lost anything more than he'd been losing already.

Clemmie, with her sourpuss and thin drawn lips, hung back and was the only person who seemed to exude on the outside what Bartholomew felt on the inside. He didn't know what she'd lost, but from the looks of her, it didn't appear to be a lot of money as her clothing was raggedy far beyond what a few months of hard times would have brought.

"I'd rather sing the songs of Krampus than Santa," Clemmie mumbled.

Bartholomew studied her. Krampus, Santa's evil counterpart, played the part of awful tormentor of naughty children. This image made him chuckle. Clemmie gave him a wink. He studied the group as though they weren't the same species. There didn't seem to be shame associated with the economic downturn, no humiliation at being grown adults sharing a home, literally paying for a room to share in a house someone else owned. They sang and laughed, except for Clemmie, and Bartholomew realized he hadn't felt this comradery with his friends even before everything went bad. He'd never been part of something so… awful and wonderful at the same time.

"You know about Krampus?" Clemmie asked.

Bartholomew nodded. "Sure."

"You look like Krampus is your kind of fun. Glad to have you here, Scrooge."

Bartholomew started to claim that although he was depressed and unmoored, he was no Scrooge. But Nathaniel interrupted when he exchanged the proper words to the song for "O Bartholomew, O Bartholomew, how lovely art thou!" The others joined in, taking Bartholomew by the shoulders, shaking him around as though that would make him join in their frivolity. Penelope shouldered past the men and swallowed Bartholomew into a bear hug.

He tried to bat her away as the singing grew louder and more obnoxious, but then their joyous song and laughter swept him into hilarity as well. Still embracing him, Penelope squeezed tighter. "Merry Christmas," she said in his ear, giving him chills. Though his mind told him again to push her away, that her behavior was far too familiar for two people who'd just met days before, something softened him and he lingered in her warm, strong arms. The moment reminded him of his mother's hugs, the way she never said much, but always hugged him tight, even when he didn't know he needed it.

Mrs. Tillman entered the kitchen and clapped her hands. "Now, now. Let's get serious."

Bartholomew was afraid to ask what she was talking about, wanting to slip into the parlor to be alone. But tea. He needed some tea for his scratchy throat. So he hung back with the rest of them. The group settled and the silence was only interrupted by the sound of a match being lit. Everyone's head snapped toward Clemmie who held a match to the end of a cigarette.

She shrugged. "My dead and buried hubby, Iggy's his name, loved his cigarettes like smoking each one was depositing gold dust in his lungs and I'd be able to mine for it later or somethin'."

Bartholomew felt his eyes go wide. He cleared his sore throat.

"Anyhow. Just got a Christmas box from my brother-in-law the other day." She circled her hand in the air, a trail of smoke circling her wrist. "The brother-in-law went ahead and sent my Iggy's yearly stash of family-made cigarettes even though Iggy's well, like I said, dead and buried." She shrugged. "Figured I'd smoke 'em just to feel like Iggy's above ground. Even for a minute I can fool myself into believing it. Special tobacco and all. Southern family blend of… well, I dunno. I'm no tobacco *connoisseur*." She waved the cigarette again. "But the smell. Just like him."

Bartholomew inhaled a deep breath, noticing that everyone in the kitchen did the same.

"Well, outside please," Mrs. Tillman said. "We don't want to introduce tobacco scents to our baking, do we?"

Clemmie's eyes watered and she cleared her throat. "I'd rather be alone with my memories anyway," she said and disappeared out the kitchen door.

Mrs. Tillman sighed. "No one wants to be alone with their memories. I'll sit with her. Penelope, you take charge. I'm an amateur baker compared to you anyway. I'd love you to use the recipes that I bookmarked," she pointed at a cookbook, "but please, use yours, too."

Nathaniel nodded. "We've got lots of baking to do if we're going to enjoy our Christmas properly. First we bake for others, then we bake for ourselves. In one week's time we'll be celebrating with all the joy and love that we can imagine."

Bartholomew narrowed his eyes on Nathaniel. Was he serious?

Mrs. Tillman pointed at Nathaniel. "That's exactly right."

"Thank you for allowing us to share in your holiday, in your home, Mrs. Tillman." Penelope hugged her so tight that she lifted the woman off her feet. Bartholomew rolled his eyes. If only he could channel such gratitude, but no, he could not.

Mrs. Tillman left to insert herself into Clemmie's memories and Penelope put an apron over her head and tied it at the waist. "First, organize the eggs. Bartholomew, please put the dozen special ones in their own bowl so I can explain what Mrs. Tillman wants us to do."

"Oh," he said going to the tea caddy. "Um, my throat. It's… I'd like to make some tea or you could make it or…"

Penelope narrowed her eyes on him and he got the message.

"I can make the tea," he said.

"No. You do the eggs like I asked, and Arnold, make some tea and coffee for all of us. Leonard, you're looking peaked. Take a seat and relax. It's going to be a long, but wonderful afternoon."

Arnold started on the beverages. Penelope continued to give orders, and Bartholomew followed her instructions. He swallowed the irritated sigh that threatened to burst out of him. "Here's the special dozen I waited in line an hour for. The eggs look just like the others."

"That's a very important dozen of eggs, Bartholomew. It's amazing what those eggs do to recipes. They're delicate but..." Penelope shrugged.

The others questioned what Penelope was talking about and they gathered around Bartholomew.

"Gotta agree with Bartholomew here. Look like ordinary eggs to me," Arnold said.

"Not those, Arnold," Penelope said as she pulled a bowl over to transfer the eggs into. "Those."

"Oh," Arnold said. "Those *are* beautiful."

"The light blues and whites—I never knew there were so many shades of white in the world," Nathaniel said.

Bartholomew felt a grimace take hold of his face and hoped no one noticed. Ridiculous people, mooning over a bunch of eggs, of all things. Anyone could make hens lay.

"Well, they're more than good-looking. They're magic," Penelope said. She kept on praising the eggs and Bartholomew started his task of transferring the special dozen to the bowl Penelope wanted them in. One by one they went into the bowl and he hoped that Mrs. Tillman wouldn't realize he had been rudely rushed by his hostile line-mates and couldn't get the "feel" for most of them.

The fourth egg was so light he stopped before putting it into the bowl.

Penelope took it from him and looked at one end then the other. "What's with the holes?"

He leaned in. Each end had a hole and he took it back. "I don't know... I didn't... what in the hell..."

The group inched closer.

Bartholomew lifted the egg up and down. "That's really light, like it's empty or something." He shook it.

Penelope took it back. "What on earth? I know people blow out the insides of eggs at Easter and decorate them, and the two holes look just like this, but there's no painting on these or… did the woman say she was selling you empty eggs?"

Bartholomew felt attacked. "*Definitely not.* I was told to…"

"Get the feel for the eggs," Mrs. Tillman stepped back into the kitchen with Clemmie. Mrs. Tillman edged closer, a look of curiosity on her face.

Nathaniel held up two more. "These have holes too. Light as feathers."

Bartholomew's heart raced. He clasped his chest. He couldn't even buy the right eggs? His cheeks burned. Had he paid for empty eggs, *premium price* for empty eggs?

"Now there's a kick in the teeth," Clemmie said, shouldering into the group, holding up one of the empty ones.

Bartholomew waited for Mrs. Tillman to scream at him, but she didn't. "If these are the eggs you selected then it was meant to be."

He started to explain how he hadn't picked them, that he'd been rudely rushed and… he bit his tongue, watching as Mrs. Tillman took the egg from Penelope and tapped it on the edge of the bowl, cracking it. She pulled the sections apart and a little piece of rolled paper fell into the bowl. Everyone drew closer still.

Penelope picked it up and unfurled it like a miniature scroll. "Look. Writing."

"Read, read," Arnold said.

"Christmas delights in so many ways. Stories and memories fill the days. If it's reading you love, please come to me. 5720 Ellsworth Avenue is where you'll practice your literacy. Come, come and you'll see."

A hush fell over the kitchen.

"Ohhh, a riddle," Nathaniel said.

"A *lovely* poem," Mrs. Tillman said.

Bartholomew couldn't believe what he was seeing and hearing. Praise for a thief? A bad poem and a thief. That's what this person was. The egg girl—a bad poetic thief.

"These can't really be empty." He cracked the second one with holes and another note tumbled out. He unrolled it. "Join me! I love books and long talks by the fire." He stopped reading aloud and groaned. "This must be a joke. This isn't—"

"Finish reading it," Penelope said. The others cheered him on.

He sighed and continued. "Send me your favorite line, one from your favorite book. Then I'll return the favor—I'll send you mine." The address was included again. "Please write me. Literature enriches the soul like nothing else."

"*Her* life's enriched, she got that right." Clemmie shook her head. "Gets to keep the egg's insides and a sucker pays for the empties. Air. Paid for nothing. You're the sucker in this scenario." She elbowed Bartholomew.

Embarrassment swamped him. A sucker. Clemmie was correct. He'd done it again. Gotten nothing in return for what he'd given. He didn't recognize any part of this life he was living. But he must have deserved it. For he selected the eggs and even in a rush he should have realized they were too light to actually have yolks in them. He should have noticed the holes. Well, he'd been made a fool of but he was not going to let it go.

Nathaniel was cracking open the third egg with the holes. Bartholomew snatched the rolled paper and read aloud. "Scrooge is alive and well in Shadyside. Let's give him the boot this Christmas season. Join me for tea and reading… Are you a Scrooge? There's no reason."

Bartholomew couldn't breathe. Who was the egg lady to scold people she didn't even know? What nerve.

He pulled on his coat and hat. "Give me that one with the address."

"Hey, you're heading off to find the love of your life? Long talks by the fire?" Leonard winked.

"Hardly. I'm going to get my—*your* money back—Mrs. Tillman. I've been to 5720 Ellsworth Avenue before and this is absolutely unacceptable. This is thievery, clear as day. Can you imagine someone doing such a thing—stealing from others—just taking their hard-earned money and…"

He scanned the faces before him. Their eyes widened, they backed away. He knew right then that they all knew he was a disgraced banker. They'd heard all about him.

"It's all right, Bartholomew." Mrs. Tillman patted his hand. "These *are* special eggs. There will be plenty for our baking. You'll see. If these eggs came to you then… they were meant for you. Beautiful magical eggs. Who would have thought they'd arrive with notes! The egg girl gets more and more interesting every single day."

He buttoned his coat with ferocity. "Magical? Like the Lord Jesus is going to bless the empty eggs and suddenly there will be enough ingredients for whatever it is you're making? As though all is right in the world because we're about to pretend we all have our lives the way they used to be and we all have our things back, our jobs back, our homes back, like this economic crash never happened and…"

The shocked looks on their faces made Bartholomew finally shut up and he unrolled the note again—5720 Ellsworth Avenue. "I'll be back, Mrs. Tillman. I won't have you taken advantage of when you're so kindly sharing your home with me."

And he stomped out of the kitchen and down the street, people sidestepping out of his way as he loped past, angry and wishing the world was enchanted. He scoffed at the idea there was some supreme majesty captured in those damn *special* eggs. The only magic he was interested in was the kind that could change everything back to how it had been when he knew who he was and what he was meant to be.

CHAPTER 7
Bella

Bella took playful strides down the winding driveway, kicking each foot forward with a flourish that lifted the hem of the magnificent sable cape so the wind could animate it like it was being lofted by a dozen Christmas elves. She couldn't stop brushing her hands over the fur, lifting the collar to caress her cheek with the furry decadence she'd never even imagined feeling until that moment.

Curving through the maple and apple and pear and pine trees, she was suddenly alive with the stories she'd invented when she was half awake and the sun nibbled at the edge of the horizon, calling her to waken for the day. Parading down the drive in that getup she was the princess, the woman rescued. She stopped abruptly and put her hands out as though she'd run into a solid object. "No." She opened her arms. She was not going to be rescued.

What was she thinking? She was more like Fanny Fern than Sleeping Beauty and that was how she liked it. She chuckled and spun around again, pirouetting along, humming "Joy to the World" as she went. She had no idea how the heroine she was always imagining might rescue herself, but the thought of it tasted delicious and set her giggling as she twirled down the lane. There would be no savior prince in the stories she wrote.

She wasn't three rotations farther down the drive when she swirled right into a tall, well-dressed man with dark eyes that drew her in and held her captive. He held her waist, her arms still outstretched to help her recapture her balance.

He growled and untangled his feet from hers, huffing and puffing before squatting down and brushing the toe of his shiny shoe with the back of his gloved hand. "Well, isn't this just the *luckiest* thing."

She dropped her arms and squatted with him. She brushed his other shoe with the back of her hand.

"Don't touch my shoes. You've done enough." He shot to standing.

She did the same, unsure what would make this man overreact to bumping into her. "*Maybe* it's lucky. I don't know. What's so lucky about running into me like Mr. McGuff's field plow?"

He glared. "You ran into *me*, spiraled right into me like some kind of tin-lidded top."

She crossed her arms, feeling protective of the property she had no right to. She was also concerned she'd be accused of being where she wasn't supposed to be. "This is private property, you know."

"Oh. I *know*." He stood. "I've been here many times, for parties and luncheons and… And I've come to find the author of this little diddy." He dug into one pocket and then another, not finding what he sought. "I know it's here. I put both of them…" He sighed, mumbled, and flung open his coat and dug in his coat pocket then his pants pockets, looking crazed as his eyes went unfocused and his cheeks blushed red.

She tapped her toe. "Look, fella. I've got lots to do before the sun sets and—"

He shoved his hand forward, a little paper pinched between his fingers flapped in the wind. She squinted and moved closer.

"Recognize the writing, do you, egg girl—no, woman? You're not a girl at all. Miss Westminster? You are one of the flock of Westminster daughters, aren't you?"

Bella stared at the paper. Of course she wasn't a Westminster. But the sight of the paper in his hand turned her mute. One side of the scrap had typewriter print on it—a letter from the Sundry Station that had been trashed then snatched up by Bella who wrote on the blank side. Her notes had landed in the hands of someone. Her heart rate sped up. It worked. She covered her mouth with one hand. *It worked.* She turned her back to him. *It worked.*

Her eggs had conjured up a handsome man as though she'd drawn up the idea in a water-colored, hardback book. She faced the man again. She was unable to stop a grin from tugging at her lips. Was she dreaming? Was she suspended between moonglow and sunrise, with Simon warming her feet? She drew her gaze up to his and her smile snapped away. This was the person the universe had brought to her? This couldn't be right. His scowl soured her mood. He was mighty irritable for the man who was to become a partner in literature and maybe even love.

He shook the paper so hard that his fingers slipped apart with a snap and the note took flight on a wind gust like a princess lifted onto a genie's magic carpet.

Bella had to know which note he'd received. So she chased it into one of the maple groves, bending to snatch it up as the wind took it again, just out of grasp. The man followed, doing the same, reaching for it just as the wind would whip it away. He lunged, huffing and grumbling, trying to stop the note by stomping on it like he was putting a spider out of its miserable life.

His groaning and missing the target made her laugh so hard she couldn't breathe. Her own misses caused her to laugh harder. And with one final attempt to snatch it up, she dove and seized it, tumbling like a rolling haybale, catching his foot and tripping him. He kept his balance long enough to dive over top of her and complete his own roll that came to a stop not even one arm span away. The two of them splayed among the snowy maple trees like kids making snow angels.

The vision of what happened repeated through Bella's mind, making her laugh all over again, so hard she couldn't breathe. When she looked to her side, his jaw was clenched and he leapt to his feet. This was one prickly man.

Remembering what had caused her hilarity and his sourpuss, she lifted the paper and read it. It asked the recipient to share a favorite line from a novel. She imagined that this man must have years of schooling and read thousands of books in his time. And this was his response? She got up on her elbows.

"I've come to exchange these paper slips for fully filled, fully yolked eggs," he said.

"But—" Bella got to her feet and shook the snow from her cloak.

"I've no interest in trading *treasured* poems like…" He threw his hands in the air. "Like I don't even know what."

Her heart sank. She definitely wasn't dreaming. Something had gone awry.

"What?" He lurched toward her. "You've gotten caught and now you're feeling the weight of your con? Discuss poems? Of all the—"

"*Literature.*"

"Litera—*what*? What's the difference?"

"It was an invitation to discuss literature, not necessarily poetry. Although if that suited you, I would be willing." How could this be happening? She'd read a story about a little girl who knitted mittens to sell five states away and asked for a doll and received it for Christmas. A doll. Someone—no, many people, as the story goes—made sure that girl got a doll. All Bella wanted was someone to talk about books with.

"Someone like you doesn't know the difference between poetry and literature? Honestly."

"I've come for my eggs."

This made her think of the kitchen where she'd deposited the last of the day's eggs for Margaret which made her remember why she'd left the house and what she'd been tasked with. She started down the drive toward Ellsworth, striding along, struck again by Margaret's plight. That's a problem. Not one egg with a nice invitation in it instead of its yolk. That was not a problem at all. He traced after her. She shouted over her shoulder. "A man with your means came all the way to Maple Grove to gripe about an egg? *One* egg?"

"No. *Three* eggs. One of the others had a quote out of *A Christmas Carol* and said Shadyside was full of Scrooges and—"

She stopped as though she'd hit a wall. She turned. "Yes, Scrooge. Hmm. Now I see. It fits perfectly. The right recipient got exactly the right note. Worked just fine, didn't it? Like magic, the egg found the right owner." She stalked away.

He lengthened his strides and caught up to her. "*I'm* a Scrooge? Me? Look at you. Sweeping into the cold with your cape and hat and a butler, of all things. I saw that butler rushing out the door to tend to you, bringing you your peacock hat and gloves like you couldn't even take the time to remember your foul weather garments. Must be something else. This decadent life you live. I've been to your house before. I knew the Westminsters were—I knew you daughters were—"

"But I'm not—"

"Supreme luxury—the mark of people who don't understand how the rest of the world lives."

"Decadent life?" She stopped, astonished that he'd mistaken her for someone worthy of a butler, that he thought she was one of the Westminster daughters.

He pulled up and threw his arms open. "Do you know that most everyone has lost their butlers except for, apparently *you*. Fire roaring inside, every chimney sending smoke out, like smoky little taunts to those who've got nothing. Yes. Look at you. Sending your cook to the market with *magic eggs*, charging for them like they were made of gold and…"

"Me? Look at *you*, buster." She brushed the back of her hand across his shoulder. "Coat's cut to your figure perfectly, isn't it? Pretty sumptuous, given the state of the country right now, I'd say. So many people with nothing, with no food, waiting in line at soup kitchens."

"You don't know anything about me," he said. "I do plenty for the poor."

"The poor? *The* poor? Like being poor empties a person of her soul and heart and very human aspect? I'm sure *the* poor are ever so grateful that you've wasted your time bickering over an egg when you could obviously buy dozens of them and share with—"

"I wasn't permitted to buy dozens of the so-called special eggs. You're running a con. Is this how your parents bought that house?" He stepped back and bent this way and that to see through the trees. She watched his eyes darting from one end of the home to the other.

"That *palace*," he said. "Get a load of your getup. That mink cape and—"

"Sable."

"What?"

"The cloak is sable." She petted it.

He growled like an angry bear, fisting his hands. "This palace of yours. Is that how the Westminster family bought it? Little by little, piecing coins together by selling empty eggs? Is your father bilking people out of hard-earned cash some other way? Empty crates of I don't know what he is pretending to sell? I can just picture scores of empty crates careening down rail lines reaching their owners completely empty."

Now her jaw was clenched. She forced her words out. "The eggs weren't empty. And the railroads are bankrupt. There's barely any shipping of anything at the moment if you haven't noticed. The country is hurting."

"The eggs were empty of what I needed, what Mrs. T—"

She glared and shook her head. "Go." She pointed toward the driveway that wound its way through the rest of the maple and apple trees to Ellsworth Avenue. "You pompous ass. You're ruining the holiday mood."

He started to back away. "You are everything you think I am." He pointed his finger on each word spoken, emphasizing his thoughts.

"You've no idea who I am," she said plugging her hands on hips.

"I know all I need to."

"Same as I know about you."

"You should be ashamed," he said. "Rich and greedy."

"Hmph. Move along, Scrooge. I'm sure you have a whole list of people's Christmases to ruin."

"You too, obviously—a real holiday wrecker."

She shoved her finger through the air again. "Go."

"Oh, I'm going."

And as he disappeared down the drive, taking long, graceful strides, she had to catch her breath. She pressed her chest, her fingers caressing the sable fur. Her breath had left her partly because of what the man didn't grasp about her life, and partly because something about him stood in opposition to what she did indeed think she knew of him. It didn't make sense. *He* didn't make sense. No more than he had that morning when she saw him standing in line, face upturned, catching fat snowflakes on his tongue in his perfect, expensive clothing.

CHAPTER 8
Bartholomew

Bartholomew paraded back toward Mrs. Tillman's boarding house. Until then, his failures had been neatly cataloged in his mind, his emotions in check, but the faster he walked, the less control he had. Humiliation, friendships severed, foreclosed upon home. Loss of control over the emotions that had been neatly tied to his failures caused the orderly mental arrangement of regrets and disappointments to explode, dizzying him with swarming, tangled thoughts. On top of this, he couldn't stop thoughts of the face of the sable-caped Miss Westminster from returning.

Her laughter when they tumbled to the ground, her lack of concern for the exquisite cape's condition after rolling around the snowy carpet. No woman he knew would be so careless. No, it wasn't carelessness. It was a sense of absolute freedom. Freedom from angst, worry, regret, loneliness. He sighed. It was the first time he realized it. He was deeply lonely. The egg-notes. Literature. She obviously loved that. Her tone with him, her... boldness. God, her soulful eyes and easy smile.

She was so... fluid, was the word that came to mind. Her feelings came over her face in ocean tides, so absolutely beautiful. He let out a full body sigh as he neared Walnut Street. Was he now destined to obsess over a woman who would never even look in the direction of someone like him? Not now, with him having nothing. How had he never noticed her before?

What was he doing thinking about such things when he had immediate needs related to just surviving? But then the image of her, the way she spun down the driveway, so lost in—whatever it was she'd been lost in—the sheer joy she embodied. He yearned for the same unworried state Miss Westminster clearly enjoyed. He used to be like that. If only he'd appreciated it at the time and made better decisions he wouldn't be in the boat—no, in the boarding house—that he was.

Though completely taken by Miss Westminster, he was still angry at her empty eggs and little notes that somehow were supposed to make up for the absent yolks. Well, it was nice to be rich and unaware, a wealthy woman toying with those who had so much less than she. His spitefulness crusted like ice that started at a pond's edge and spread to the center, freezing everything it touched. He wondered how long it would take before his heart was completely frozen over, petrifying even his memories of a tranquil, happy life full of possibilities.

Nearly to the boarding house, Bartholomew saw Arnold and Nathaniel on the front porch. Nathaniel played a violin. The sweet strains of music hit Bartholomew as sorrowful and rich, and he knew he couldn't join them. He might burst right into tears if he did. Instead of stopping at the home that sat nestled between two other tall, skinny houses on Walnut Street, he passed it, waving at Arnold and Nathaniel as he did. "Be right back," he yelled after they shouted for him to come listen to the music.

He broke into a jog and turned up Aiken Avenue, hit Fifth, and ran and ran and ran for miles into Oakland, through Friendship, back through Oakland, the Hill District, and was halfway into Pittsburgh's city center when he forced his feet back in the direction of Shadyside. With blistered heels and heaving breath it took him a few minutes to realize what he was seeing when he reached the boarding house on Walnut.

Red and orange flares shot from the windows of Mrs. Tillman's and the house to its right. He'd never seen such enormous flames. Red, orange and purple heat licked the structure, emerging from windows like giants had taken over the inside, devouring the two structures from the inside out. Thick, black smoke belched from the attic and sank, choking everyone who'd gathered in the street.

"Bartholomew!" He startled and saw Mrs. Tillman rushing toward him, arms outstretched. She flung herself into him and clamped on as though he were a life preserver keeping her above water. "I thought you'd been swallowed up by the fire. Nathaniel said he thought you went into the house through the back and... oh, you're alive. Oh, thank heavens."

He patted her back and drew away, studying her face. "Your home..." was all he could say. This woman who'd offered him a place to stay was witnessing everything she owned incinerate and yet she'd been worried about him. He was struck with the urge to run into the house and drag out anything he could of her belongings. The parlor where she'd let him stay was full of furniture and books and items that she'd clearly spent a lifetime collecting. It wasn't that she had Van Goghs hanging on the walls or Ming Dynasty vases gracing delicate tabletops, but he had learned that it was the oddest things that sometimes meant the most when you were watching your entire life dissolve in front of you.

For him it had been his mother's book collection. It was the first thing he sold off in a desperate attempt to stop the financial hemorrhage. He should have at least kept her fairy-tale collection. At least those. But he hadn't. And now it haunted him. He so carelessly sold them off not realizing he would eventually want those back to remember her by, to remember his childhood and her reading to him.

Mrs. Tillman patted his cheeks. "Don't despair. Leonard had a massive burst of energy and he pulled out your trunk and your briefcase and your satchel."

"He did?"

"Since your things were in the first-floor parlor and the fire leapt from the attic next door to my attic… well, we saved more of your things than most. Leonard did."

Bartholomew looked over to see Leonard sitting on the stoop a couple doors down, and someone with a doctor's bag was examining him. Bartholomew went to him and thanked him, pacing back and forth while he was checked. Leonard waved Bartholomew off, saying anyone would have done it. And when he was back on his feet, Bartholomew guided him back down toward Mrs. Tillman and the other boarders.

Firefighters and neighbors were helping to put the fire out as the boarders coughed and supported Mrs. Tillman.

Nathaniel had rescued his violin and Penelope saved her baking books and a bowl. Leonard had also gone upstairs and gotten Clemmie's suitcase out before the flames got too strong.

"Lost my ciggies, though. Whole crate of 'em." She inhaled deeply. "I can smell 'em, though. Fire took 'em and the whole block smells like my dead husband. When he was alive I mean… 'course that's what I mean. Fire took 'em all." She inhaled deeply, red eyes watering, sooty cheeks revealing tear streaks. Everyone standing there inhaled the scent of Iggy, but Clemmie was the only one who seemed moved by the scent of fire.

Firemen shouted at one another as they kept the blaze from leaping from Mrs. Tillman's to the home on its other side.

Bartholomew couldn't believe what he was watching.

"There goes the bread for the poor," Penelope said.

"Now we're the poor," Clemmie said.

Mrs. Tillman wrapped her arm around Clemmie. "No. No. We're alive. We have each other."

Clemmie scoffed, but didn't pull out of Mrs. Tillman's embrace.

It was then, through the smoke, that a flash of movement cloaked in a sable cape caught Bartholomew's eye. Miss Westminster. Was it her? He craned to see better. It was. She was heaving buckets of water onto the porch next door to the boarding house to help keep flames at bay.

"Bella Darling," Mrs. Tillman said as she followed Bartholomew's gaze.

"What?"

"Bella Darling. The egg lady."

"*What?*"

"She was here when the fire started next door. Needed to buy my ginger tea."

"Miss Westminster?"

"Miss who? No. Bella lives in the barn at the Westminster place. A long story." Mrs. Tillman pointed to the beautiful girl who'd spun into Bartholomew's life earlier that day. "That's *Bella Darling*. She raises spent hens and gets them to produce the most wonderful—you *know*. You met her at the market, right?"

"The *egg* lady? You mean she's not—"

"You bought those eggs for me. From her. The special ones. The ones with the notes. You stormed off to see her. Didn't you answer the riddles? Didn't you meet her?"

He shook his head. "She followed me?"

"Followed you? She came to me for some tea for a maid at the Westminster place." A look of understanding came over Mrs. Tillman.

"Oh." She crinkled her nose. "Oh. You're the man who yelled at her today? She told me. But she didn't know we knew you or that... well, that was just before the house next door went up. The flames leapt to my place quick as the dickens."

Bartholomew shoved his hand through his hair, confused and embarrassed. "I went to get your money back and... I'm sorry I wasn't here to help you put the fire out." He looked back at the house. "You've lost everything."

She shrugged. "Not everything." But her denial was punctured by the reality of what was in front of them and she broke into heaving sobs.

Bartholomew drew her into his arms and held her tight, keeping her from collapsing.

"What will we do?" she said into his chest. He gave her a handkerchief and watched as the flames retracted into the house, dying a slow death, heat pulsating off the wood heaps. He'd never seen anything so awful. His losses had come in the form of invisible structures, only alive on paper. Yes, his assets walked out the door as depositors withdrew funds at an alarming rate, but he didn't have to watch it all go up in flames. The worst of his losses lived in his mind.

"What will we do?" Penelope said.

Bartholomew had no answer. But he could help with the fire. So he relieved a fireman from his bucket and tossed as much water as he could on the sparks and embers that would threaten to reignite if not fully extinguished.

When the rested fireman took back over, Bartholomew joined Mrs. Tillman, checking on her.

"Everything will be fine. Life always gets to be fine," she said.

Bartholomew shook his head. He had the most things pulled from the house by people he barely knew. He felt heavy guilt that his things were so readily saved. He looked to his left and right. The boarders all stood in a row to either side of him, arms entwined, the few belongings each managed to haul out of the house at their feet. Not one item was placed at Mrs. Tillman's feet.

"Were any of your things saved, Mrs. Tillman?" Bartholomew asked, shoving his hands in his pockets.

She cocked her head and then met his gaze. "Why yes, Bartholomew. Now that I consider it. My friends. All my friends have been saved." She roped her arm through his and leaned into him.

"I just wish things could go back to how they were," he said, watching the front wall of the house collapse. "When everything was better." Although he meant the statement for himself, he also felt the heavy seepage of pain from the others. He wished he had some means to take away what they were about to experience. He wished, for the second time in his life that he could make a real difference in the lives of others.

"Starting again isn't always worse, Bartholomew," Mrs. Tillman said.

He wanted to vomit. He couldn't agree with that. Starting again was hopeless. But they had no choice. Again, new, was all they had.

Nathaniel started to sing "O Christmas Tree" in a whisper. Just hours before, the boarders were light and cheerful, belting out the song and he'd been completely irritated at their joy sung loud. And now the same happy song narrated awful loss. Bartholomew's stomach filled with acid. He knew what Mrs. Tillman said was true—it was most important that lives were saved. But what was next for these souls? The poorhouse? That, he wasn't sure he could bear. That was just too much. The thought of it brought to mind the idea of life and death being completely intertwined, a poorhouse, the place where souls went to pretend to live and wait to die.

With the flames extinguished and the firemen still keeping everyone back from the rubble, the egg lady—Bella Darling, apparently—went to Penelope and they examined something inside a leather bag. He eyed the two, marveling at how he'd completely mistaken this woman for the wealthy daughter of the owners of the beautiful palace on Ellsworth Avenue—Maple Grove. He guessed his mistake made sense—she was decked out in a sable fur, with a peacock hat and fine gloves. And she didn't correct him. Although thinking back, he realized she may have been trying to explain and he just locomotived right over her words. And he never did see her from the front at the market so he shouldn't feel so embarrassed. He ran his words through his mind again, accusing her of running a con. But what was she doing in that outfit? Was she a thief?

Bella dug through the satchel with Penelope and as the crowd dispersed she glanced over at Bartholomew twice before recognition spread over her face. Then confusion. She wrinkled her nose and shook her head as she sauntered toward him.

"You." Bella crossed her arms. She opened her mouth as though she was going to go at him all over again, but then she looked down the line of people standing together and her expression softened. "Oh. Are you? I mean. You own Mrs. Tillman's Boarding House and she runs it for you?"

"Oh my, no, dear. I own the home," Mrs. Tillman said.

Bartholomew cleared his throat which had gone from scratchy to painful due to the smoke that coated it. "Staying here, well there, I mean. Well, not anymore I suppose."

"This young man has been living with me—"

"*Staying*—"

"He lived there, yes," Nathaniel leaned in. "With us."

Bartholomew grimaced, feeling exposed all over again. What was the point of hiding it? But his reaction was to defend his position. "I never received mail at Mrs. Tillman's and that's the defining element that denotes a person as living somewhere."

A man with a mail sack stopped and dealt out mail to the group. "Mr. Baines?"

He sighed and accepted the envelope. He jammed it into his breast pocket, defeated. "All right. Yes. I live—lived there but…"

This brought a rumble of laughter to the downtrodden group. There was no denying it. Bartholomew was one of them.

"So you're poor?" Bella asked.

He looked away.

"I'm poor, too." She chuckled and he looked at her. "No. Not really. I don't own anything, even borrow all my books. But I'm not poor. No, sir. Certainly not."

He narrowed his gaze on her, unable to grasp how she could own nothing yet claim not to be poor. To him it was black and white—enormous stores of cash and property or not. No other way to see it.

They all turned to watch flames shrink to embers that shook off their orange glow in exchange for quiet charcoal heat rising in waves off the debris.

Arnold shook his head. "I don't want to split up. Me at the poorhouse for men. Penelope and the other women at the Home for the Friendless. Leonard at the asylum. The holidays were meant to be… us together. This year was supposed to be…"

They stared into the black holes of Mrs. Tillman's boarding house. Bartholomew imagined all her things sooty and soggy. They must have stood silent for half an hour.

It was Bella who finally moved. She turned to Mrs. Tillman, her eyes filling. Bella swiped at tears as they dropped down her soot-covered cheeks. She shrugged. "Come with me."

"With you?" Nathaniel asked.

Bella nodded.

"Surely there's not enough room in your barn. Palatial as it must be if the Westminsters own it. But I can't leave them," Mrs. Tillman said, sweeping her hand toward her boarders.

Bella looked at each of them, stopping at last on Bartholomew. "You need a place to stay. The Westminsters have a… well, palace, I've heard it called by some."

Bartholomew's cheeks heated.

"We couldn't. It's not your house," Mrs. Tillman said.

"The Westminsters are stranded in Europe. Who even knows where at this point? I have to get this tea and ointment back to Margaret and it's a palace, for goodness sake. The Westminsters took me in and allowed me to stay in the barn as long as the hens continued to lay, and they lay like rabbits have babies." She let out a sigh. "This is urgent and it's Christmastime and it's the right thing. I can't imagine the Westminsters wouldn't be proud to lend a hand to those in need. They aren't using the house. Not one room."

Bartholomew couldn't imagine just stealing into someone else's house. Not the way he'd been bred.

"Besides," Clemmie shoved a thumb toward Bartholomew. "This one used to go to balls and parties there. So he's one of them. I read the papers. I'm in the know."

A fresh wave of humiliation swept over Bartholomew. Added to that, the weight of being dragged into squatting in someone's house sickened him. "I did attend parties there, but only because I donated to their causes. I certainly wasn't one of them. Not like you're thinking. I have no right to invite or even agree to go with you to stay in that home."

They all sighed.

It was as though they expected him to decide for the group. He looked at their blackened faces and listened to Leonard start to cough uncontrollably. For Leonard. Maybe that was enough. It was that or the poorhouse. And that wasn't fair to Leonard.

CHAPTER 9
Bella

The boarding house crew traipsed to Maple Grove and pushed through the kitchen door to find Margaret and James by the fire. They leapt up and apart. Bella wasn't sure if it was merely the shock of having an unfamiliar posse steamroll into the kitchen, or if, again, their closeness was something they viewed as "wrong."

Bella apologized for her lateness in getting back with the tea and liniment and introduced the gang. She collected coats and hats from their guests and hung their things in the cloakroom to air out. "I'll explain everything as soon as I get the hens and Simon into the barn. Meanwhile, have a nice chat."

She moved quickly to settle the girls and Simon inside, giving them dry oats until she returned with warm dinner. Back at Maple Grove she walked into an awkward hush and immediately went to work smoothing things over, explaining their day as she shook out of the sable coat, peacock hat, and leather gloves.

Margaret only interrupted the story of what all these soot-covered people were doing in the Westminster house once, and that was to assure Bella she didn't have to make the tea, that she and James had dug some peppermint lozenges out of the powder room attached to Mr. Westminster's study and that had calmed her nausea.

But Bella made the ginger tea anyway to help soothe everyone else's sooty throats. None of the three original Maple Grove residents—James, Bella, or Margaret—corrected anyone's assumption that Margaret and James must be married. And sharing that secret made Bella think the two would be more agreeable to sharing the home with this group of strangers.

Margaret wiggled her finger at Bartholomew. "You, I've seen before."

Bartholomew went white.

Mrs. Tillman laced her arm through Bartholomew's. "This fella, Bartholomew Baines, is a successful banker. He's stumbled onto hard times, but I don't take that as a mark of failure. Failure is just another name for opportunity. So you might have seen him here before. As a guest. And so we hope his presence in our little group lends us credit and standing and that his presence is all the more reason we're hoping you agree to let us stay here. Please. Just until I get my insurance check. We'll make ourselves small and useful. We promise not to break or steal anything. I personally vouch for all of them. Every single one of them."

Margaret and James exchanged glances. "Even the banker?" Margaret flung her hand toward Bartholomew. "You know bankers are all about what's for them, and we can't have him taking off for his friends in high places tattling on us—"

Mrs. Tillman walked over to Margaret and took her hand. Bella wasn't sure how Margaret would respond to that. But she simply gazed up at the older woman, mesmerized. "Even the banker. This one's different. He's a fine soul." Mrs. Tillman patted Margaret's hand then let it go.

Bartholomew looked as though he was going to unbutton his skin and melt into the floor. Bella was impressed by Mrs. Tillman's heartfelt recommendation of a man who'd seemed so awful just hours before.

"If you say so," Margaret said.

The comment about Bartholomew the banker was more along the line of Margaret's typical snootiness Bella knew well. Yes, it was odd for someone holding what was seen as a lesser position in society as being snooty to those "above" her, but Margaret managed just that feat. She held people's riches against them and she held others' lack of money against them as well. Bella couldn't say exactly who Margaret thought of as being fine people other than those exactly like her. Margaret must have really been feeling better to have regained some of her sass.

"Please," Mrs. Tillman said.

James whispered something to Margaret, too quiet for Bella to hear, and then he stood. "We welcome you here for as long as we can rightfully allow you to stay—meaning the Westminsters are apparently stranded or they've abandoned us—but for now we are still tasked with being here. And if you're going to really be moving on as soon as you can, I don't see how we could possibly turn away strangers in need when we have this large home with—"

"Estate," Clemmie said. "This is an estate."

James cleared his throat as though he might disagree and then nodded. "With just the two of us staying at Maple Grove and Bella in the barn. But we'll need to erase our footprints every day. We don't want to take advantage or leave one bit of evidence you were ever here."

That sounded difficult. Bella wished she had enough room in the barn for all of them to stay there so they wouldn't have to worry. And so, with exhaustion settling in, each of the guests took turns washing up in the servant's cloakroom. Margaret sent Bella to the attic to dig through trunks of old clothing that the Westminsters had deemed too worn for mending but not yet repurposed or passed along.

With everyone in fresh clothes, Bella organized what they'd removed, setting items that could be washed in one pile and those that had been too damaged into a rag pile.

"Thank you, Bella." Mrs. Tillman waved just before disappearing into the back staircase with Margaret, Clemmie, and Penelope, heading where they would sleep. James took the men to their room, leaving Bella in the kitchen, the sudden silence surrounding her, reminding her that most of her days were spent alone.

She sighed, exhausted as well. She told herself not to be down, that she hadn't suffered a single loss that day, and her thoughts turned to her hens. She had no idea what the next day would bring, but she did know her girls would have been missing their dinner by now and missing Bella as well. And so, she pulled some oatmeal from the cold storage in the cellar, added a splash of water and milk and heated it on the stove. When the oats were warm she shook her stash of foraged berries and nuts into the pot. She added some pepper and took her pot outside, trudging through the snowy courtyard, into the lane that led to the barn.

Once in the barn she fed the animals. While they ate, she told them the day's story, adjusted the bench covered in hay and petted the hens until they were calm and drowsy. Finally she cleaned up for bed. Nestling into her covers never felt so good. Simon purred and curled into her legs and when she felt herself falling toward sleep, she realized

she hadn't been able to keep her eyes open to read even ten words of
Mrs. Perkins' Ball.

Bella woke and when she recalled what had happened the day
before, that she had guests staying at the big house, she felt a surge of
happiness that nearly knocked her over. Then when she remembered
why Mrs. Tillman and the others were there she felt sadness for them
having experienced the fire. Still, they were on the property and Bella
was suddenly excited at the idea of having people to share her world
with. And so she quickly fed the hens, gathered their eggs, set them
outside for the day, and headed for Maple Grove. When she entered,
only Mrs. Tillman was in the kitchen. She was opening cabinets,
wearing a velvety wrapper and slippers. The toes of the rose-hued
slippers were festooned with three-dimensional roses that jutted out
from under the hem of the robe.

"Nice slippers," Bella said.

Mrs. Tillman lifted the hem past her ankle and turned her foot,
revealing that her heel hung over the end of the shoe. "These beauties
were made for a child's foot or a dainty creature more delicate than I,
but Miss Margaret woke nauseated again so I threw on the first things
I could find and rushed down to make her the ginger tea."

Bella set her eggs down, realizing that if the velvet wrapper and
fancy mules were at arm's length in Margaret's room, then she must
have been borrowing clothing from the Westminsters' daughters
because those night clothes—loungewear that the public never saw—
were finer than any clothing a maid would have to wear out into the
world, let alone wear in the privacy of her own room.

"I can help get you situated," Bella said, opening cabinets, drawers,
and boxes. "Teacups and mugs are here, teas are kept in these boxes,
honey there. And I could whip up some cracker dough to settle
Margaret's belly. And an egg pie. I'm no fancy chef, but I can make a
very savory egg pie." Bella opened the oven to assess the coal situation.

One by one, Bella and Mrs. Tillman welcomed each of the boarders
into the kitchen as they wakened with coffee, tea, and egg pie. Each

new member of the household came tentatively, unsure about their presence in such a grand home.

"Kitchen's plenty big for all of us to sit around the table. And we've got the fireplace and the settee and chairs. We'll be right at home in here," Mrs. Tillman said.

Bartholomew flinched at the comment.

Bella set a coffee mug in front of him. "Oh, Bart, come on. You must have something you can build your life on again? You must have hidden away something from your bank. I've heard of banks collapsing, but never the banker himself. You should look the least glum of all."

"Bartholomew."

She smiled. "You're more of a Bart these days, aren't you?"

He stood and took his coffee mug. "You can't just rename a fellow because you think you ought to, like you've scooped up a stray dog."

"I like Bart better and it suits your current situation."

He lifted his gaze to her and he appeared hurt by what she said, which unsettled her. She put her hand to her throat. She'd never seen a man of his former stature impacted by the words of a woman who sold eggs for a living. She'd expected him to launch into a diatribe on how he wasn't responsible for his losses or those of the depositors who'd entrusted him with their money, to explain how it was he who'd ended up with nothing. She wished she could take the words back. She hadn't meant to hurt him. But she hadn't said them harshly. Now she wanted to make him feel better. "Would you prefer your coffee in the study?"

With that statement, his sad eyes turned hard and he narrowed his gaze on her.

She reached out. "I didn't mean to be mean, I was just—"

Bartholomew took his coffee, waltzed through the cloakroom and right outside, slamming the door, too irritated to even accept Bella's apology.

James entered the kitchen with a stout, mustached man beside him. "I've got someone—um… this is Mr. Buchanan and he's got something important for us. He says… he…" James's face went white and he coughed into a closed fist as though he had information he didn't want to share. "He holds the mortgage on Maple Grove Cottage."

Bella's throat grew so tight she could barely get a breath down. Another banker.

"Oh, Mr. Buchanan, please sit. Have some egg pie," Mrs. Tillman said. "A guest for breakfast. How lovely for us." She offered Bartholomew's abandoned seat and Mr. Buchanan sat, hat in his lap, briefcase at his feet.

"Does smell good," Mr. Buchanan said.

Leonard entered the kitchen, shuffling along, hacking away. All eyes turned to him and Bella ran to him just as his legs nearly gave out. Mr. Buchanan stood. "I believe this man needs the seat and the food more than I."

Leonard sat and patted Bella's hand. "Thank you." He smiled, his grizzled chin indicating he hadn't shaved that morning.

Bella brought him a glass of water, coffee, and a slice of pie.

The man cleared his throat. "That does smell good. Maybe I could have a bit."

"'Course." Arnold popped up and gave the man his seat. "Sit, please."

Silence while Mrs. Tillman prepared his plate created sharp, shifting, awkwardness that no one seemed to know how to soften.

Mr. Buchanan ate a bite of the egg pie and relaxed back in his chair. "That is splendid."

"'Course it is. Made with the best eggs in the land," Mrs. Tillman said glancing at Bella.

"An egg's an egg," he grumbled and pulled a stack of papers from the pocket of his leather case.

"No, sir." Penelope set a water glass at Mr. Buchanan's place. "Bella's hens lay very special eggs."

"Humph," he said as he spread the documents beside his plate. He read a couple words from them aloud then stopped, gobbling up more of the egg pie. He moaned with food-inspired ecstasy and shook his head. "I'm sorry to enjoy this wonderful pie and have to say what I'm going to say but…" He pulled spectacles out of his breast pocket and continued. "Well, I'm not one to mince words so I'll just move ahead." He drew a deep breath, exhaled, then took another bite of pie. He dabbed his mouth with the napkin. "On this day, December nineteenth, 1893, at this home at 5720 Ellsworth Avenue, Shadyside, Pennsylvania, these papers serve as the eviction notice on the Archibald Westminster property. Failed payments and delinquent taxes have resulted in foreclosure. Every inhabitant should evacuate the premises immediately and the Westminster property will be surrendered to the sheriff as partial payment for..."

"Stop." James held up his hand. "We understand. We aren't even—"

Mrs. Tillman interrupted, dishing another slice of egg pie onto his plate. "You can't mean to throw us out six days before Christmas? You *can't* be so… I just won't believe a clearly fine man like you would do such a thing. My home—our home—just burned to the ground."

He grumbled, devouring more pie.

Mrs. Tillman topped off his coffee. "What on earth do you plan to do with this property in the remaining days of the year? Certainly no one's buying it today. Certainly."

He closed his eyes, enjoying the food.

Mrs. Tillman gestured to Bella to cut even more. She served another plate and added slices of fresh bread. He slathered butter on the bread, gobbled it all up, and asked for more. Passing glances and shrugs, they watched, not wanting to break into his satisfied happiness.

Bella scanned the faces of her newfound associates, seeing sadness and worry etch deeper, their smiles turned fully upside down.

When Mr. Buchanan stopped shoveling food into his mouth, he leaned back and surveyed the room. Bella's mind raced. She couldn't just up and leave the barn with her hens and Simon. They would freeze to death or worse. Any poorhouse would only welcome the hens with the promise they could appear on the table for the next meal. Her eyes burned and she swallowed rising tears. She'd trusted things would simply work out. But now… with other beings to care for? Well, crying wouldn't help.

Leonard bent over, coughing, interrupting the tension. Bella scurried to refill his glass and rubbed circles into his back, hoping to relieve some of his discomfort.

"Like Mrs. Tillman said. Her home burned down yesterday," Bella said. "This man rescued the few belongings these people had to their names. He helped Clemmie here escape with her suitcase and only the back of her skirt getting singed. Please, Mr. Buchanan. Please don't do this."

He lifted a fist. "I've been lenient. Surely the Westminsters alerted you to their lack of payments. Surely this isn't a surprise. Where *is* old Archibald? I'd like to deliver the paperwork to him personally."

"It surely *is* a surprise. Mr. Westminster's indisposed," Margaret said stepping into view. She rubbed her belly and Mr. Buchanan's gaze fell on her hands cradling her full belly.

"You mean still out of the country," Mr. Buchanan said.

The lack of response was all the confirmation he needed.

Margaret's posture straightened. "James and I have worked for the Westminsters for a decade. We are charged with caring for the home."

He closed his eyes and scratched his sideburns. "And yet you've invited this cluster of folks into the fold?"

Bella held her breath, waiting for Margaret to toss them all out to save herself.

"I have. And I take responsibility for anything that—"

He held his hand up to stop her.

Bella moved a dozen eggs from yesterday's bowl into a basket and set them in front of Mr. Buchanan. "Please. Take these eggs to your wife and just let us be until the new year. Please. We can't be costing you money. I've been told I can stay at the property until the hens stop laying. And they haven't. I've got them laying many times the normal amount for older hens, even more than a dozen young pullets."

He leaned on his forearms, plucking egg and crust crumbs from his plate into his mouth. He sighed and scratched his chin. "That crust is unbelievable."

"It's the rosemary seasoning blend." Bella put a full pie plate next to the basket of eggs in front of Mr. Buchanan.

"They're special—the eggs," Mrs. Tillman said. "Will be worth your while to trade. You can trust us to care for the home like it was ours."

"Let you all just squat here, willy-nilly? No way."

"We're fine people," Clemmie said in her scratchy low-toned voice.

The silence in the kitchen made Mr. Buchanan look away from the group. He stared at the eggs and ran his fingers over the orbs. "You want me to trade time in a foreclosed estate for a dozen eggs? A measly dozen eggs?" He traced his gaze from one person to the next.

"Yes," Bella said. "These eggs aren't measly."

"They're magic," Penelope added.

"You'll see," Bella said.

"And you'll be doing the Lord's work," Mrs. Tillman said. "Think of it. You're making room at the inn for those who need it most. At Christmastime."

He sighed again and twisted his mouth then pushed to standing. "You've softened me with this remarkable pie. I'll take the eggs and give you two days maximum. That will give you time to relocate, the hens laying eggs or not."

"Well." Mrs. Tillman turned her back. "Thank you for that."

"That's more than generous." He walked back through the pantry just as Bartholomew reentered through the cloakroom.

Bella saw that Mr. Buchanan had forgotten the basket of eggs. She scooped it up and hurried after him, catching him as he was opening the front door. "Your eggs," she said holding the basket out to him.

He put his hat on. "You keep them. Sounds like you'll need them."

She shook her head. "Nonsense. We made a deal and the eggs are part of it. Surely your wife will look kindly on fresh eggs at the holidays."

"The missus hasn't been looking kindly on much of anything I've done lately." His gaze lingered on Bella. She gave an understanding nod. Instead of him walking away, his posture loosened and he took on the tone of a close friend. "Truth is, nothing's good enough or even satisfying. I can't get anything right anymore."

The confession moved Bella. She felt his disappointment as though it was her own. His soft sadness disarmed her—something she hadn't noticed in the kitchen. She reminded herself that money didn't solve all problems, that sometimes money just made problems bigger or spread them out among more people. It was something that she comforted herself with since she could remember. "Take them. Eggs are a symbol of new life and prosperity. Something everyone needs these days. Everyone."

He cocked his head. "You're right. Eggs as a present are as good as anything I've dreamed up as of yet. I'll give it a try."

And so he was gone, leaving Bella to shake off the dread he'd brought with him.

As soon as Bella returned to the barn, to her animals, her mood shifted. She turned her thinking upside down. She had animals to protect and so she would fully trust that she'd find a way to do so. There was always a way. She'd managed to land in soft spots throughout her life and this would be no different.

As she was heating up oats and melting snow to water her pets, someone knocked at the door. She yanked the door aside and peered outside.

"Bart. What brings you calling?"

"Do you have to keep saying Bart instead of Bartholomew?"

"I do. It fits you. And I don't think a person should gallivant about with the wrong name as though it doesn't matter."

He shifted his feet and removed his hat. "I'd like to come in. To talk."

"Well, I—"

He stepped past Bella, through the opening. "I guess if you're going to be bold and change my name I will be bold and just invite myself in."

She tapped her chin with a finger then shrugged. "That's fair as anything I've ever heard."

She pulled a rocking chair in front of the fire and offered it to him. She knelt at the pot and stirred the oats.

"You're setting a luncheon for yourself?"

She raised her eyebrows. "Nope. For the hens and Simon, my cat."

"They're in here?"

"They're outside right now, but I've set up quarters for the hens in here for nights for now. Trouble with coyotes put me on high alert."

He picked up a stack of books and looked through them. "How can you afford books?"

She looked over her shoulder. "Can't. Borrowed them from a lady who's associated with the wife of Mr. Carnegie who's planning to make a lending library for all of Pittsburgh to use freely. It's going to be a palace to house thousands of books and welcome readers of every part of society. Anyone who signs up can borrow books. Can you imagine?"

"You really love reading, don't you? The notes? The borrowing?"

"Love reading, love stories told right out of people's mouths. Love all stories. And someday I'm going to write them myself. My friend Ada even gave me paper and ink just yesterday for that very thing."

Bartholomew leaned back in the chair and rocked. "You've made me remember."

"Remember what?"

"My mother loved stories the way you do. We had a library in our house and she would walk along the shelves, running her finger over the book spines then snatch one out to read to me. All the time. Thinking of it now—it really was the thing she and I did together most." He chuckled. "Way she talked about the characters, you'd have thought they were as real as you and me."

Bella was filled with a sense of wonder. "You had a library? With floor-to-ceiling shelves and… I bet you did."

He nodded.

"So what's your favorite?"

"Ah, back to our first meeting. You wanted to know my favorite line from my favorite book…"

She nodded, pleased that he was finally playing along. His silence startled her. "So?"

"Don't have a favorite story or book or line. The memories of being with my mom while she read to me are wonderful, but as I grew up I'd read the news or play with numbers while she read her stories. We were still enjoying that time in the library together, but I loved different things than she did."

"Everyone who's ever heard a story has a favorite. Surely you remember one you love?"

He scrunched up his face like she had begun to speak in another language.

She sighed and spooned the soft oats into several bowls. "Can't be fully rich if you don't have a favorite book. Just can't be. Sounds like each of us is half rich. Me with my books and you with your money."

He flinched at that statement.

"I'm sorry. I keep saying rude things. Talking about your mother and the library made me forget you're no longer rich with money."

"So you think I'm completely poor then?"

"Well, I think you can start cherishing books like your mother, then fall in love with a couple and be at least half rich like me. You're not helpless, you know. You don't have to live poor forever."

KATHLEEN SHOOP

He shook his head, studying her, and she knew he was trying to decide if she was serious. She grasped that most people viewed money as the defining element of wealth.

He narrowed his eyes on her suspiciously. "You are so…" He shook his head again. "I don't know what you are but you…" He drew a deep breath.

"I what?"

"I don't know."

"Well, you can decide what I am while you help me with the animals." She spooned oatmeal into bowls and handed two to him.

He set the bowls where she directed. "You've got one thing right," he said wiping his hands on his pant legs. "I can't think of one thing in my life that might be considered symbolic of or actually a mark of wealth. Not rich, not anymore."

Bella scratched Simon behind the ears as he ate. Bart stood and dug his hands into his pockets.

"Or never was rich. Not really. Perhaps if you'd captured the true riches in your life with stories then you'd still have something worth having."

"You really think you're rich because you have stories you love, because you read?"

"I've got stories of all kinds. Mine and others—those written down by famous people and those told to me as I worked my way through life. Yes. How can you even ask that? I'd like more money, of course. I'm saving up for a small, cozy place, maybe a home set in the bend of a river or stream."

"Filled with books," he said.

"Top to bottom." She stood and took the empty oat pot off the fire.

He sat in the rocking chair watching her as she cleaned.

"I still don't get it," he said. "What's *your* story? Where's your family? What's so great about your story that you don't feel poor even though you…" He looked around. "Live in a barn."

She puffed out air. "And not even my *own* barn. I see what you mean about that. It's comical at a certain level. But, yes. I feel rich most of the time—a contentment, I guess. To me that's equal to wealth. You know when I don't feel content? When I feel poorest?"

"When?"

72

"When someone else needs something and I don't have a way to help them. Poor mothers with starving children at the market. I feel their desperation to my toes. A widow who loses her house and can't fathom what to do next. When I'm around those people I feel poor because I can't help them."

"Hmm, yes, if you don't have money you can't be helpful."

"I'm not an idiot, Bart. I realize I can't eat stories, or give them to someone else to eat but… well, I am proud to feel a level of satisfaction in the world that clearly others who had everything, even someone like you, can't claim."

"Who said I wasn't content before—when I was rich?"

She tilted her head. It's possible he was, but it didn't seem to fit with this corked-up irritation, always threatening to build and blow the lid off, like when he'd been so angry about the egg notes. She could feel his unrest from five feet away.

"I shouldn't assume you weren't content."

"I wasn't just content. I was stinkin' happy. Elated. Loving my life."

She drew back. "That's a lot of joy," she said. "For me, contentment feels like the best thing in the world. I suppose I've never said it aloud. I understand how the world views me, but that's not how I view myself. And I'm proud of my very pleasurable life."

"You surely made your life fit your definition of wealth."

She tossed some logs on the fire and sat in the rocking chair across from him. "Well, I was lucky enough to be born into a world where we had so little that I never felt like I had nothing."

He leaned back in the chair and began to rock. She could see he was considering what she said.

She gestured toward the book to his left. "That one. Read aloud while I sweep up after the girls and Simon."

He pulled the book onto his lap and the crack of the spine excited her as he started to read *Vanity Fair*.

Listening to his deep poetic voice narrate as she worked made her feel as though one of her fantasies had come to life. When she finished sweeping and emptying her dustpan out the side door she finally turned back to Bart. And when she did she covered her mouth at the sight.

He'd stopped rocking, but continued to read. One hen sat on his knee, another on one shoulder, the cat on the other, and the other hens on his feet.

"Bella?" he said.

She moved to where he could see her.

"Help."

"Help what?"

"Look at them."

"I see."

"Help me with them."

"They love you."

"No. I just met them and I'm not an animal person. There's no love at first sight for me and animals. They're going to attack, aren't they?"

"This is love at first nuzzle, not first sight. I get the feeling they didn't like you at all at first sight."

He looked away, his cheeks blazing red. This made her smile even more.

"Animals never like me."

"Maybe that was the old you. The Bartholomew. These animals definitely love Bart."

"The old me?"

"The one who cared more about money than people."

"What? How can you possibly say that? You don't know me."

She cocked her head. She was being rude. That wasn't something she liked to be. "You're right. I'm sorry. I'm lumping you in with all the bankers who put personal profit above all else. I don't know you and maybe you're a new breed of banker with philanthropy at the center of your workday."

He stiffened further, the hens and Simon seeming to grow antsy. "Bankers are valuable members of society. And I attend many philanthropic events. Why, just the week before the May 23 crash, I attended the Ladies Relief Association's musical benefit for the poor of Allegheny City."

There he went with "the poor" again. She tapped her toe. "Well, bankers might give some money to causes and the like, but think about the creators in the world. Engineers. You know, builders and makers and artists who see how their work betters humanity. Or people who coax old biddies to lay untold eggs for the benefit of others."

His breath caught. "That's unfair. Look at Nathaniel. He's a brilliant musician. I would know because I attend musical evenings as I just mentioned. I've heard all the best. And he's living in a boarding home, jobless, now homeless. They fare no better than people like… me. At least I had something before… all of *this*. Yes. Bankers care. We get all the best invitations to prove it. Think of it. I've been to parties here, yet I've never been near the Westminsters' level of wealth for myself. Not yet. I was on my way there. And I certainly will achieve that kind of wealth someday. But the Westminsters saw my value. I wouldn't get invitations to galas and fundraisers for—"

"The poor?"

He groaned. "If I wasn't a valuable member of society." He whispered the words. Matilda shook her wings causing a feather to fall and brush past Bart's nose, making him even more unsettled.

Bella stifled a giggle, surprised she could evoke such a reaction in him. "I don't want to upset you. I really want to know. *Do* bankers care? I assume Mrs. Tillman and the others told you what happened with that Mr. Buchanan. He's putting us out of here in two days. Just before Christmas. You understand that. He could let us stay here until the new year, yet he says somehow not kicking us out will cost him money. He doesn't care."

"*I* did. Care, I mean. I do. I—" He shifted abruptly and the cat leapt away with a hiss, the hens squawking as they took flight into the rafters. He stood brushing at his clothing. "Told you animals don't like me."

"And yet there they were, wedged into every crevice and perched on every plane of your body. Until you got ornery."

He stopped fussing and stared at her. She crossed her arms, her gaze lingering on his. His brown eyes conveyed something different than any other time she'd looked at him. Maybe she hadn't really looked at him before. Maybe, like Margaret, his hard times were softening him. She stuck her hand out to offer a handshake. "I'm sorry. I really am. I was rude to a person in need and I shouldn't have been."

He stood, looked at her hand then took it. The warmth of his palm against hers sent electrical jolts through her. Her mouth dropped open and she froze. Then to avoid the urge to nestle herself into him like the animals had just been doing, she patted his hand like a grandmother would to an acquaintance she didn't really want to be near. "And I hope you'll accept my apology and we can part ways day after tomorrow with goodness in our hearts."

Bart looked down at their hands as she bobbed them up and down.

And then it was like he snapped out of a dream and made eye contact again. "I accept your apology. If you mean it. As long as you're not just offering some sort of single suture over a gaping wound kind of apology that the patient and doctor both realize can't close the gap in the least. And eventually the patient dies of gangrene or something worse."

"Something worse?"

He shrugged, but still held her hand, his thumb brushing over her skin, lighting her on fire all over again.

She reached to pull her cuff down completely over her wrist. "Something's worse than gangrene?"

"Has to be something."

"Crushed under boulders?"

"Drowning."

"Run over by an angry steer."

"Been chased by one before. Scared the life out of me."

She cocked her head and let a giant grin cross her face. "*Me too*. Me too. Can you believe that? That must mean something. We've had the exact same near-death experience."

Bart's gaze slipped to their hands again. Bella knew he must be thinking he was holding her hand in a way that was far more intimate than the original handshake.

"This is getting very strange," he said. "So I'm going to see what I can do to help Leonard with his breathing. He's not doing well."

"Well, I'm going to finish with my beasts."

And finally he pulled his hand away without another word. He was still looking at her when she turned away, hoping he wouldn't see that he'd left her breathless and flushed. She regarded her hand and retraced where he'd been caressing her skin, then pulled her cuffs down further, hoping he hadn't noticed the scarring that sometimes showed under a shirtwaist when she stretched her arms too far. That was one story she didn't like to tell.

She heard the door slide open and turned to see him closing it, looking right at her with the most sublime expression of curiosity. She almost begged him to come back and sit again. She wanted him to hold her hand again, to conjure up what she'd just felt. And she wondered how this man could possibly not have a favorite book. Someone so powerfully and subtly soulful who could evoke such emotion in her must have a favorite story he told himself over and over again.

CHAPTER 10
Bartholomew

Bartholomew was last to waken for breakfast. He'd slept little the night before. After his visit with Bella in the barn, he spent the evening alternating between helping Leonard move about to keep his lungs clear and helping Margaret with her nausea. Walking gave Leonard and Margaret some comfort. But Leonard was so bad that night that Bartholomew wondered how the man would continue to go on with his raspy breathing and racing heart.

The smoke from the housefire had exacerbated whatever illness had been hounding him for years. Throughout the night, with support, Leonard had walked around the first floor, circling, just fine and then it would be as though he'd walked into a wall and his legs couldn't even keep him standing. So Bartholomew would scoop him up, sit him on the settee near the fire to rest, and then they'd try that all over again.

Bartholomew helped with the teas and even made up a bed for Leonard in the kitchen near the fire so when he was ready to sleep they could take turns sitting with him without disturbing the others in the men's bedroom. Helping Leonard gave Bartholomew's body something to do while his mind spun around Bella. He had to leave her in the barn the previous day because the simple act of accepting her handshake kindled something inside him he'd never felt before.

My God, he found himself caressing her hand, wanting to pull her into him to hold her, and he'd even been overwhelmed with the urge to kiss her. She had beautiful lips and though he hung on every word she said, there were moments when her voice faded into the background and all he could think about was swallowing her into his arms and brushing his lips over hers.

Completely inappropriate for so many reasons. But Bella stirred him. Her spare, unflinching assessments cut astonishingly close and picked open wounds, fears, his very own failures. It was as though she saw into his heart and soul and plucked the threads that were anchored in humiliation and regret, causing all the awfulness to unspool at his feet. And though he did get defensive at the suggestion that being a banker made him morally bankrupt, the way she was so matter of fact about how she saw him, not mean or spiteful, softened his armor and turned him curious, letting his anger fade away.

Bella had put his shortcomings into sharp relief and he couldn't forget what she'd said. But he didn't know what to do with the realizations except to double down on remaking his life to be what it once had been, so busy and wonderful that he could ignore any further contemplation on the meaning of it. He would donate more money once he had something to give again. Determined, he felt more powerfully that bouncing from friends' homes to boarding houses to poorhouses was no way to live.

He entered the kitchen and found Bella cooking with Mrs. Tillman. Leonard and the men were seated and Penelope was setting an enormous platter of pancakes in the center of the table.

"Bart!" they all yelled in unison and he stopped himself from correcting them about his name.

Clemmie scooched her chair over and he sat beside her. "Keeping bankers' hours this morning?" she said.

"What? No, I—"

She elbowed him. He rubbed his arm where Clemmie's sharp bone had made contact yet again.

"Canoodling at Bella's, were you?" Clemmie stared at him. The group leaned in, waiting for a reply.

He couldn't speak. How did they know that he'd been to her barn and that he'd have loved to sit with her all day, arms wrapped around her?

"With the hens and the cat." Penelope set two small pitchers of syrup on the table. "You know, nuzzling them."

"Oh," he said through a relieved laugh. "Yes, the animals."

"Bella said you're a natural, that the animals loved you instantly. The girls laid extra today and just for you," Margaret said.

He relaxed into the chair. They weren't aware that it was Bella he wanted to wrap into a canoodle. "Oh, yeah. They did sort of take to me." He caught Bella's gaze from across the room. She smiled and lifted her spatula in some sort of salute. His hands turned sweaty and his neck heated up. He forced his mind to go to Leonard. "You're feeling better, Leonard? Your coloring's much, much pinker."

Leonard cleared his throat, indicating it wasn't as though he'd suddenly rid himself of all his ailments. "Much better. Must have been all the extra attention you've arranged for me. You're all quite gifted at doctoring."

Mrs. Tillman laughed a hearty laugh and looked over her shoulder even as she kept doing the dishes. "It's all a plan to get attention. I've seen this act before."

Leonard laughed so hard he fell into another coughing fit. "Enough of the jocularity, Mrs. Tillman. You'll have me in my grave yet if you keep up with your comedy routine."

Though this was only moderately funny, Mrs. Tillman's and Leonard's laughter was catching and caused the entire gang to fall apart over their coffee.

"That feels so good," Leonard said. "Laughter cures just about anything. Always a good prescription."

This made Mrs. Tillman turn fully around. "No grave for you, Leonard. I couldn't imagine a day without your smiling face."

And as the last bit of laughter trailed off, they made room for Bella and Mrs. Tillman at the table.

"The world's a beautiful place," Leonard said with a sigh. "Truly."

Everyone agreed as food was passed and passed again.

Bartholomew could have devoured the entire stack of pancakes, but he chewed slowly to refrain from making a pig of himself. He was about to take another bite when the doorbell rang.

They froze, only their gazes slipping from one to the other, eyebrows raised. "Who would that be?" Bella asked.

Margaret shrugged. "Dunno."

James rose and disappeared through the butler's pantry. They sat quietly, listening for some hint of what was happening. Tension gripped Bartholomew's stomach, suddenly feeling his former position in life again—here he was, a respected banker, squatting in a home where he once attended parties.

Voices grew louder and they turned to watch James enter with the banker, Mr. Buchanan.

Clemmie shot to standing. "You gave us two days. We have until tomorrow. You said. You promised."

Her voice boomed and Bartholomew instinctively reached for her hand, pulling her back into her seat. He turned and focused.

"Oh." Recognition flashed across Mr. Buchanan's face. "Bartholomew Baines. What brings you here to this gathering of…"

"Gathering, yes." He stood, hoping to cut off anything insulting the man might say. And he realized because he knew what might come out of Buchanan's mouth that it was further evidence of the vapid life he'd lived before, just as Bella had noted. "Gathering of friends who I'm quite sure, though I wasn't here at the time, you traded some eggs for two days' reprieve from foreclosure. I can assure you that none of us have broken the conditions of the deal."

Mr. Buchanan appeared confused. "Well, new friends for you, is it. That's fitting considering the state of your bank and… well, no matter. I suppose my neighbors will recover from your decision making." He held his hat to his belly. "I didn't come to throw you out early. In fact, I've come with good news."

The gang looked at each other, hope lighting their eyes.

"Yes," Bartholomew said, feeling more like one of them than a colleague to Mr. Buchanan. "Go on."

Mr. Buchanan gestured toward the food and eyed Mrs. Tillman who sprang up and offered her chair. She filled a plate of pancakes and slid the syrup pitcher to him.

"Oh my goodness. Did you use those special eggs for these? So fluffy. And the syrup."

"Bella made the syrup."

He stopped his fork midway to his mouth. "Well, you are quite the little livestock and agriculture artist, aren't you?"

Bella's face lit up and Bartholomew felt pride on her behalf.

"Turns out, it's because of you, Bella, that I'm back here with a new set of conditions."

He pulled a set of papers from his breast pocket and handed them to Bartholomew. "Open those up, son. You're accustomed to reading contracts."

Bartholomew unfolded the papers.

"Well, go on, read aloud," Clemmie said.

"Foreclosure on 5720 Ellsworth Avenue is set for…"

Bartholomew looked up with a grin. "January second."

A cheer went up and Bella wrapped her arms around Mr. Buchanan from behind. His face went red and he shimmied out of her grip. "Don't you want to know what caused this change in dates?"

"Yes, yes," Mrs. Tillman said putting steaming hot, fresh pancakes on his plate. The group quieted and he swallowed his food.

"Well, I took those eggs home and presented them like they were made of gold. I'm embarrassed to say her initial reaction wasn't what I hoped for. But that's the life we've been living—high on the hog, silver fork to silver plate—well, you know. I'm rich."

Mumbles of agreement filled the kitchen. "But in being so flush with treasure and luxury it appears we've lost the appreciation for the little things. Her exact words, not mine, but I listened and figured she might have a point. Suddenly. I knew—this was it. She picked up two eggs and was standing there bouncing them in her palm, up and down, up and down, and I got the distinct sense that she was going to pelt me with them. But instead she studied them closer and looked at me hard, like the kind of stone-cold look that turns your blood to ice and makes you wonder if the grim reaper might have entered the room with your name on his list."

Bella set a coffee mug in front of him. Bartholomew noticed she was still smiling like she knew what was coming next.

"Well, she didn't toss the eggs at me, she cracked one and then the other and they were empty of yolks. And I have to say I nearly bolted right back here to deliver an earful and toss you out on your behinds posthaste. But luckily for us all I've got a cool head and natural curiosity, so I stayed and watched my Misha pluck a tiny scroll from the bowl and unfurl it."

Everyone gasped. Bartholomew glanced at Bella, his own grin coming fast and wide. He couldn't wait to hear what Mr. Buchanan's little scroll said.

"So I'm thinking, what in the blue hell is going on here? And she reads the first note." He pulled a tiny note out of his pocket. "'We had our breakfasts—whatever happens in a house, robbery or murder, it doesn't matter, you must have your breakfast.' And the next one Misha read said, 'And earth was heaven a little the worse for wear. And heaven was earth, done up again to look like new.'"

Bartholomew saw Bella mouthing the quotes word for word.

"Well, next thing I know the wife's burst into tears, waterfalls worth just pouring down her face. And she flings herself at me like… like she used to when we were spry and feisty, if you know what I mean?"

Bella beamed and rubbed her arms as though she'd been struck with a chill of some sort.

"And when I got my lovely wife to stop blubbering long enough to talk, she looked at me with this softness, this long lost, but familiar love… in her eyes."

Everyone leaned toward Mr. Buchanan, every word magnetic.

"I stared into her eyes deeply and it was like my young wife was looking back at me. And I could see my youthful self in her gaze. And she says, 'Neddy'—she hasn't called me Neddy in twenty years— 'you've finally done it. You've finally heard what I was saying.'"

A collective "awww" filled the kitchen.

"Oh my, that's wonderful," Bella said, adding more coffee to his mug.

He grabbed her wrist. "That's not all. First, those quotes—"

"From *The Moonstone* by Wilkie Collins, 1868," Bella said.

"Well, turns out my dearest had been blabbering to me for years about that book and quoting this and that and I started to remember when we were first married she used to say, 'Whatever happens in a house, you must have your breakfast.' It was a joke and the son and I said it too, but didn't know it was from a book. It became sort of a daily vow we took, saying that no matter what happened between us we would meet every morning at breakfast to start again." He paused and Bartholomew couldn't believe what he was witnessing.

"It was… I don't know, business took off, more kids came, got loud, sick, laughing, wonderful, I don't know but somehow we stopped saying that to each other and we stopped thinking anything bad would ever happen to us. And nothing had, except that we forgot to meet each morning to set the little things right. That was the big bad thing that we hadn't even realized came between us."

"A tale for the ages," Clemmie said.

Mr. Buchanan nodded. "When she read the first note she burst out happy and tearful over that, and then the other quote about the world being heaven and just needing to be done up again she took to mean that the troubles of the world were going to give way to newness, goodness, the old way we were together. These quotes... and then the rest of the eggs! My goodness she butted the chef right out of the kitchen and started baking and cooking all my favorites. She made enough food to feed the soup kitchen in Oakland. And so we took it to them. The whole dinner crowd ate off her cooking, your eggs, Bella. And last night, Misha came back to me. I was the old me. I can't explain how this nonsense came to be real, the magic of these, well... so I re-examined what I was doing and you were right. There is no reason for me to take this house until January. You are free to stay. But with some conditions. Don't steal anything, and take some time to sweep up the outbuildings. Worthless garbage in the carriage house and blacksmith's shed—broken glass and old wood, but I need this place ready to go for buyers on January second."

They all looked at each other. "Agreed." It was difficult to believe any of this was happening.

Everyone shook Mr. Buchanan's hand. And when it came to be Bella's turn, he grabbed her tight and didn't let go. "Thank you, Bella Darling. Thank you for this enchanted moment. A new start. I couldn't have imagined something like this ever happening. Like Santa himself put his hand right into my life. This is going to be the best Christmas I've ever had."

"I'm so happy for you," Bella said.

"Misha thinks I finally listened to her and dug back through that book to find those quotes. She actually announced to the entire household that for at least one moment, for at least one Christmas, I would no longer be known as the resident Scrooge."

Bella hugged him hard. "You have no idea how happy that makes me."

"Really glad your life's on the upswing," Clemmie grumbled. "Others are still waiting for the magic."

"Well, because of Bella here, you have two weeks of a reprieve for you and your band of merry travelers. I'd file that under a little bit of magic."

They all nodded.

"Suppose that's a smidge of magic," Clemmie said with a grumble.

"Why not stop in for Christmas Eve?" Mrs. Tillman invited. "I'm sure we'll find something to make for dinner, before midnight services."

The rest of the group seemed panicked by that idea.

"Well, I doubt we'll be able to do that. We have our own party. Bartholomew—you've attended it before, right?"

"I have," he said, wanting to swallow his tongue and disappear into the crevices of the stone floor. A new flood of embarrassment swept in as he felt the gazes of his compatriots settle on him.

"Well, then you understand why I won't be able to break away for the evening. Especially with how depressed the city is right now. The city needs the Buchanan Christmas Eve Bash more than ever."

"Of course," Bartholomew said. "So many in need." He looked at his hands, then straightened. He wasn't the one who should feel shame in this case. The tension in the room from the irony of Mr. Buchanan's suggestion that the grand Christmas bash held for wealthy friends who'd maintained their positions and much of their wealth was serving those in need was laughable. But with the group having just been given their two-week reprieve, he wasn't going to poke at the man. Not right then.

James saw Mr. Buchanan out and returned to the kitchen. The crew let out whoops and cheers, hugging each other, Penelope yanking Bartholomew into the group of laughing, embracing misfits. He let himself feel grateful, lucky to have stumbled into the world of this group of strangers who were beginning to feel like more than that. When he conceded this notion, he was swept by sadness that his family didn't exist anymore and that the friends he'd thought would stand in as family hadn't when they had the first chance to kick him out of their circle.

James led Margaret to the settee by the fire. "You're looking pale. Maybe it's getting close to your time?"

Margaret shrugged. "Suppose it might be."

Leonard shuffled over and knelt beside Margaret, taking her hand and turning it over, putting his fingers at her wrist. "Your heart rate's good."

Margaret sank further into the settee, her breath turning even and relaxed. "Thank you, Leonard. You must have children, I suppose."

"I did have some. You rest here and we'll…" He stood and opened his arms. "We'll make a Christmas to remember."

Another cheer went up.

James smacked his hands together and then rubbed his palms, excitement seeping from every bit of him. "Arnold—you're our resident gardener. The property in the back is lined with holly. Evergreens everywhere. We need fresh greens for decorating. The Westminsters always cut their Christmas trees from the property so let's do that. Just one big one—let's not be greedy—for the foyer."

"Marvelous! This is exactly what we need. No use thinking about two weeks from now when we have a beautiful holiday to celebrate! I can show Arnold where the trees and holly bushes are," Bella said as she slipped on the sable cape, her eyes lighting up as she hugged herself with glee.

Bartholomew's stomach fluttered when he made eye contact with her. He wanted to go with Bella and Arnold.

"Margaret," Bella said. "You rest and when you feel better you can let us know how you want to help."

Bartholomew was about to suggest he go with Bella and Arnold to get the tree and greens when James patted his shoulder.

"Nathaniel, Bart, Penelope, and I will go to the attic and haul down decorations for the foyer and front rooms. Just enough to give us the flavor of Christmas this year. We don't want to take advantage. It isn't our home, after all."

Leonard raised his hand. "I'd like to contribute something to the festivities, but I'll need Bart's help."

Mrs. Tillman gazed at Leonard and confirmed for Bartholomew that Leonard meant something more to her than simply a decades-long boarder. She took his hand and held it between both of hers. "What do you mean?" she asked.

"A skating rink," Leonard said.

Silence draped over the kitchen.

"A what?" Bartholomew said.

"A rink," Leonard repeated. "We used to make one every year when my children were young and when… It was *wonderful*."

Mrs. Tillman craned to see out the window. "Suppose it's cold enough."

"It's a simple thing, really. But I promise it will be worth it," Leonard said.

James pulled a face and groaned a little. "I don't know."

Arnold went to the window. "Right there—the property just beyond the courtyard is as flat as I've ever seen in Pittsburgh."

Leonard smiled. "I'll take Bart with me. He can help me along so we can actually get it done."

"Shouldn't I go with Bella and Arnold? Taking down a Christmas tree is no small endeavor."

Bella lifted one arm and bent it, touching her bicep. "No need. I'm strong as an ox."

Leonard patted Bartholomew's back. "I promise the completion of a simple skating rink offers returns you can't imagine. *Divine* is the only word I can think to describe it."

Bartholomew wasn't buying that. But he'd begun to feel protective toward Leonard and certainly didn't want the older man to go back down the road where he couldn't even breathe or walk unsupported again.

Mrs. Tillman sighed. "I'll go to the insurance man to file my claim on the house."

James smacked his hands together again. "So it's settled. Our celebration may be simple and rustic compared to anything Mr. Buchanan is about to give, or that the Westminsters would have, but ours will be…"

"Full of love." Mrs. Tillman pulled Leonard's hand to her.

"Full of magic," Penelope said heading toward the back staircase.

"Full of beauty!" Bella said pushing her hand into the air.

She dug her arm through Arnold's and pulled him out the door, taking Bartholomew's breath with her. How he wished he was on the errand to cut the tree and gather the boughs.

Instead, Leonard was pulling him out the door. "James! I'll need some string to mark off the walls for where the rink will go. We've got four days until Christmas Eve!"

With that, another cheer went up and they scattered like Christmas mice—some racing into the attic, others trailing outdoors, and others to town.

And Bartholomew put his arm out for Leonard to take and they went to survey the area for the rink, Bartholomew wondering when the sheer joy the others seemed to feel was going to take him, too. What if it never did? What if he wasn't capable of feeling simple bliss that didn't sprout from the sight of growing funds written on a bank statement? Relief for the moment—he felt that strong and sure. But seeing the others, the gladness at what they were about to create, was ephemeral and temporary. How could it be worth the energy when after they left, none of what they'd celebrated or created would matter? He scoffed. It wasn't any more ephemeral than the very dollar bills and bank notes he'd lost for himself and others. If only he could feel the pleasure that he knew he should. If only.

CHAPTER 11
Bella

Bella and Arnold grabbed a pull wagon and tramped through the snow. They stopped to water and feed the hens the mixed nuts and oats she'd put in a pouch and tied around her waist. Then with wagon in tow and an ax and shears ready for chopping and clipping, she led Arnold around the grounds, pointing out any growth that might be used in festive ways. He oohed and awed at the beauty of the Westminster property. "The Reynolds had more land, but this, in the city, is grand and peaceful, and wow... I would have loved to work land like this."

When Arnold wasn't moving fast enough, Bella took the wagon handle and turned to pull it with her back toward where they were going, chattering at Arnold. They reached the holly bushes and he taught her how to clip them to get the largest bounty but also ensure that they would continue to grow full and lush. He explained that at the Reynolds' home they used to get Christmas trees with the root ball and then plant them on the property when the holiday was over.

"I can tell you love your work."

"I did. I do, I mean if I could get hired onto a property again. I assume this depression will lift soon. It just has to. I tried to talk to Bart about the state of economics, but he went white at the gills and I just let it go."

She tugged on the wagon and he pushed it. "Handsome Bart doesn't seem to be open about his banking affairs."

"*Handsome* Bart?" Arnold chuckled.

"Oh my, yes. Anyone can see that."

"So you're sweet on him?"

"Sweet on him? No. Just stating the obvious. And interested in what's not obvious. He's mysterious. But his dark eyes and dark hair and... he's handsome by any standard."

"He definitely cuts a fine figure, no doubt. But he's not fond of the position he's found himself in and I think he's embarrassed and quiet as a result of that. Not mysterious. Same old bank collapse story, same old banker."

"Hmmm," Bella said. "I don't know. There's something off about his story. Even if you account for him not having been as rich as a Frick or a Craig or even a Westminster—he should have options to stay other places with people he loves and… well, people like him may fall down, but they rarely end up crawling into boarding homes with a bunch of craftspeople and musicians and… well, something's not right."

"It's you who are mysterious. How is it you found yourself with nothing but some hens, a cat, and a barn to live in?"

There wasn't much of a story. And the bad parts weren't worth telling. She wasn't one to wallow and she'd long buried the details. "It's just my life. One thing rolls into another and the only thing I've had steady is a love for reading and people along the way who lend me books and I do odd jobs in return. I've been lucky. People do nice things for me and for that I am always grateful. And then the next person does something nice for me. And so on."

"Well, you undersell your own goodness. You're a good soul and people respond to your appreciation of them."

She sighed. "Suppose so. There was one job I wasn't so appreciative of. I was a laundress."

"That does sound like hard work."

"It was. But isn't that a wonderful word for doing back-breaking, strip your hands of its skin, work?" She giggled and turned, tugging the wagon along behind her. "Laundress. I love the word. But I must admit, I'm glad I don't do that anymore."

"I love how you look at things, Bella."

"And I love how you love the natural world. You should write nature stories for people to read."

"There." He stopped pushing and Bella's gaze followed where he was pointing.

"Ooooh. Yes," she said. "It's tall and fat and… well, just look at it—a perfect triangle." The evergreen loomed over them, serene and wondrous. "I almost don't want to cut it down."

"A Fraser fir," Arnold said. "My favorite."

She looked at the wagon already stuffed with greens.

"I know," he said. "You drag that back to the house, empty it, and send Nathaniel and James to help me with this wonderful tree. I'll prepare for its removal."

Bella let Nathaniel and James know Arnold needed their help. She assisted in organizing the decorations, but followed James's orders to let them be until he returned to direct their placement. While waiting for the tree to arrive, she went into the kitchen. Margaret had baked bread and was napping near the fire. From outside she heard voices and looked out the window to see that Bart and Leonard had staked off the dimensions of the rink. The thought of it made her heart speed up. She'd skated before and loved the feel of wind whipping through her hair, turning her cheeks red, imbuing a sense of life in her. Having a rink right outside the back door was as decadent as anything she'd considered for a home.

She put water on for tea and coffee and headed out to join the men. But when she got outside they were gone. Her eye caught a glimpse of footprints in the snow leading to the carriage house. She stepped into the prints, first using Leonard's then Bart's widely spaced treads, nearly doing splits to measure up. When she got to the carriage house she entered the dark space. The two men stood down the way near stacked crates, wood, and wagons. They had a lantern between them as they talked, not noticing her. She moved forward, and when they still didn't notice her approaching she stopped to listen.

"Now, Bart. Why on earth are you so negative about this venture? I can tell you that skating under the stars with a fire and marshmallows—"

"We don't have money for marshmallows—"

"That's beside the point. It's the idea of having a gathering place for people to do something fun and…"

"But all this work. You're not feeling well and then what? We all pack up and leave on January 2nd and it's like none of this ever happened. There's nothing to show for this. We should all be out beating the streets for work or a new boarding house or—"

Leonard took Bart's shoulder. "Let me tell you a story about a young man… younger, anyway. A doctor, an engineer. During the Civil War he helped raise money for Pittsburgh Sanitary Commission—$322,000 through a bazaar in Allegheny City. No one thought they could raise a dime during such hard times, but in just *eighteen days*, they raised that incredible amount. Musicians played the 'Relief Polka' and 'When This Civil War Is Over' and so many more. Singers sang, potters donated their wares, glassmakers made goblets and stained-glass ornaments and windows, clothiers and crafters of every type brought their things to sell. And then the doctor bought supplies with the funds and headed to the front lines, enlarging hospitals and caring for soldiers. And eventually he was captured and sent to Libby Prison."

"In Richmond?"

"Right there." Leonard sighed. "Thankfully the engineer created a little funnel that captured water and hosed it into the jail for fresh drinking water for his fellow prisoners. The prison was so tightly packed with men that the guards never got close enough to the windows to see the water funnels he'd made. But making them sliced his hand good, right up between thumb and forefinger, and he thought for sure it would be the end of him, that infection would set in."

"Wait. Engineer? I thought the doctor was the man who got captured."

"Oh… I wasn't clear. The engineer and the doctor were the same man."

"Wow, he was both? That's impressive."

Leonard gripped Bart's hand. "Some might have thought the doctor wasted his skills in taking all the supplies to the front and then getting captured. But the engineer in him saved even more lives once he arrived."

Bella was touched by the story and nearly broke her silence, but Bart's voice stopped her.

He lifted Leonard's hand and was looking closely at it—the scars snaking between finger and thumb. "You? You're the doctor *and* the engineer?"

Leonard nodded. "I am. My life has taken so many turns and tumbles. You might think something like a skating rink being so important to me is silly, but I promise. You'll see."

From outside the barn Bella heard the shouts of James and the others and so she bolted without Leonard and Bart even seeing she'd been there.

CHAPTER 12

Bartholomew

Bartholomew was so engrossed in Leonard's story of the Civil War that he almost felt like he needed a rest. He had so many questions but instead of asking them, he was moved to explain something to Leonard. This brave, industrious man had lived an extraordinary life that no one was even aware of and suddenly it meant everything for Leonard to understand that although Bartholomew had lost his bank and everything else, that he had not behaved dishonorably.

Leonard pointed to some lumber. "Pull those aside and stack them. They should work nicely for the retaining walls."

Their quiet work made talking seem less threatening to Bartholomew. "Can I tell you something?"

"Sure."

"Bella and Margaret said something about a bankers' type of mind. And Nathaniel joked about bankers' hours. And boy, oh boy, hearing your story about the things you've done, I can see why people have decided bankers don't offer real value, they just…"

Bartholomew tossed a board on the pile and leaned forward, hands onto his knees. "I didn't steal from anyone. And although I've recently joined the Duquesne Club, I'm not one of the Number 6 Luncheon Group."

"Oh, Shoyer, Herron, Jones, Chalfant—those fellas?"

"The very ones."

"Successful fellows." Leonard leaned against the wagon catching his breath as Bartholomew continued moving lumber into the pile.

"Though I dreamed of being invited into that group that's well over six men now, I had nowhere near their money. Just barely opened my banking doors when it all—"

"Crashed."

"That's right. And I'm not saying I've built anything like you did. I just go to galas and support causes and I donate money to pay for things like sanitary items for a war. But I'm not a scoundrel or a thief. I'm not a heartless lout."

Leonard coughed and then caught his breath again, sitting on the side plank of the wagon. "Yet you feel like one? Why does it sound like you think maybe others think you're a scoundrel or a thief or a lout?"

Bartholomew's throat tightened. Perhaps he shouldn't confess. Perhaps it was best to just let Leonard think whatever he chose. "Because when someone came to ask me for help I didn't do it until it was too late."

"What was too late?" Leonard asked.

Bartholomew's breath came shallow.

Leonard gestured toward the back of the garage. "Bring those little iron pipes over here. Keep talking."

Bartholomew took three trips back and forth before the words just tumbled out of him. "When this whole thing happened in May I couldn't believe it was going to be what it turned into. I just couldn't believe that the railroads would fail and that people would rush to withdraw their money or that the market would bottom out."

"Happened before. But yes, it's hard to fathom," Leonard said.

"And so at first when depositors came, I doled out a little to everyone. And then my own mortgage came into question and I had to pay on that. And then…"

"And then?"

"Mrs. Franks shows up one day and tells me her husband has put most of the cash from the loan I'd made to them into a grocery business specializing in fruits. They still had some silver in the vault. So she's nervous and pacing, telling me he's got orders on bananas from Jamaica, oranges from Los Angeles, avocados from Hawaii, pineapples and lemons, and she went on and on saying how they were also growing berries and fruits that were native to Pennsylvania, but that just before the crash, Mr. Franks had ordered the foreign fruits with every last penny they had. And now the farmers had sent word that they could not honor their deal. They had spent the money with their own creditors and they couldn't ship the fruit, if there was anyone even shipping at all. Their entire world, Mrs. Franks's world, was collapsing."

"And she wanted what they'd deposited in the bank to help tide them over?"

Bartholomew nodded. "And she needed another loan." He sat across from Leonard, sorting the iron pipes. "But I'd already promised to parcel out fair amounts to others—all the depositors, hoping no one would lose everything. She started crying. Not sobbing, still talking, but just this flood of tears down her face and I couldn't help her with more. I could see her desperation. She explained that her husband was threatening to harm himself if something didn't change. He was unable to see that their own fruits would come into season and they could at least sell those until the world sorted out. And then there were my own problems. My own mortgage and…"

"You said no."

He nodded. "No to lending her more."

"And so she came back a week later." Bartholomew's voice cracked.

Leonard gave a reassuring nod.

"Her husband was dead. He'd gotten enraged, chased the children around the house and yard, threatening everyone. And then when the kids hid in the cellar, he dug stones from beneath the berry bushes and stuffed his pockets with them and leapt from the Smithfield Street Bridge. This time Mrs. Franks wasn't even crying. She was like this empty shell. She didn't have to finish the parts about a funeral or the children or anything else. She just wanted me to know how it ended. She didn't ask for a thing and I didn't have to tell her no this time."

"And so you have to deal with having spent the money on yourself instead of the desperate family?"

"No. I emptied every last dollar and dime from the vault for her and her children. And that is how my mortgage went belly up. And the rest of the depositors, including good friends, lost everything they'd put with me because I gave it to her. As if that could somehow bring her husband back. And now no one wants anything to do with me. The story was in the papers in July. And I just… I don't know. I helped the Franks family too late, and helping them at all bankrupted the people closest to me. I thought my friends could weather it. If I was going to suffer I figured we could suffer together. But… no."

Leonard scratched the back of his neck. "I see how complicated all of that is. You gave away the money you needed and still lost everything else. Friends and… support."

Bartholomew felt tears rising. "I don't blame any of them really. How could I? I let all of them down in different ways. And now just before I fall asleep or just as I'm waking up all I can envision is Mr. Franks standing on that bridge, pockets stuffed full of rocks. Just picturing it is unbearable for me. I can't imagine how his family feels."

"I understand nightmares that come on the fringes of awake and asleep. I sure do."

"But you did so much good," Bartholomew said. "Real good. Not good works that came too late."

"You're young, Bart. You've a chance to figure your life out. You've been caught up in this machine, this grand market that's supposed to work one way, and it does until… well, until it breaks down and people are left to see they depend on networks of goods and services and paper notes, and like you've seen, some of us haven't built anything that can feed us when all the papers have been taken on the winds."

"And bankers are certainly part of that machine."

"They are."

"I am."

The two men stared at each other.

"You are."

Bartholomew swallowed hard.

"But you did the best you could at the time. You tried to help everyone, and when things got worse you tried to help the person in the most need. But now you need to help yourself. Create a life that's meaningful even if you never make another bank deposit, let alone own another bank. What is it you can create for the world that is important even if small?"

Bartholomew scoffed and tears splashed onto his shirt. He swiped at his cheeks with the backs of his hands. "Nothing. I don't even know how to make a simple ice rink. How much easier can a project be? The earth itself is literally an ice rink right now and I'm not sure I can make anything at all."

Leonard pushed to standing, his wheezing louder than it had been all that morning. "Well, we better change that then. No time like the present."

Bartholomew drew a deep breath and stood hands on hips looking at the assembled materials. "First we pound in the pipes?"

"Very good. See. You have instincts."

This made Bartholomew laugh. "That's ridiculous."

"Well, maybe. But you have to start somewhere and it sounds like until that happened with the Franks family, you just never bothered to listen to your instincts before, to respond rather than dictate. You did a good thing when you realized it needed to be done."

Leonard withdrew a piece of paper and pencil from his pocket. "Now, it's time to let go of what went wrong with the banks, the crash, the Franks family, your friends. Everyone's just scared and lashing out and grasping for whatever solid thing they can latch on to. Your friends will come around. Someday. You should always remember what you learned, but you can't let it harden you over like an eggshell or numb you like a good bourbon. You want to live fully and that means feeling all the things that you've been through, then embracing what's to come and what's right in front of you. Like Bella Darling. She's as soft and open as a person can be."

Bartholomew nodded. "Bella Darling. She doesn't have a care in the world."

"Oh, she does. She cares more than most."

"But it's not like she lost—well, she never said she lost anyone or anything."

"You just met her. Heck, I just met her. So maybe you're right. Or maybe she's simply figured out what's important."

Bartholomew thought of their conversation in the barn, that he'd assumed she was simple and silly even as she had expressed profound ideas. He bent down to adjust his shoe. The blisters that had started to form when he went on his great pilgrimage the day of the fire had gotten worse.

"When we get back to the house, I'll put my doctoring to use and tend to your feet. And maybe you can find some boots suitable for outdoor activity in the cloakroom. Those shoes weren't constructed for making ice rinks."

"Guess not."

"You get the pipe and boards to the rink area and I'll sketch out the plans just so we have it down. Just in case."

Bartholomew picked up a load of boards and put them over his head. He was exiting the barn when Leonard's words hit him. He turned. "Just in case of what?"

Leonard hesitated then shrugged. "In case of all the things we can't imagine happening until they do."

Bartholomew saw how weak Leonard appeared in that moment and hoped one of those things that might happen wasn't connected to the health and well-being of his new friend.

CHAPTER 13
Bella

Bella swept open Maple Grove's mammoth front doors to make room for the beautiful Christmas tree. She watched in awe as Nathaniel, Arnold, and Bartholomew carried the grand lady into the foyer. They moved in synchronized steps, directed by Leonard, quietly coaching, "Little higher, watch the boughs on the doorjamb, careful, *careful*." The men nimbly and gently worked as though the tree were a person, not just some thing that would stand as the symbol of the most magnificent day of the year.

It was then Bella realized that the men had managed to shovel around the root ball and it was still attached to the tree. She could tell by Arnold's grip on the root end of things that he was both pleased and concerned. Bella covered her mouth, smiling behind her hands. The tree was alive. How wonderful that they didn't simply chop it down. It hadn't looked so enormous in its outdoor home, among its even taller friends. Arnold had crafted a plywood platform with a hole cut into its center and put a bucket underneath to hold the root ball and keep it watered.

When they got it into its spot, they backed away, gingerly stepping, arms extended as though they might have to catch it suddenly. When it looked as though the tree was settled, they seemed to all exhale simultaneously. Nathaniel dramatically dragged his hanky across his forehead.

Bella took Arnold's hand and squeezed it. "She's alive."

"She's too beautiful to just chop down. We've got to take her back home after the holiday, on New Year's Day, since we have to…"

They all knew what he didn't add to the sentence.

"She," Bartholomew said. "Agreed. She's a she for sure."

Arnold sighed. He lifted his hands and gestured for everyone to come closer. "You all okay with me naming this robust lady?"

"She's yours." Bella patted his arm.

"Margarite. After my mother. Christmas was her favorite time of year."

They stood there staring up at the evergreen honoring Arnold's mother.

"Margarite. A beautiful name," Bart said, his gaze falling to Bella and Arnold's clasped hands.

Bella thought she saw a look of discomfort flash across his face and she released Arnold.

"I almost don't want to decorate her she's so perfect just like this," Arnold said.

"Nonsense." Clemmie shuffled closer, gently taking a bough in her hand. She leaned in and drew a deep breath. "Every lady needs to dress for the holidays. A little sparkle here, a dash of color there."

Everyone stared at Clemmie, surprised.

When she noticed she was being watched she dropped the bough and straightened. "What? You think Martin and I didn't swirl around a dancefloor or two in the good old days? You think Bart here's the only one who's gone calling at the Olivers' on New Year's Day?"

Bart studied her. "You went to their New Year's Day Festival of Friends and Family?"

"Henry Oliver's place? The coal man?" Leonard asked.

Clemmie nodded. "The very one."

"It's good to be in coal," Margaret said.

The group gave a collective sigh as though they'd all agreed.

Bella saw Bart's confused expression. "Clemmie—" he said, but Leonard started coughing and Bart turned toward him.

Leonard batted Bart's coddling hands away and began to work with Arnold to give orders in further securing Margarite. "Tie off tighter there—no, not there—yes, there! But gentle with the binding, gentle, gentle," he said. And on and on.

Bella sorted some ornaments and heard her name being called. "Bella?"

She turned to see Ada Pritt, the woman's husband, and their three children standing on the threshold of the front doors.

Their faces were bright with the sight of the grand Margarite.

Ada finally put her attention back on Bella. "I heard about the fire and thought you all could use some beans, at least, something. The doors were open and so we just…"

Bella took Ada's hand and that of one of the children. "Come, come. Help us decorate."

And they did just that. Ada's husband Bruce hauled a wagon full of bean sacks around the house to the kitchen. And the group tenderly added glass balls of red, silver, and gold, providing spangling and bangling worthy of the stunning tree.

The children never stopped smiling and when it was time for them to leave, Ada reminded Bella to soak the beans overnight so they could be slow cooked the next day. "I know it's not a fabulous meal—*beans*—but it's something."

"It's more than something, Ada," Margaret said. "We'll eat for a week on what you brought us. In fact, why don't you come back for Christmas Eve supper?"

Everyone eyed each other, concerned. They didn't want to risk breaking one of Mr. Buchanan's conditions.

Bella spread her arms wide. "Mr. Buchanan said *no stealing*. Not *no inviting others to enjoy supper* on one of the most glorious nights of the year."

They nodded.

"And a bonfire," Leonard said. "We'll build a fire pit near the skating rink. It will be wonderful."

Bart let out a big exhale.

"What's wrong, Scroogie?" Clemmie batted his chest.

"Scroogie?" Bart looked offended. "I didn't say a word."

"Didn't have to. What's got you all bristly now?"

He shook his head. "Nothing, but." He looked toward the door. "Warmed up quite a bit today and I don't think the ice will be ready if temperatures stay like this."

Leonard pulled himself up straighter. "It's all right. We'll have the bonfire at least. At least that."

"I guess," Bart said, staring into the yard wishing he could will the temperature to drop again.

"A holiday gathering." Mrs. Tillman clutched her hands to her chest. "Holiday merrymaking. I could not be more pleased." She stalked off to the butler's pantry. "Those beans aren't going to soak themselves."

Bella and the gang bedecked the foyer, the two front parlors, and the dining room with boughs of spruce, fir of every kind, and holly. Bart carried a crate of cast-off branches around back and swept the needles and leaves that had fallen to the floor.

Bella saw him limping as he finished up.

"What's wrong with your foot, Bart?"

He lifted one then the other. "Blisters. Started a good set the day of the fire, after I met you and thought you were…"

She felt a gurgle of laughter rising up in her. "Oh, my gosh, so much has happened. I forgot that you thought I was one of the Westminster daughters."

"Well, I was so angry at… well, everything, that I ran for miles. So stupid. And by the time I got back to Mrs. Tillman's my feet were raw and the fire was raging."

She imagined his blisters must be worse after how he helped extinguish the fire and all the work he'd been doing at Maple Grove.

Leonard appeared with a small bag. "Found this in the pantry. Got to be some bandaging in it and some tinctures or ointments. Got to be." He coughed again, bent over.

"I'll bandage his feet," Bella said. "You go lie down, Leonard. You'll be no use tomorrow if you don't get some rest."

He agreed to let Bella do the nursing but said he needed to get some water. And so they went into the kitchen and dug through the bag to see what they could use. Leonard told his doctoring and war stories. After he'd had his third glass of water he looked over his shoulder at Margaret who'd settled back onto the settee near the fire. "You okay, mama bear?"

Margaret rubbed her belly. "I feel better than I have in weeks."

"A family will do that," Leonard said and none of them disagreed. "I think I'm going to head up for an early night. Lungs are tight again."

And he refused any support as he disappeared up the back staircase. "I'm not dead yet, folks," his disembodied voice came strong and loud.

No one responded.

"You can laugh," Leonard's voice came as his feet shuffled upward. "That was a joke. Don't lose your humor. Not this close to Christmas. Jesus had a wonderful sense of humor."

And so they let the laughter fill the room as Mrs. Tillman and Penelope filled the vats with water to soak the beans. Bella sat across from Bart, a towel over her lap, one foot on top of that.

"You've managed to make blisters along the side of your feet and on the heels. That's quite a feat."

"I'm a very talented man," he said, seeming to be less uncomfortable in her presence than when he'd come to the barn.

Arnold sauntered in, showing them a glass bottle. "Made this for blisters I get from work." He dumped a yellowed liquid into the bowl Bella had prepared. "Put your feet in it for a soak. Fifteen minutes should do it. Better than anything in that bag Leonard dug up."

Bart flinched as he dunked his feet into the bowl between him and Bella.

Arnold stared at Bart's feet as though he was waiting to see something happen. "I've gotten my formula down, and though it stings, a bowl of water infused with apple cider vinegar will heal you fast. Then when you've let your feet air dry, add a little of this." Arnold drew a little jar from his pocket. "I was telling Bella earlier how the Reynolds family took an active interest in their gardens and property and greenhouse. And they even had some exotic plants brought in. One of them was aloe vera. And that plump plant produces an incredible salve. So after your feet dry, dab some of that onto the wounds, then let the air do more work. Then bandage them loosely for the night. That should have you healed whip-fast."

They thanked Arnold. He lifted one hand above his head. "Welcome. Back to the greenhouse for me. There's a treasure at every turn."

When they were alone Bart broke the silence. "Tell me about your family." He swished the water around with his feet.

Bella folded and refolded the gauzy bandaging. "My family." She didn't talk about family often. She had enough literary stories at her fingertips that she rarely got cornered into discussing her own family, the lack of stories they inspired.

"Yes, tell me about them."

She looked at the ceiling. She didn't know where to start. She knew what people liked to hear about family and that wasn't a story she had wrapped up nice and neat with velvet ribbon.

"Tell me your favorite line in your favorite story and I'll tell you about my family."

"Bella. You're hellbent on embarrassing me, aren't you?"

"What?"

"I don't have any stories cataloged in my mind. I told you, my mom read to me often, but I'm ashamed that I don't remember any lines in particular. I remember the nursery rhymes and fairy tales and that she never went without a book in hand. But I am devoid of literary interest or information."

Bella sighed. "That's a shame. I really thought maybe you were—"

"What? The man who likes long talks by the fire? Who carries literary words in his mind and unfurls them like magic carpets for his true love to step onto and take to the sky for adventure and riches beyond belief?"

She leaned forward. "How about just laying the literary words across a small stream like stepping stones?"

He looked away.

"You *don't* like talks by the fire? Or walks across streams? I realize we can't reserve a magic carpet, but talks by the fire? That's hardly extravagant."

He looked over his shoulder. Margaret was asleep, the fire blazing. "I love talks by the fire. Look at us here. I'd prefer not needing medical intervention while talking but… Of course. I just thought it was curious that you thought you might catch a soul mate by putting notes in eggs. Like a fly fisherman of love."

She giggled. She liked that image. "Yet here you are." She crossed her arms and stared at him. His cheeks reddened and he shifted, making the water slosh onto the floor.

He covered his mouth looking concerned.

She bent and wiped the wet floor with a rag. "Oh, don't worry, Bart. It's not like you entered into a contract to marry me because you read my notes and hunted me down and then wounded yourself after being so unsettled by my very existence. It's not like my presence means anything at all to you. I wouldn't expect it to. We aren't anything alike."

"I didn't say I thought—"

"It's all right. Foot up," she said then patted it dry in her lap.

"Air dry," he said.

She narrowed her eyes on him.

"Arnold said to let my feet air dry."

"Well, pull the other one out and set it on the towel with the first." He followed instructions. She studied the blisters to be able to measure the difference the next day. "Feel any better at all?"

"Little," he said.

When they'd sat in strange silence for a bit, discussing the weather and anything insignificant that they could, she pressed her fingertips over his skin to check for dryness. Next she dabbed the aloe vera onto his skin.

He flinched.

"That hurt?"

"A little."

"Well, pain's part of life, isn't it?"

"So brave when you're not talking about yourself," he said, winking at her.

She couldn't really argue with that.

"Tell me about your family. I explained why I couldn't tell you what you wanted to hear. That deserves something in return."

She nodded. "You've got nice feet for a man."

"Bella. Tell me why you're here living alone in a barn coaxing hens to lay more eggs than should be possible? Where are all your people?"

She began to wrap the one foot, checking it for the right looseness as she layered the gauze. "Once upon a time, there was a baby whose parents died of the grippe. A couple years later her grandparents died of old age and she was just lucky enough to get shuffled from one nice person's home into the next until she ended up here. People have been good to her so she's happy wherever she lands. She has to be. Because the alternative would be…"

She searched for the right word.

"What?"

She stopped wrapping and paused, thinking. "Unthinkable. To slide into the sadness of it all would be awful and she'd be full of hopelessness and angst and simply never—"

"But aren't you lonely?"

"Aren't you?"

He studied her but didn't reply.

She knew it must be hard for someone like him to admit to loneliness. Heck, it was hard for her to admit she might, just might, feel lonely at times. She gestured for him to set his wrapped foot down and she started on the other. "I can imagine that your life, once full of invitations to the Phipps' home, the Magees' and Childs' and Scaifes', could fill a lot of gaps in what might be missing in your life."

She stopped dabbing the ointment and met his gaze. "So tell me the truth. For I spend an inordinate amount of time reading about fairy-tale families with untold wealth and every convenience known to man, and love tales that end with happy people having every single thing they need. Tell me the truth. Do all those people living in all those fairy-tale mansions seem any happier than I am in my barn?"

He shifted in his seat. She was quite sure if Bart could have gotten up and stalked away, he would have. His discomfort with their conversation made her keep a gentle but firm hold on him. When he didn't answer she continued with the ointment and then the wrapping. She glanced up to see him watching her. The intensity caused her to bobble the gauze, but she caught it before it fell into the bowl.

Heat crept up her neck and another glance at him filled her stomach with butterflies. She supposed he might not want to spoil her sense of a fairy tale happy ending by admitting that none of those people were as wonderfully gleeful as the stories told. Or he didn't want to admit to himself the answer was that Bella was just as happy with nothing as all those people with everything. She shook her head and finished.

"Arnold said for you not to put shoes back on until morning. And I'd appreciate it if you waited for me tomorrow morning before you take off the bandages so I can see the results."

He agreed to that and stood. "Wait. You can't go in the dark. Alone, I mean."

She squinted at him. "I do it all the time, Bart. Haven't had a chaperone since… well, never." She lidded the vinegar bottle and ointment jars and set them on the windowsill before washing her hands. She could feel Bart's scrutiny and she almost gave into the urge to stay for some tea, to be with Bart longer.

Mrs. Tillman and Penelope emerged from the cellar with the crocks to cook the beans in after they'd soaked for the night. "You leaving?" Mrs. Tillman asked. She set down her crocks and took Bella's face in her hands. "Stay, enjoy a feast of bread and butter with us."

Bella thought of her animals, her loyal companions. "Gotta feed the girls and Simon. He must be livid at my absence. Tomorrow I have to take eggs to market." Her life was simple, but her little animals were dependent on her.

She tossed on what she'd now come to think of as her sable cloak, lit a small skating lantern, and trekked back to the barn. The ground was swampy and she passed by the staked-off skating rink area and felt a tug at her heart. The temperatures kept rising after being frigid. Leonard was so excited about that rink and she hoped that Bart's weather fears were unfounded, that it would freeze deeply enough for the ice to be ready for Christmas Eve.

She listened for coyotes. Silence. They must have made their way to other sections of the city or been managed by one of the property owners down the way. Still, she didn't want the hens in the coop. She called for them and they appeared one after the other, seeming irritated with the now muddied land. Simon was peeved as well, stopping short of her, offering a scolding meow. She turned toward the barn, hens trailing behind her. The silence made room for the clear sound of laughter coming from the big house. Penelope's laugh rang out, then Nathaniel's, then… music. The strains of a violin made Bella stop. She looked over her shoulder. The notes were slow and beautiful and carried a sense of sadness. She wasn't schooled in music the way she'd managed to become with books. And for the first time, the feeling she felt at being separate from others, the group at the house, made her want to cry. She choked back her surprise at that along with a sob. What was happening to her?

The music stopped and more laughter came. An upbeat polka followed and a whoop came from Arnold, or at least she thought it was his whoop. She didn't believe Bart was the whooping type. She slid open the door to the barn and led her animals inside. She set the fire and lit it, pulling her book onto her lap—the same one Bart had been reading when he came to call the other day. She laughed at the image of him with the hens and Simon sitting on every surface of him that they could. "Oh, Bart," she said to no one.

She shook her head, wanting to rid herself of this new longing for the company of others. Especially because January 2nd would mean splintering. The very sound of the word was painful. She didn't want to layer in any more discomfort than she was feeling already. What was the use of yearning for togetherness when they were soon to only remember each other as short-lived acquaintances who happened to share a hard time together, who were lucky enough to come together to make their worlds momentarily better? If she kept the idea of her pending aloneness at the forefront of her mind, at the center of her heart, then when they finally left the Westminsters', it would be like they never lived together at all. It would feel like nothing had been different from the life she'd been living before she'd met them.

She washed up, and climbed to her loft with Simon. Like always she turned on her side to study the stars out the window. But the clouds were low and dark and before she could open the book on the bedside table, she'd fallen into deep, peaceful sleep.

CHAPTER 14
Bartholomew

Even though he was sharing a bedroom with other grown men, Bartholomew slept better the night his feet were bandaged than he had in ages. He rose before daylight, refreshed and ready to be as useful as possible. Though he was no closer to figuring out how to rebuild his life, he was inspired by the physical work they'd been engaging in at the Westminsters'. No solid plan was forming in his mind, but the energy around ideas sprouting when he least expected it lifted his spirits and told him that he would indeed figure something out soon. Instead of worrying about the lack of plan at the moment, he simply jotted down anything that came to him, scrawling on scrap paper the family had left by their no-longer-working telephone. He could have dug his own pocket notebook out of his briefcase but he didn't want to open it and be reminded of all that had gone wrong. Not yet.

Remembering his promise to not unwrap the bandages until Bella returned that morning, he told Mrs. Tillman he'd drain the soaking beans just as soon as Bella arrived. Until then, he helped Mrs. Tillman ready the ingredients. They cut onions, measured salt and pepper.

Mrs. Tillman pointed to the cabinet above the sink. "Up there. Can't reach the ketchup bottles."

He got a couple down.

"Supposed to use tomato paste in the beans, but ketchup will do in a pinch. 'Specially if it's Heinz."

"Good people," he said as he removed the lid from one bottle.

"The Heinzes?"

"I've had a few cocktails with the mister and missus."

He measured out the ketchup in increments of two tablespoons. "That family's always looking out for those in need and… Sarah Heinz is quick with a donation or a kind word. Yeah. They're really good people."

Mentions of the Heinzes made Bartholomew consider what people might say about him in his absence. He knew what most thought of him at that moment—they didn't understand that he'd let his friends down in an attempt to help those in more dire need, that he'd also lost everything that once lent him comfort, that told the world who he was, the kind of person he had been. Successful. Fun. A good fellow. He imagined people mentioning his name at that moment weren't characterizing him as "good people."

The sun was barely up when Bella arrived with a basket of eggs in her arms and Simon perched on her shoulder like a parrot.

Bartholomew couldn't ignore the surge of glee that hit him when she appeared. He relieved her of the basket and set it on the counter.

"You've brought us a friend," Mrs. Tillman said.

"He's a little peeved that I was gone so long yesterday, so I figured I'd bring him along."

Mrs. Tillman smiled. "Check your patient's twinkle-toes so we can get these beans mixed and into the oven. Lots to do today."

Bartholomew sat and Bella removed the bandages. She gasped when she revealed the skin on the first foot.

He lifted it. "Well. Look at that."

Bella lifted his foot, turning it back and forth, her touch sending excited chills through him. She was nurturing and warm and suddenly he wanted her touching him all over. If only that were appropriate or possible.

"Still a little red but no oozing, no seeping," Bella said. She set the foot down and reached for the other. "Does it *feel* healed?"

"Sure does." His voice was full of the same wonder she felt as well.

She nodded at what she saw when she unveiled the second foot. "Looks like our Arnold's not only a gifted gardener, he's an apothecary, too."

"Sure looks that way."

Bella wiped her hands and rewrapped the feet. "Suppose you ought to take it easy on those feet for now. Maybe there's a pair of broken-in boots in the cloakroom. Don't think your dressy shoes will be forgiving to your newly healed heels."

"Don't suppose." He pulled on the fresh socks Mrs. Tillman set on his lap.

"Oh, Mrs. Tillman," Bella said on the way to the cloakroom, "I brought you the last of my maple syrup stores. Bottom of the basket. Three jars. Big, though. And I thought we could make maple bread and use the rest for anything we might need. Don't suppose I'll be able to travel with jars of syrup once we're booted out."

Her words draped a cloak of silence over the kitchen.

"Don't suppose," Bartholomew said. He pressed his chest. The aching there stole his breath.

The sound of a violin startled them.

Nathaniel sauntered in. "Don't get all glum on me, folks. I've written up a storm all night—five songs, and they're cheerful and snappy like the season, because we're all together in this mansion…" He sighed. "I want to live the next eleven days like they're never going to end."

Leonard shuffled in, taking Nathaniel by the shoulder. He looked weaker than the day before. "That's what I like to hear. Didn't survive doctoring at the front and a stint in Libby prison to live any other way. Joy to the beautiful world."

Leonard's cheeriness made it easy to ignore his pale coloring and wheezy breathing.

"Heck, I'll even give up on my skating rink if it means being in good humor. But not just yet. I feel cold, bone biting weather on its way. I just know it. All in good time."

Bella reappeared with two sets of boots. "Let's try these, Bart."

She knelt and loosened the laces on one.

Bartholomew leaned forward and put a hand on her shoulder. A tendril of her hair brushed the back of his hand. "Call me Bartholomew." How could he tell her that he longed to hear his full name roll off her tongue? That he wanted to remember how it sounded when she said it when the group went their separate ways.

She pulled a face. "You're a Bart around here. Around us anyway. You'll get used to it."

He grumbled.

Bella focused on the boot. "Lift," she said.

He followed orders, wiggling his foot into the kind of boot he'd never tried before. It was made for someone who worked in a forest or a garden or a field. Even as a boy, his play boots hadn't been this rustic.

Bella held the mouth open as far as she could. "Careful now. Don't want to agitate the wounds."

He wiggled his foot into the boot and he exhaled. Relief. He stood. It felt good, comfortable even. He circled his foot in the air. "These are *great*. My goodness, if I'd known boots like this were so comfortable I might have bought myself a pair a long time ago."

"So they're a fit?" Her face brightened as her eyes met his. Electricity shot through him. He wished he had a full body's worth of injuries for her to bring back to health.

"I can't believe it," Bartholomew said. "It's like they were made for me. They *really* fit."

"All right, Cinderella." She tied the boot even when he told her he could do it. She looked up at him with a mischievous smile, a light in her eyes reminding him of the first day they'd met, the easy laugh when she rolled in the snow and they'd grappled for the paper that had soared with the wind.

"Cinder-*fella*, starring Bart Baines." She laughed and laughed at her joke. She stood, hands on hips. "Back to work then, Cinder—no. Bar-thol-o-mew."

She laughed again, hands over her mouth. "Nope. You're a Bart."

Her presence tied his tongue and he marveled at how someone like her could have that effect on him. It wasn't like she was special. It wasn't like he could court her because when he got his old life back, then what? Yet the attraction. He watched her waltz away, skirts flouncing in a way that made him wonder what her unclothed hips looked like as she moved. He may have been enraptured by her, but once she was finished with fussing over his feet, she seemed to have forgotten he was alive.

What was he thinking? Bella *was* special. She was the definition of it. And right there with the admission of her uniqueness and her ability to utterly weaken and inspire him, excite him, lure him, he found that he couldn't breathe. He reached for his chest again. *What's happening to me?* He couldn't stop watching her as she sorted the eggs—some for Mrs. Tillman, some for the market. And he found himself praying to God that she hadn't slipped any more notes into any more eggs.

He realized right then, he wanted to be the one she wanted. He wanted to be the man she'd hoped for when she slipped the teeny scrolls into the magic eggs and imagined just the right man showing up at her door.

CHAPTER 15
Bella

Bella quickly sold her eggs at the market and bought the things that Penelope, Margaret, and Mrs. Tillman suggested the household would need to survive, to help celebrate the impending holiday.

Feeling good about the day, she was on her way to remind Ada Pritt to bring her family on Christmas Eve to enjoy a bonfire and skating if it got cold enough. She neared Ada's table and saw her draping a woman in a scarf and hat set. The woman nodded and handed Ada money.

Almost to the table, a ruckus down the aisle made Bella stop. Several women were shouting at a vendor. The man's eyes were wide and for a moment, Bella feared for his safety. But then he wound up and swung at one of the women and Bella ran toward them. Before she reached them, a woman lunged and took him by the collar. This fueled the fracas and suddenly twenty women were snatching up everything they could see.

"My child's starving and you sold me rancid flour. I want it replaced." The man declared it impossible for flour to go bad.

"Then it was never good. Crushed stone, that's what you sold me."

"You made my son sick with what you sold me last week!" another woman yelled.

Suddenly barrels of flour were tipped to their sides and women with babies in arms started kicking the barrels down the aisle, claiming reparations for the bad product the week before. One of the barrels hit the back of a wagon wheel and split open. With that a stream of women appeared out of every crevice of the market scooping up flour into aprons and skirts held like bowls to keep it all. Faces red and crazed, Bella backed away, frightened at the scene, at the desperation. The scavenging crowd grew larger and louder, and before she could do

119

anything to help, she was running the other direction, helping Ada pack her things and escape without anyone stealing from her.

The two made it back to where Mr. Hansen's wagon was waiting and he offered to drive Ada home, too. Bella was quiet, the spectacle horrifying her. Then as Mr. Hansen was pulling up in front of Ada's tiny home, Ada reached over and patted Bella's knee. "You're crying."

Bella grimaced and touched her cheeks. They were sodden, but Bella hadn't even realized she'd been weeping.

"It's all right. You're all right."

Bella wasn't worried about herself. She simply ached for the despair that turned those women rabid. She thought of Margaret being with child. When you had children to keep, you turned different when threatened. Bella worried that would be Margaret soon. Unmarried, a baby, no means to survive. A year from now would Bella see Margaret at the market, stealing a barrel of flour, kicking it along with her baby in arms, desperate just to bake a loaf of bread?

"I'm all right. It's the others who…"

Ada patted her knee again. "I know, I know." She hopped out of the wagon. "See you tomorrow." She gathered her things from the back, and entered her fenced yard.

"What's tomorrow?" Mr. Hansen asked.

His question helped pull Bella away from her dread about what she'd seen at the market. "Just some beans and a bonfire and maybe ice-skating for Christmas Eve." She held out her hand. "If it gets colder."

"Oh, that sounds wonderful."

She turned to him, still feeling heavy inside. "You should come. Bring your family."

He looked at her. "To the Westminsters'?"

She nodded. "We've got permission to be there. The banker who's foreclosing opened his heart to us."

Mr. Hansen shook the reins and steered the horses into traffic. "You know. That might be just the thing we need to feel festive. We normally host a houseful, but no one can make the trek this year. Ruth's sad and cranky. The girls are all right, but… It's just not the same with this pall over everyone."

"Oh yes, please come. I think Nathaniel, the musician who used to play at the Monongahela House, will play music. We'll sing carols. Your girls can run around with Ada Pritt's children."

He was quiet for a moment. "Only if you take that bacon off my hands."

She pulled back. "Bacon?"

"No one bought it. As you saw from the women wrestling one another to scoop flour off the ground, people don't have much money for anything. And if I'm bringing my family to a party, we're going to bring something. I've heard Penelope can bake up a storm, so you don't need baked goods, I imagine."

Bella nodded, grinning, but that darkness came rushing back. She looked over her shoulder, back toward the market. Another woman was kicking a barrel of flour down the road, her peers and the vendor chasing after her. "Oh my, another barrel on the loose."

This turned her stomach and worried Bella again. *Were* she and her friends just another turn of bad luck from grappling over the very basic things? She played with the clasp at the neck of the cloak. She knew no matter what, she'd be fine—somehow she always was, but what about her friends? They weren't so used to having nothing.

"Bella? Changing your mind about inviting us to Christmas Eve?"

She swatted his shoulder. "'Course not."

"It's a date, then."

And so when Mr. Hansen dropped Bella at the Westminsters', he helped her carry in the supplies she'd bought with the proceeds from the egg sales and his bacon contribution. They pushed through the door and the scent of maple baked beans filled the air.

"Well," Mr. Hansen said. "The bacon'll be perfect for the beans. Those are beans you're baking, right?"

Mrs. Tillman turned and smiled. Bella would have thought they'd brought her crumbled gold nuggets for how thrilled Mrs. Tillman got over the bacon. They told her about the women and the barrels of flour and Mrs. Tillman grew serious. She folded her hands and whispered a little prayer for the world's desperate souls.

Leonard's coughing interrupted their bacon celebration. He was asleep on the settee near the fire. Even though coughing madly, it didn't pull him from his slumber.

Mrs. Tillman dashed to Leonard and tucked the quilt in around him. Her movements were sweet and loving and made Bella smile. She and Mr. Hansen moved closer toward each other.

Mrs. Tillman patted Leonard, retucking the quilt. "The Cupper just left. Must have put fourteen cups on Leonard's back. Man said that alone will increase circulation and oxygen intake. Leeched him, too. Then sunk him in a hot bath. Said he'd cough up half a lung for a few hours and then he'd be good as new."

Mrs. Tillman studied him, then pulled the quilt up to his chin, before retucking yet again.

Bella nodded. "Hope so. Sounds terrible right now."

Mrs. Tillman nodded. "He's got plans for that rink out back so I'm hoping… No, I'm going to believe. Leonard will be spry as the day I met him. Heck, he moved in twenty years ago and was coughing like a madman even then. It's just what he contends with. We all have crosses to bear…" she said with a sigh.

It was evident that Mrs. Tillman felt special affection for Leonard and he for her. Bella wondered why the two never married. She put an arm around Mrs. Tillman. "He's going to be just fine," Bella said. "He'll finish that rink and it'll freeze in time for the Christmas Eve gathering. Just like he wants."

Mrs. Tillman looked deep into Bella's eyes like she wasn't convinced. "You're just like Leonard. Always seeing the good, the hope, the promise of tomorrow. Of Christmas."

Bella squeezed Mrs. Tillman, feeling lighter than she had since leaving the market. "What else do we have if not that?"

"Nothing," Mr. Hansen said. "Nothing at all."

CHAPTER 16

Bartholomew

Christmas Eve

Bartholomew watched Bella with Mr. Hansen and Mrs. Tillman. He smiled at how she encouraged Mrs. Tillman, telling her that the rink would be completed and Leonard would be just fine. That thinking was partly what drew him to Bella, what filled his head with thoughts of her. A thrill worked through him and his hands trembled at the sight of her. Seeing her smile or laugh or comfort someone made him want to hold her tight, to share in a little of the magic that was spilled out of this penniless, beautiful woman who claimed she liked to be alone more than with others. He simply didn't believe it.

He shook his head trying to calm the quivering that came with simply being in the same room as Bella. He reminded himself that the countdown was on to when he probably would never see her again. Allowing himself the pleasure of her presence in his mind would only be painful later. If only time would stop.

Adding to his wish that the two weeks wouldn't end, he wasn't so sure the cupping, leeching, and bathing could cure Leonard of the smoke-filled lungs he'd acquired during the fire. Thinking of that reminded him he should go through his belongings to see if any of the smoke had seeped into the trunk or briefcase and ruined what little he had left to his name.

But instead of doing that, Bartholomew, Bella, Mrs. Tillman, and Penelope kept an eye on Leonard while they decided how to use the modest market ingredients they'd acquired.

Nathaniel joined them, sitting at the table to write his music.

Arnold rummaged in the cellar for anything that might be useful as their resources would surely be drained in the next day or so. He appeared at the top of the cellar stairs with another vat. He lifted it.

"Candle making. I've found exactly what I need to make some as we're out of candle and kerosene money."

He dragged the vat into the yard to the bonfire area where they'd celebrate later that evening.

So much joy in the kitchen. Bartholomew felt useless compared to the others, but was willing to follow their directions. And when Arnold entered with a courier by his side, they rushed with excitement to see what the man had brought. They were careful not to reveal that none of them were actually Westminsters and James signed for the crates as he always did when deliveries arrived.

The delivery man inhaled deeply as he set one crate in the kitchen. "Smells wonderful. What is that? Maple beans?"

"Yes," Mrs. Tillman said.

He rubbed his belly. "An old favorite."

"Well," Mrs. Tillman turned and shifted the crocks from the front of the oven to the back and the back to front so they would cook evenly. "Stop back this evening for a plate of them."

"Oh… really?"

"Surely," Mrs. Tillman said. "We're going to have a bonfire and some food. We'll be serving up happiness."

"Thank you, thank you," he said and he was gone.

Bartholomew pried open the crate and removed paper shreds. James and Margaret studied the return address.

Bartholomew opened smaller boxes and lifted several large, round objects from inside. "Camembert cheese," he said with unexpected glee. "Oh my, this cheese. Is this crate from France?"

Margaret nodded. "From the Blanchets. They send a crate every year."

"Which means…" James shouldered past the others and fished around in the crate. He lifted another two boxes out of it. He dug into the first, breathing hard, smiling like a child after Santa arrived. At the table he cut through the string. Everyone leaned in to see. He lifted paper bundles out and unwrapped one revealing something white and shaped like evergreen trees.

"What are those?" Bella asked.

The scent of sugar filled Bartholomew's nose. He knew what they were.

"Marshmallows," Margaret said tearing off the top of one of the trees. She passed it around so everyone could tear off a bough or the trunk. The sugary delight made Bartholomew smile as the others who'd never eaten one before bore blissful expressions as the pieces melted in their mouths.

"A treat for the fire," Leonard said, shuffling toward them. "Nothing like sugar to pull a man out of a dead sleep. We'll get that rink finished yet."

Bartholomew looked past the group to see what looked like rain coming down outside. That wouldn't bode well for the ice rink.

Leonard laughed. "Rain'll stop, Bart. I promise. That rink is going to be built if it's the last thing I do."

They pulled out a seat at the table for him to sit.

"Yes, every year the Westminsters toast marshmallows in the fireplace, drink chocolate, and dream of all the gifts to come," Margaret said. "We can always roast marshmallows in here if the rain keeps up."

"Remember what Mr. Buchanan said. We can't steal," Bella said.

"We aren't stealing. We're using something before it goes stale," Margaret said.

The crew agreed without hesitation.

"Hmmm," Bartholomew said. Enough people were accusing him of stealing, or at least of gross mismanagement of other people's money. Did he really want to prove them right just to enjoy some marshmallows?

"The Westminsters wouldn't mind," James said. "They aren't here to eat them."

"We are using all their other stuff. Heck, I just made four dozen candles using their wax and molds and…. What's the difference?"

"The Westminsters have been generous to others over the years. We're just the latest recipients of their generosity. That's how we should view it," Margaret said.

They looked at each other, all but Bart shouting yes to the rationalization.

"What if we vow right now," Bella said, "that in the future every one of us will give a fair turn to others no matter what? We'll share our bounties and give what we can. If we eat these marshmallows, we'll promise to someday be as giving as we are taking right now."

Clemmie grumbled. "I could vow to that. Guess so."

Bella sighed. "An easy vow for me."

Bartholomew wasn't sure about this logic. "What if I run some numbers for us? If we eat the marshmallows we'll pay it back in some way with interest."

Nathaniel nodded. "I knew a banker would come in handy eventually."

"Well, the Westminsters can't toast marshmallows from London," James said. "I'll make that vow. I'm in on being generous any time I can and we'll pay the Westminsters back within reason."

That satisfied Bartholomew. The Westminsters were about to lose their home and everything in it, so what was the harm in enjoying something that would go stale in a month? "Let's enjoy them. I'll come up with a decent trade for eating food that isn't ours."

"We've already invited Ada and her family."

"And the delivery fella," Mrs. Tillman said.

"That's generous of us," Margaret said with a smile.

Penelope dug through the rest of the crate. "The cheese will go beautifully with maple bread. I'll make that tomorrow."

The excited conversation faded into the back of Bartholomew's mind as he wrestled with what they were doing in eating the treats that arrived. He couldn't imagine just eating someone else's food in another time or place. His inclination now surprised him. Was he being a good steward? He reminded himself it wasn't his job to manage this household's bounty. His agreement to the plan was granting people who had nothing, something wonderful, just for one night. What Bella had said about a banker's mindset when he'd visited her in the barn had stuck with him, nudged him. The idea that he couldn't create anything or make anything that was valuable had sunk deeper into his skin ever since. It was true. The least he could do was let these people enjoy a couple of pleasant holiday moments.

The others didn't seem conflicted. They immediately leapt at the idea they'd somehow pass some future bounty on to someone else and that would make it all okay. Like a team of Robin Hoods. His initial reaction—the opposite of theirs—struck him. A bitter taste bubbled up on his tongue. Their hand-to-mouth, survival mindset that saw each bit of "luck" as something to celebrate, was new to him and he'd yet to embrace it. Or surrender to it—that was the accurate term.

No one *chose* to live like this. In fact, when he stopped to consider his place in this potpourri of squatters, he wanted to step outside of his skin and pretend none of it was happening. Though he'd agreed to the idea of paying back with interest and paying forward with good deeds, he wasn't so sure anything good could come from this. And the sooner he embraced *that* fully, the sooner he could fully set his mind to fixing what was broken in his life.

CHAPTER 17
Bella

Bella reveled in the holiday preparations, the music, the singing, the preparing of delectable food. After the cheese and marshmallows arrived, a crate of walnuts came from Oregon and another box of oranges arrived from Florida. Bella was so moved by the excitement emanating from each new edible arrival and the comradery in preparing everything that she took a few minutes to write a tiny Christmas story. Each of the boarders brought something lovely and wonderful to the group, to the holiday, and she hoped to capture that.

The state of contentment that she'd bragged to Bart about was still her foundation, but she had to admit that this time, with people she now saw as friends, something wonderful had been added to her life. With her story started, and more work to do, she folded the paper and tucked it in between the sugar and flour canisters near the window.

Penelope feverishly flipped back and forth through her recipe book, scribbling menus and ideas onto the pages, planning the dishes that she would make. Her glee was contagious.

It was only when Bella was helping Penelope measure out the flour for several recipes that she was reminded of the plight of the mothers at the market. She explained to Penelope the sadness that came from witnessing the melee.

Penelope put her hand over Bella's. "I understand. I've seen that before where a seller discovers his flour is cut with gypsum, or who knows what, and tries to throw it out and people swarm the garbage, even knowing it will hurt them. Hunger can make people do things we would say were appalling in other circumstances. There's something horrific in seeing that level of desperation, like they've gone feral. Heartrending to see. Worse to actually feel, though."

"Thinking of those mothers, I wonder if maybe we shouldn't be doing all this for ourselves. Maybe we aren't being generous like we promised."

Penelope shrugged. "It's not like we can invite them all to Christmas Eve. Sometimes we have to settle for the small bit we can do, what we can do for each other. It's complicated."

"I don't know," Bella said. "That feels…"

"I know, I know. Not enough."

Bella added a cup of flour to Penelope's bowl.

"Go on," Penelope said. "Get some fresh air and tend the hens. We're going to need your magic touch to get enough eggs for what I plan to make. You'll feel better after that."

Bella chuckled. She didn't feel much like chatting up her hens. "Guess I better pull out *Jane Eyre* and get reading to them. They love that book. Believe it or not."

"You love your stories, don't you?"

"I do."

"This is the first time I've seen you down in the dumps."

"Me? No, no. I'm not. I don't generally visit the dumps. All of what's happening is making me see things differently. Just thinking about the way I've always wanted my life to be. Things have changed and I'm confused and… I just want to keep my simple life, the easiness, the expected. Everything I found here in the barn. I want that to go on forever. Just that simple contentment."

"Sometimes a good dose of unexpected elation is worth as much as contentment. You can live off the memory of elation for a good long time. And us. Aren't you glad we're all here?"

"Oh my, yes. I was just thinking that, too. This. It feels like family. I mean what I imagine family would feel like."

"Well, go on, then. Let's both take care of this little ramshackle family. For today, let's pretend this is our home and we'll get to live together forever."

That idea pulled Bella out of her worrying and so she bundled up and left.

The rain had cleared just as Leonard had promised. Once in the courtyard, Bella heard Bart and Leonard talking. Drawing closer she saw them huddled, heads bent as Leonard gestured at a paper and then at the space they'd cordoned off with string.

She held her hand out gauging the temperature. It was biting cold, but not bone-chilling. With the sun poking through fat clouds the temperature probably wouldn't be consistently low enough to freeze the rink even if they completed the structure that afternoon.

It certainly wouldn't be frozen in time for the Pritts and Hansens to arrive later that evening. Arnold, just a little beyond the rink area, was setting and notching logs to be used as benches around the bonfire. And seeing this activity, Bella submerged further into holiday bliss.

She smiled and waved at Bart. He didn't see her as he was completely absorbed in Leonard's plans. The sight made her stop. He seemed completely different to her at that moment. His hard mask had gone soft, his expressions animated, exuding warmth and interest. And when Leonard started to cough into his mittened hand, Bart roped his arm around Leonard's back and led him to one of the log benches Arnold had finished setting up.

The three men sat on the bench studying the plans, their gazes snapping up from the paper to the rink space and then back to the paper. At one point Bart caught sight of Bella and his face lit up with an enormous smile. Electricity pulsed through her. A smile like that just for her. She froze in place, stunned by intense attraction. And it took a bit to realize Bart was motioning for her to join them.

She sat on the log beside him, his long, muscular leg brushing against hers. Even through the sable cloak she could feel his body heat, his closeness bringing a fresh spicy scent that filled her nose, dizzying her. The men went on and on explaining the rink plans. Words like *transit* and sighting rods, carpenter's level, yardstick, elevation, retaining wall, pipe straps, lumber, burlap to wrap the base of the tree that would be part of the rink… On and on they talked, but Bella couldn't take her eyes off of Bart. And then he turned from the men and focused on her.

"What?" he asked.

She opened her mouth to say something. What she would say, she didn't know, so she shut her mouth again. He leaned toward her, his forehead brushing past hers, as though he was going to… kiss her?

That was the thought that came to mind, but he simply plucked a twig from her shoulder and leaned back into his own space. Every nerve in her body was alive. She could have counted every last one of them if asked to. If she'd been alone with Bart, she feared she might have thrown her arms around him and initiated the kiss that she obviously wanted so badly.

"Bella?"

She raised her eyebrows and brushed her fingers over her throat, still unable to find her voice.

"You look… sick," Bart said, brow furrowed. "Or something. You're not coming down with Leonard's cough are you?"

She glanced at Arnold and Leonard who hadn't noticed Bart had pulled his attention from them. She looked back at Bart. She wanted to run her finger over his lips. The thought was bizarre and startling. What was happening? The desire to touch him finally got her moving. "No. Fine. Fine, fine. Just have stuff to do." She hopped up. She had to get away from Bart for fear she'd do something untoward right in front of everyone. "Hens. I've got to—" She stomped away. "Gotta go." And the farther she got away from Bart the faster and fuller her breath came back.

Bella spent late afternoon cleaning her loft, spending time with the hens and Simon and promising them she'd be back soon. Once she'd finished with the care of the animals she took care of herself, spending extra time scrubbing and freshening up. She put on her best shirtwaist and skirt, the one she'd been given at the last home where she worked, the one hemmed with velvet so dark that most people probably didn't even notice it was there. But she knew and the little touch made her feel decadent. The lace collar on the shirtwaist was the prettiest thing she owned and she was grateful she'd been able to keep it clean and fresh and hadn't had to wear it except a couple times a year.

She fussed with the neckline that traced along her collarbones, feeling pretty as she braided and looped her hair into intricate ropes that formed a low bun at the nape of her neck. A knock at the door startled her.

"Penelope," Bella said as she slid open the barn door enough for the woman to enter.

Penelope pranced into the barn and turned down her skater's lantern. "Barely needed the light with the clear skies and full moon." She stopped and took in Bella from head to toe. "Your hair is magnificent."

"Thank you," Bella said touching the bun, pleased with the reaction it garnered, but surprised that she'd managed to create anything magnificent. Hairstyling wasn't exactly her area of expertise.

Penelope eyed the space. "Lovely," she said. "I can see why you adore this cozy place."

"What's wrong? Is something wrong?" Bella couldn't imagine Penelope visiting if something wasn't wrong and she immediately thought of Leonard.

"All's well. Except for the weather. Leonard's gone outside and back in a thousand times, muttering curse words about the uncooperative temperatures. But, here." Penelope pulled a little jar from her drawstring bag. "This is why I'm here. Where's your mirror?"

Bella pulled Penelope toward the corner where she washed up and did her hair.

Penelope unscrewed the lid from the little jar. "Put this on your lips. I made it this summer before the hotel let me go."

"What is it?" Bella slid her fingertip across the surface of the reddish jelly-like substance as Penelope showed her.

"Lip shine. My kitchen girlfriends and I made strawberry dye from the superb *seven hundred* strawberries grown on Reverend Knox's farm on Mt. Washington. Then we mixed it with Vaseline. You can put some on your lips and a little on your cheeks. Makes a woman feel beautiful."

Bella brushed the salve over her lips and immediately loved how the subtle color with the Vaseline softened her skin and highlighted the fullness of her lips. "Thank you. But you shouldn't have done this."

"Well." Penelope turned Bella by the shoulders and looked straight at her. She pulled a tiny bottle from her bag. "Perfume." She unscrewed the lid as she explained. "I've been noticing Bart noticing you, and I've seen you lost in his gaze like you're envisioning one of those stories you love so much come to life right in front of your eyes."

"Oh, no—" Bella said.

"Oh, yes. And if it were me having such a handsome man take an interest, I'd want to be sure I was soft and shiny." Penelope dabbed the perfume behind Bella's ears and ran her finger down Bella's neck. "You have the most graceful neckline. I can't imagine being as beautiful as you."

Bella's cheeks heated. "Thank you," she said. No one had ever said that about her. Not ever.

Penelope turned Bella's hand palm up and pushed the cuff of her shirtwaist sleeve up. She looked down and gasped. "Bella. What happened?"

She yanked her arm away.

Penelope took her hand again. "Does it hurt?"

Bella shook her head and let Penelope dab perfume on one wrist then the other. "No. I don't even remember when it happened. I was a toddler. Think so, anyway."

"Burns?"

"Well, hot scalding water burns, not fire."

"Oh, I'm so sorry."

Bella felt a little self-deprecating laugh roll through her. "Just a chapter of life. Gone, past, don't even remember. Some people have their scars tucked inside their skin. Mine are on top."

"Your parents must have been horrified."

"Oh, they were already gone by then."

"Gone?"

"Well, gone to their new life, or dead or… I'm not even sure." Bella tugged the cuffs down. "Dead is what I was told. Sometimes I wonder if the real story is different. But not something I dwell on. Life is about what's happening now and what will happen soon. And that's how I look at things. I focus on all that's wonderful, and if nothing seems wonderful, I pull out a book and step between the pages and…"

"Bella." Penelope took her hand again. "You're a marvel. In every way. No wonder those hens lay for you like they do. They must absolutely bathe in your goodness."

Bella put her hand over her mouth. "Thank you, again, Penelope. I'm rich in compliments tonight."

"You deserve every one of them," Penelope said and looked toward the barn door. "Let's go."

"I've got to refill the water for the girls and Simon." She pulled the watering can in from the side door, where it'd caught plenty of earlier rain falling down the rain chain that dangled from the overhang. Bella glanced at Penelope who waited at the main door. Bella couldn't believe Penelope had noticed that she'd been looking at Bart. But more so, that Penelope was claiming that he'd been looking at her. She hadn't been imagining what she felt pulsing in the air when she was near him. Was it possible that he might feel something for her, too?

She thought of her scarred arms and the slightly short shirtwaist sleeves. They'd be outside most of the night and she'd have her cloak on. With only bonfire and bright moonlight there should be little chance of anyone noticing her scars even if the cuffs rode up her forearms a bit.

"Almost finished?" Penelope asked. "I've got to get the oranges in the oven to bake."

"Baked oranges? Oh my, that sounds like heaven."

"Oh, it is. Quite the miracle that all these luxurious ingredients just popped up at the door. Another little dose of luck just for us."

"Wait," Bella said as Penelope tugged at the heavy door. "Your perfume and lip shine."

"*Your* perfume and lip shine. Merry Christmas, Bella."

And before Bella could turn down the gifts, Penelope was traipsing down the winding lane, her lantern light bouncing toward the house.

Bella pulled on the cape and headed after her friend. *Friend*. What a lovely word. "Thank you, Penelope!" Bella said when she caught up. "I can't imagine more thoughtful gifts than what you brought me."

"You're welcome!" Penelope hummed carols along the way.

Bella smiled at Penelope's happiness and then fully shared in it. It was going to be a good night.

Laughter rose over the trees—coming from the house, no doubt. Bella was struck again with a sense of being left out since she wasn't staying with the rest of them, comforted that Penelope was with her right then. The barn, Bella's sanctuary, her nest that cocooned her in satisfied aloneness since arriving at Maple Grove, now gave her a twinge of missing out, despite what she'd told Bart. She had to admit that a yearning to be around people more often had started to grow. *Bart*. She exhaled at the thought of him. She couldn't deny all the preening for the evening had been more for him than for the gathering in general.

January 2nd wasn't far off. She pictured Margaret and James, Clemmie, Leonard, Mrs. Tillman, Arnold, Nathaniel, Penelope, and Bart folded into the Westminsters' place like family. And then she imagined how they'd scatter with the wind at the stroke of noon. A sharp stone of regret lodged inside her at the thought.

Bart. When she pictured him, he was the only one of them she couldn't fathom ever seeing again. Their lives were too different and even in his absolute loss and devastation of all things that used to be, he carried the richness of his former existence with him. He didn't really seem to notice it. But every word, every gesture, even his bearing was of another class and experience than the rest of them. And she reminded herself that he wouldn't be able to imagine her in his future any more than she could imagine him in hers.

And yet. Thoughts of what his hand might feel like wrapped around hers, their fingers intertwined, returned. He'd had the feel of her hands tending his feet. Shouldn't she at least have a feel of his hands on her before they went their separate ways?

Strains of Nathaniel's violin music grew louder. The scent of burning wood filled Bella's nose and she knew the fire must have been lit. She wanted to be part of the festivities, to be with her accidental family more than anything. So she linked her arm into Penelope's and the two ran the rest of the way to the house, excited to get Christmas Eve under way.

When they arrived at the house, the bonfire was raging and Bart was standing near the rink, pointing and explaining something to a group who'd gathered with him. Ada Pritt and her family were there along with the Hansens and the delivery man who brought the marshmallows.

"Bella!" Arnold called. "Meet Reverend Carlson. He's agreed to do a candlelight service right here at midnight. Imagine! We'll be remembering the birth of Jesus right here in the open air!"

Bella greeted them then went into the kitchen to help Penelope and Mrs. Tillman ready the food.

Mrs. Tillman was quieter than normal. Bella got her a glass of water. "Is everything all right?"

Leonard entered and squeezed Mrs. Tillman's shoulder. Then he kissed her cheek and pulled her tight. She hugged him right back, hard and long, and when she pulled away, Bella saw her face was wet with tears. Though the intimacy between the two was evident in the way they talked and joked with one another, this was the first time Bella'd seen them embrace as though a couple in the full bloom of love.

"Can I help, Mrs. Tillman? What's wrong?" Bella asked.

Mrs. Tillman waved her hand through the air. "It's nothing."

"It's not nothing." Leonard brushed his hand over her hair. She gripped his wrist as though she wanted to stay connected.

Mrs. Tillman led Leonard to the table. "You sit, have your tea and clear those lungs so you're ready for tonight."

Bella poured the hot water and added tea. Mrs. Tillman's hands shook as she took the honey from the cupboard. "I just got word from my insurance agent after trying to track him down earlier. Knew something was wrong when he wasn't in his storefront. Apparently his business is gone. He's got nothing to pay out. Twenty-five years of paying into his company and there's nothing in return. Nothing to cover my losses."

Leonard held a box up to show Bella. "She found this wedged under the stairs when she stopped by the house to see if anything was recoverable. Maybe there's something valuable inside?"

Mrs. Tillman nodded and chuckled. "I doubt it. Thomas put everything we could into the house and its upkeep. Once he died I did the same. She took the box and jiggled the lock hinge, but it didn't budge. He must have tucked it into the wall under the stairs when we built the house. The collapsed stairs bent it and it's locked tighter than if we'd sealed it up that way on purpose." She slid it into the cupboard under the dry sink.

Leonard smiled from his seat at the table. "The box will keep, dear Melody Tillman. You are the most valuable thing to me. Have been for two decades."

"A gift to all of us," Bella said.

"And I promise," Leonard said, "we'll enjoy tonight and tomorrow and then we'll find a way for you to rebuild. There's always a way.

Tonight we share Christmas with the world. Let's see those children's eyes light up and their parents laugh and lighten up even as times are hard."

Mrs. Tillman bent down to Leonard, latching her arms around his neck. "I love you, Leonard. I feel so lucky that you decided to board at my home. I can't imagine life without you. Especially the last ten years."

He buried his hand in her hair and whispered something that made her giggle. She nodded as they let each other go and she pulled Leonard to standing. "Let's share Christmas with the world."

"At least with the neighborhood," Bella said, thinking of all the mothers fighting over the flour at the market. "I should have invited them."

Margaret rubbed her belly and looked pained, making Bella rush to her. Margaret said she was fine but accepted a glass of water.

"With all the treats delivered today we just might have enough for this crew," Penelope said pointing out the window as more people trailed into the courtyard outside the kitchen. "The marshmallows are a winner. Look at those kids."

The sight of the smiling children, many more than just the Hansens and Pritts, made Bella burst with elation. Warmth spread through her like she'd been given new life right then and there. Glee. That's what it was coursing through her. She'd never thought pure happiness could be as wonderful as even-keeled contentment, her treasured aloneness without loneliness, but it was. It truly was. Penelope had been right. Moments of elation were more than worth a string of contented days cementing weeks and months together. She finally understood what she had meant.

"Go on," Penelope said. "Go say hello to Bart."

And so she did. She took two mugs of chocolate and found him staring at the soggy rink when she got outside. "Come on," she said. "The rink'll wait. You can't will it to freeze itself. Let's enjoy the fire and a nice melty marshmallow." She held one mug out to him.

He took it and shivered. "This feels good against my hands. It's not cold enough to freeze the rink, but it certainly isn't warm either. Left my gloves inside."

"Well, how about we sit near the fire and get you all toasty warm?"

He shrugged, still staring at the rink.

"It'll get colder, Bart. I can smell it. In three days it'll be frozen. And you and Leonard can dance a little jig around it in celebration."

He leaned into her with his shoulder, playfully bumping her. "Dance a jig? I'm going to sprint around it on skates."

"You can skate? You? Mr. Serious Businessman? You like to skate? You've actually done something for fun for no reason other than just because?"

"I do fun things. Plenty of times on the ice. A little hockey. Oh, yes. I can skate, Miss Bella Darling."

"Well, a new side to the man I thought I'd known everything about."

"I bicycle too, you know. With the cycling club. I used to anyway."

"You? On a bicycle?"

"Yep. But not anymore. Sold the bike. Sort of out of the club now. Every club."

"Well, I'd never have guessed you were one for having a little fun."

The two sat on a bench near the fire. Bart sipped his hot chocolate, the fire reflecting in his dark eyes. "Oh I was fun all right. In an organized kind of way. Before, well, you know."

Bella lifted her mug toward the rink off to the side of the bonfire. "You and Leonard did all the hard stuff. Walls are built, ground's level, hose is ready. Mother Nature will bring the cold and snow. You'll see."

He shrugged and smiled at her.

She laughed when she saw it.

"What?" he asked.

She wasn't going to say it. She wasn't going to do it, but as she looked at him, floating on the strength of his affectionate gaze, she reached toward his face.

He winced.

She pulled her hand back. "Chocolate, just… right there."

"Oh."

She reached closer again. "Let me…"

He leaned in and she swept the corner of his mouth with her forefinger then her thumb, her fingertips brushing along his fresh-shaven jaw, his smooth skin smelling of lime aftershave. His lips parted and for the second time that day she wanted to wrap her arms around him and kiss him. She wanted the easy way with him that she'd seen between Mrs. Tillman and Leonard. She wanted that so badly, so suddenly, that it dizzied her. And under the gentle moon rays and starlit sky she pushed the word *insanity* from her mind. For those moments she let herself believe the two of them could absolutely love each other.

"Bella," he whispered, moving closer still.

A whoop from children chasing each other right past them startled Bella and Bart apart.

The spell broken, Bart cleared his throat. "Yes, it will get cold. But Leonard wanted it for tonight, not later. Time's ticking away."

"Any amount of time we get on the ice will be worth it. If anyone can accept a delay it's Leonard. Seems like he's always a good sport. He's a doer. That story of how he saw a need for medical supplies so he raised the money and took the things right to where the soldiers needed it. I mean, he has the perfect blend of action and patience. He's an amazing man."

"Just hate to feel disappointed," Bart said. "For Leonard, I mean. He really wanted the kids to have fun. He even brought out the Westminsters' skates from the cellar, insisting that it would get cold enough. I just don't want him to be sad. So much work, for what?"

"For the joy of it, Bart. For even five minutes if we're lucky. I see that now, myself. It feels good to be included in all this revelry, to be out of my nest."

He was quiet.

"Bart?"

He grimaced.

She turned toward him, her knees hitting the side of his thigh. "You still don't see yourself as a Bart? Even Leonard calls you Bart. Or is it… what? You're sorry you're with us, still?"

"I don't know. I just…"

She didn't want his answer to ruin how she'd softened toward him. She stood and pulled him by the hand. "Come on, Scrooge. Let's embrace the moment—a marshmallow moment. Can't imagine anything sweeter."

Clemmie came up beside them. "Looky here. The minister yanked me over to the fire. I was thinking he's about to deliver a hellfire lecture on me not attending church services on the regular, but instead he pulls out these graham crackers, hands 'em to me, then takes and toasts a marshmallow till it nearly dropped from the stick and again I'm thinking there's a lesson about dropping into the fires of hell or some such thing, but then, he plops a piece of chocolate onto one cracker, presses the drippy marshmallow on top, onto the cracker and lids the whole thing, making the most delectable sandwich I ever tasted. So I say, 'Reverend Carlson, I feel like I've gone on to heaven.' Then I explained that I wasn't so sure I'd be going to heaven but if there were sandwiches like these there, maybe I'd consider reigniting my relationship with the Lord. And then he looks right at me and says, 'See you there, then, Clemmie. See you there.'"

She let out a rolling laugh and Bella joined in. Clemmie offered her a bite of the sandwich and when she swallowed, Bella had to agree it was delicious.

"I want one of those. You too, Bart?"

He shrugged. "Sure."

"Krampus," Clemmie said jerking her head toward Bart. "This Bart's got a good dose of Krampus in him. Even more than me."

"Sure does," Bella laughed.

Bart frowned.

Bella nudged him. "Come on, Bart, we're just kidding. We know you can't possibly be a Scrooge this year—you're as poor as us now."

He stopped and looked down at her. Instead of wearing one of the expressions that had recently made her insides melt when he looked at her, this time he clenched his jaw. "I'm not a Scrooge."

"We're all a little bit Scrooge," Clemmie said. "Deep down, at least. 'Cept Bella here. She's full of life and love like none of us." Clemmie cocked her head at Bella then shook her finger. "No. I'll bet even Bella's got a little Scrooge in her."

"Well, I don't appreciate the constant Scroogy references," Bart said. "That is not who I am. I promise you that. I'd swear in court I'm not. No matter what you all think of bankers or what you think I've done to end up here. I'm different than the others."

Bella pushed her arm through his. "Come on. We're joking."

"Well, sometimes… it's not any of that, really. I just don't want to see Leonard disappointed. He's my concern right now."

Bart's worry for Leonard was obvious but Bella didn't quite grasp the negativity. It wasn't like he was dying or something. Bella froze. "Is something wrong with Leonard? I mean more than his cough and whatever's been troubling him for years?"

The sound of sleigh bells interrupted Bart. The group turned toward the jingling. It grew louder and then a distinct ho-ho-ho rang out. Squealing and cheering grew louder as a sleigh came into view through the trees.

"A sleigh!" Bella squealed.

"But how? There's no snow," Bart said.

"Mrs. Gusky came through. How about that? There is good in the world," Clemmie said moving forward.

A bearded man in a red suit sat up front, ho-ho-hoing louder and louder as he pulled closer. Screeching children rushed the sleigh, jumping and reaching up to try and touch Santa.

"Leonard," Bart said.

Bella squinted into the darkness, watching as the parents' lanterns lit the sleigh better as they drew closer. "Oh, it *is* Leonard. He's the perfect Santa."

"Look at that smile," Mrs. Tillman said as they joined her. "Share Christmas with the world," she said in a low whisper. And that was exactly what they did.

"Jacob Gusky's wife lent Leonard a wagon for the night. It's got to get back to the department store to be loaded with gifts for the orphans," Clemmie said. "But it's ours for now. See, it's a wagon, made to look like a sleigh. See that?"

Bella couldn't believe it. Even Clemmie was animated at the sight of children swept up in the Christmas magic. Seeing their excitement made Bella feel the wonder as a child might, as though it were new. The children's bright faces matched Leonard's as he passed out small sacks, telling the kids not to open them until they wakened in the morning. By the time each child had a sack, the last marshmallow had been toasted, last walnut roasted, last baked, stuffed orange and bowl of baked beans, egg pies, and hot chocolate served, there were a hundred people singing and then sitting for Reverend Carlson's midnight service.

Bart and Bella sat together, holding the candles that Arnold had made. "How do you suppose these people knew to come?" Bart asked.

Bella smiled up at him.

"You? More notes in eggs?"

She nodded. "I should have invited all those mothers from the market, too, but…"

He slipped his arm around her and pulled her close as they waited for the service to begin. "This is wonderful as it is."

Bella agreed. Every sense was alive, cataloging the warmth of his leg against hers, the quiet movements of breath lifting his chest, the way his fingers at her shoulder gently moved over her cloak. Every little thing brought a thrill she wanted to remember.

And as the service went on she only registered part of what Reverend Carlson said, but wholly reveled in the music and singing. The pure hope she felt during "Silent Night," just before the end, filled her like nothing ever had before. She knew the hushed exhilaration would stay with her for a lifetime.

When the service was over and everyone had greeted Reverend Carlson, the guests trailed along the drive toward Ellsworth, voices lifted on the notes of Christmas carols old and new. Children asleep on their fathers' shoulders as they were carried away, sugarplum dreams had already begun. Mothers carried sacks of presents, grateful to have gifts for the morning. Nathaniel played them off the premises, his fiddle filling the calm left behind.

"Those eggs," Bart said as he and Bella watched the last of the guests disappear into the trees. "I can't believe people just do what the notes say. Just show up because they read a note in an egg from someone they didn't even know. That you manage to draw people where they belong just with a few hints on paper scraps."

She looked at him and made a face.

"Oh, Bella, I'm complimenting you. I'm sorry that I can't play along like the others."

She felt a heaviness in her chest, reminding her of her initial thoughts on her attraction to Bart—that it was useless. All the more reason for candor.

"You don't believe in the magic of *anything*, really. Do you?"

He looked away.

She put her hand on his arm. "Everything can't just be figured out with a bunch of numbers on paper. Haven't you discovered that yet? Some things just have to be felt."

He looked at his feet and started to say something when Mrs. Tillman's panicked voice cut him off.

"Leonard, Leonard," she cried.

Bart and Bella turned toward the sound coming from the other side of the sleigh.

Then she was screaming. "He's not breathing."

They ran toward the sleigh and found Leonard on the ground, Mrs. Tillman shaking him by the shoulders, repeating his name, the sharp sadness in her voice contrasting what had been jubilance just minutes before.

Bella removed her cloak and covered Leonard with it, hoping added warmth might help him breathe again. She rubbed his arms and tried to rouse him along with Mrs. Tillman.

Bart knelt beside Bella. "Move Mrs. Tillman away."

Bella nodded and tucked the cloak around Leonard's shoulders. "Keep him warm," she said looking up at Bart. She followed his gaze to her now exposed arms. A questioning look appeared on his face, but she ignored it and guided Mrs. Tillman away from Leonard's body. Bart's gaze refocused on Leonard.

The whole gang gathered as Bart tried to rouse their friend, Nathaniel's music stopping abruptly as he returned to find the chaos. Suggestions to get Leonard breathing again, his heart pounding again, were given and tried.

Mrs. Tillman pulled away from Bella and dropped beside Leonard. She lay her head on his chest. "No, no, no." She took his face in her hands. "Oh no, Leonard. Not yet. No." She buried her face in his chest.

Bella rubbed her back and let the older woman release her cries.

After some time, Mrs. Tillman turned her head so her ear was above his heart. "Maybe there's still a heartbeat," she said. "Maybe."

The others wept as gasping breaths came with heavy sobs, letting their sadness out, lifting prayers into the night air. Then utter despair surrendered to silence.

And then snow. A few flakes, then huge flakes the size of gold pieces fell.

They turned their faces upward.

"Leonard's snow," Bella said as she noted how quickly the air had turned sharply cold, as though a drape had been laid over them.

She patted Mrs. Tillman's shoulder. "Look."

Mrs. Tillman straightened and looked skyward. She let out something between a groan and a laugh. "Leonard's snow." She looked down at him, removed his Santa hat, and brushed his hair back from his face. She nodded as though answering a question she'd asked herself. "He's gone."

She struggled to stand. Bart got her under her arms and then Penelope led her toward the back door.

The rest of them stood together but alone with their thoughts. All the hoping and coaxing life back into his body had stopped. Leonard was dead, the silence now crushing instead of peaceful. Most of them hadn't known Leonard long, but his death felt like the end of a lifelong friendship to Bella. And between everyone's sniffling and mutterings of disbelief, Bella swallowed her own sobs, not wanting to fall apart in front of all of them, not wanting to have to deal with putting herself back together if she fully felt his death.

Bart scooped Leonard up, cradling him like he might a child. "Let's get him into the carriage house."

Margaret held a lantern up to light the way. Arnold reached to help carry Leonard, but Bart shook him off. Nathaniel played his violin, following Bart. And it was then Bella saw Bart's soundless tears dropping onto Leonard's coat, fast as the rain had fallen earlier that day.

It was indeed a silent night.

CHAPTER 18

Bartholomew

Bartholomew settled Leonard's body in the carriage house in peaceful repose. He added a wool horse blanket over the sable cloak. Then, unable to do anything else, he ran all the way to Reverend Carlson's house in Oakland. The one thing he learned from his parents' deaths was that family needed clergy around. He realized he saw the group at the Westminsters' as family, especially Mrs. Tillman, the first to welcome him, asking nothing in return.

Reverend Carlson drove Bartholomew back in his wagon, deep night sky pulling tight around them. In the carriage house, they lit lanterns and the minister went about the business of blessing the body and reassuring Bartholomew. They went to the kitchen expecting to find it full to the brim with people. But only Mrs. Tillman and Penelope were there, cleaning up after the Christmas Eve gathering. Strains of piano music filtered into the kitchen and Bartholomew knew Nathaniel had abandoned his fiddle for the larger instrument in the parlor.

"Can't stop moving," Mrs. Tillman said through tears. "Can't imagine closing my eyes and having to envision the world without Leonard. So if I keep cleaning and talking to Penelope here, then I don't have to accept Leonard is gone."

Reverend Carlson nodded and pulled her into a hug. "Night's often the most difficult time for grieving."

"Well, morning's not too far off and I'm not feeling any better for it," she said.

"Is there anyone else I can provide comfort to?" Reverend Carlson asked.

"Not right now. Everyone scrambled off. Suppose for them, being together reminded them of Leonard most so…" She moved her shoulders in a half shrug. "Nathaniel took his music to the piano,

Arnold took to his bed. Bella just left for the barn a bit ago. Said she needed to check in on the hens…" Her voice faded away.

A shotgun blast interrupted the quiet that had swept in.

"What was that?" Penelope asked.

"Gunshot," Bartholomew and the reverend said at the same time. Another came and Bartholomew realized the noise was from the direction of the barn. He remembered Bella describing the coyotes, but she'd said they stopped coming around.

"The hens," Penelope said.

Bartholomew told the others to stay at the house and he sprinted for the barn, the full moon lighting his way through the snow that was piling up. When he got close to the barn he found Bella kneeling beside one of her girls bloodied in the snow. He glanced around for the others and heard them fussing above in a pine tree.

He dropped to his knees.

Bella sobbed against him. "I must not have closed the barn door all the way. The coyote got Mississippi and I let it happen."

He held her close, kissing the top of her head. "That doesn't sound right."

"I was in such a hurry to get to the bonfire that I must have let the door bounce back open. Something."

He glanced around, unsure of how to make her feel better.

"And Leonard. Poor Leonard. I can't… I just… I can't breathe."

He embraced her and saw over her shoulder that she'd shot the coyote.

"You got the coyote. You got him."

She curled into Bartholomew, sobbing harder. "That's awful, too."

He lifted her out of the snow and carried her to the barn, settling her on the little settee across from the fireplace.

"The hens." She got up and rushed toward the door.

He caught her around the waist and swooped her back onto the settee.

She struggled. "We can't just leave them out there. We can't…"

"They're safe. You shot the coyote."

"Stop saying that as though it's a good thing."

He gripped her shoulders. "You stay here."

He grabbed a blanket from the back of the settee and wrapped it around her. "You're frozen."

"My cloak… I put it around…"

"I know, I know." He pulled her tight to stop her from mentioning how she'd wrapped it around Leonard. "I'll get the hens." Snatching up a basket, he left the barn and dashed for the tree. His first move was to climb as quickly as he could, but his aggressive movements agitated the hens and they fluttered farther up.

"Bart?"

Bella's voice came from behind him.

"Simon's up there, too."

He looked over his shoulder to see Bella wrapped in the blanket holding a lantern high.

He tried to climb again, more gently, but again the bucking of the branches sent the hens into hysterics. He turned back again. He wanted to convince Bella that the hens were safe, that even if there were more coyotes they would never reach the hens so high up. But that wasn't good enough. Not that night.

He looked into the tree and registered where each of the hens were. He couldn't make out where Simon was perched. And then he called to them one by one. "Matilda, Mabel, Simon." He explained that Bella needed them with her, that she'd had a bad night and she needed them to come down. Nothing.

And when the silence nearly choked him, and he reached for the branch to try climbing again, the hens dropped out of the trees one at a time. One on each of Bartholomew's shoulders, Simon plopping onto his head.

When he was sure they weren't going to flee, he slowly rotated and started back toward the barn, toward Bella.

She backed into the barn, never taking her eyes off of him until he entered. The hens flapped to the ground, Simon springing off Bartholomew's head, all of the animals running back and forth then circling Bella's feet as though they'd been waiting to see her all day, as though they were somehow more than animals waiting for the person who fed them.

She got on her knees and bundled them up, embracing them, then feeding them.

"Let me help," Bartholomew said. He lifted the water jug, feeling it was empty. "I'll melt snow for water or go to the well or whatever you need."

She didn't respond so he lit the fire and set a bucket full of snow on the grate. Then he went out and dug shallow holes to bury the hen and the coyote. Luckily the ground was still soft from all the rain the past couple days.

When he reentered the barn, he stoked the fire and watched Bella give the hens and Simon more water and then groom them, checking for injuries. She petted them as they drank more. The stretching and retracting of her arm exposed the scarring he'd noticed earlier in the night. In the lantern light he saw how painful they must have been at one time. The sight hit him in the solar plexus.

And yet this woman was never anything but cheerful and practical.

He added more wood to the fire and covered her shoulders with the blanket again. "Go on to sleep. I'll stay by the fire and keep it going. You're shivering."

She shook his hand off her shoulder.

"You shouldn't be alone," he said.

"You mean *you* shouldn't be alone. I'm always alone. Alone is good for me."

"No one should be alone after Leonard and the hen and—"

"Go," she said.

"Bella—"

"This is why I keep my life small and simple. I'm happy and content and I have these beautiful animals and my borrowed books, and if I hadn't been so distracted by the party and looking pretty for you and—"

"Me?" He barely found his voice. The thought that she'd been thinking of him to distraction sent his heart pounding.

"Stupid, I know," she said. "But I must not have shut the door tight. I must have—"

He took her in his arms again. "I'll stay by the fire. You *shouldn't* be here alone."

She pulled the blanket tight across her, blocking him out. "I don't need you, Bartholomew. You are free to go."

Hearing Bella say his full name came like a punch. He'd wanted her to call him Bartholomew since she first mockingly called him Bart. But now hearing the name, the simplicity of such a thing, well, he knew what she meant in using it. She turned away. He stared at the back of her as she drew deep, stuttering breaths. Perhaps she was right. Perhaps it was better to clarify their circumstance right that moment.

He certainly wasn't interested in inviting pain in the form of a woman who would soon be out of his life permanently. She was right. Her use of his full name said it all. The two of them would never be a *them*, never see each other once the group fragmented. He'd been so absorbed in helping Leonard build the rink and also thinking what a waste of time and energy it was that he didn't stop to consider what it might feel like when they all separated. To truly feel that stole his breath for a moment.

He looked around the space, deciding that Bella would be safe if he left, even if something made him want to stay just in case. She'd lived alone her whole life, survived whatever gave her the scars on her arms, probably more. He eyed a small open box on the table. Buckshot shells. He reloaded her gun and left without another word. It wasn't as though he had the means or energy to worry about another human being. He had nothing, nothing to offer, nothing worth a woman's attention, not even someone like Bella.

He pulled the door tight, making sure it didn't bounce back open. He stared at the overlap where the sliding door covered the wall, unable to make himself leave. Blood rushed loud in his ears and he resisted the urge to go back in and demand to stay overnight, to convince her that there *was* a two of them, there was a *them*. Where were these thoughts even coming from? It made no sense to think like he was, to feel what was spreading through him, startling him, turning him numb. "Go back in," he said in a whisper.

But before he could wrench the door open, it jerked and slammed. The sound of a bolt crashing into place echoed in the night. So that was that? He gripped the door handle and gave it a tug. Locked. He backed away, taking in the barn, its smallness, its modesty just as Bella described it.

Bartholomew's throat tightened. With Bella's use of his full name and her sliding of the dead bolt, the realization hit him hard. He loved that woman. But he knew. They would never be together. And that understanding smashed into him like Leonard's sudden death or the tearing apart of the hen. It sank into him, dizzying him, making him weak.

Christmas morning came soundless. He would have thought it to be tranquil if not for all that churned inside him, if not for all that happened since the Christmas Eve service ended. Bartholomew had returned from Bella's and helped Penelope and Mrs. Tillman transition from Christmas Eve cleanup to heating the maple beans and bacon for sandwiches and maple toast they would eat for a noon meal. Arnold, Nathaniel, Margaret, James, and Clemmie appeared in the kitchen one at a time, none of them having slept. The reverend had returned to Oakland for Christmas service at his church. He would send word for when they could move ahead with a funeral.

Bartholomew didn't reveal that Bella had booted him from her barn, but he did explain her sadness at the attack and death of one hen and the coyote. She didn't seem content with the fact she'd killed to save the other animals. "Don't imagine the hens will lay much after all that," he said.

"We'll manage with the eggs left from yesterday," Mrs. Tillman said.

The hours clicked by and the crew squooshed around the kitchen table for noonday meal and Bartholomew could not have fathomed that Bella would not come to the house to share in the grief they were all feeling about Leonard's dying.

Mrs. Tillman squeezed his hand. "Give her time, Bart. She's the kind of person who's used to having a nice cushion between her and the folks in her life."

He nodded and reached for the beans to make his sandwich. It was then he realized they were all looking at him funny. "What?"

The group muttered, no one actually explaining their weird reaction until Clemmie spoke up. "We're just watching your heart break over the girl in the barn. You're in love. That's all. Wondering if you're just going to let Mama Hen go when this all falls apart on January 2nd or if you're going to make a life with her."

He flinched and felt his eyes go wide.

"I put two dimes on you doing nothing," Clemmie said.

Bartholomew's mouth dropped open.

Arnold pointed his fork at Clemmie. "I'm with you."

Bartholomew shut his mouth and grappled for words to respond but didn't know how to converse with the same candor. Talk of love and leaving and falling apart were not conversations he had willy-nilly. In his social circles, people didn't just accuse others of being in love with this person or that.

"Hmmm," Penelope said, staring at Bartholomew. "I've got a quarter on you declaring your love for her. And I'm in need of a quarter to replace my kitchen implements that went up in flames the other day. So how about you let me win? I'd be embarrassed to default on my losing hand."

"I think we've all defaulted enough for the year, haven't we?" Nathaniel said, causing them all to erupt in laughter. Little by little the laughter trickled away with Mrs. Tillman's being the last to stop.

She wiped her eyes. "Feels like Leonard's here when we take to laughing like that."

"It does," Margaret said. "He was so kind to me, helping me feel better about the birth coming up and…" She drew a deep breath.

"I've got something pleasant," Nathaniel said. "In honor of Leonard. I've written a song." He played his violin, the tune starting up-tempo and slowing into a rich ballad that filled their eyes with happy and sad tears. The song perfectly expressed the way they saw Leonard and felt about him as he entered their lives then left it.

"Well, I've got something, too," Arnold said.

Mrs. Tillman poured more coffee.

Arnold brought a box from the cloakroom and set it in the middle of the table. "I've put together a seed box—enough specimens to keep a master collection and enough for all of us to take a set." He lifted the lid and pushed his finger into shallow compartments. "I found some seeds laying around the property. Others were in the greenhouse. Got some acorns in there. The oak probably makes me think of Leonard the most—to hear his story about the war and his generosity, how his injuries stuck with him, but he just kept doing the best he could. The oak fits. But see here—maple tree whirlers for Leonard's sweetness. And I've taken a few seeds from the more exotic plants in the greenhouse to remember Leonard's inventiveness. The water story when he was in prison at Libby. I mean… he was simply more than I can ever imagine being." Arnold pulled little drawstring sacks from his pocket. "Go on and fill yours with ways to remember Leonard. Plant them when you get where you're going."

This statement brought the silence back. "That's a wonderful idea, Arnold. We'll hold these dear and plant them with much love," Margaret said.

"I've got a gift," Clemmie said.

Bartholomew wiped a tear, hoping no one saw it fall.

"But just for Margaret. Unfortunately for the rest of you, the level of my creativity is about as flush as your bank accounts." She shifted in her seat and took a swig of coffee. "Got to thinking about babies and how hard it is to raise them and how sometimes it's the smallest comfort that makes a difference over long nights or troubled days and when, when all the good and bad is just… gone."

Margaret placed a hand over her chest, her eyes lit with anticipation. Clemmie pulled a bundle out from under her chair.

Margaret's graceful fingers picked the strings loose and she unwrapped the brown paper to reveal a pillow. It was quilted with a blend of fanciful shaped cotton and velvet patches. Margaret hugged it to her midsection.

"Pattern there's called *crazy*, for the essence of motherhood. Most of the time motherhood isn't soft and quiet and warm. So you have a soft, warm pillow. Crazy quilt pattern from your crazy lady friend. You can lay it on your lap when the baby nurses, or put it in the small of your back against the chair when you've had too much. There is nothing like a trusty, soft pillow to help you catch your breath when you most need it."

Bartholomew admired the practicality and humor.

"Well, I could use a pillow after a hard day in the garden," Arnold said with a joking laugh.

"When you birth a human being I'll make you a pillow," Clemmie said.

"Oh, that's all I have to do? Suppose life isn't fair, is it?"

"It's definitely not fair," Clemmie said. "Maybe if you help coax my acorn into a sturdy oak I'll make you a pillow." She winked at Arnold.

"I'll hold you to it."

"Write that down," Nathaniel said. "Don't want any arguments on the promise later."

"Later…" Mrs. Tillman said. And the silence came again, reminding them of the sorrowful part of remembering a person gone to the grave.

"I've got nothing to give," Penelope said.

"You've made Leonard's favorite bread for the bean sandwiches. That's something," Nathaniel said.

This made Penelope smile as the others agreed. "Well, let me write the recipe to include with Arnold's seeds. That all right, Arnold?"

"That would be perfect," he said.

"I've made something," James said.

He dashed into the butler's pantry and reentered the kitchen with his hands behind his back. "I've been working on this all fall, when things were slow and it was just Margaret and me in the house. I explored the blacksmith's shop. And last night when I couldn't sleep I went there to finish and decided this particular bit of work would be in memory of Leonard so I added some final pieces."

"Enough of the rigamarole," Clemmie said. "Show us."

He moved toward the kitchen window still hiding the gift, then he raised the object up and daylight exposed it more fully. "It's a window."

"Stained glass?" Margaret said. "That's what you've been doing back there?"

He chuckled and handed it to Mrs. Tillman. She ran her fingers over the pieces.

"Not stained glass the way you'd see in a church. Just scraps of glass I found in the carriage house—broken bottles, old windows…"

"James," Nathaniel said when Mrs. Tillman passed him the glass. "Is this a manger scene in the center?"

He nodded.

"Wow," Bartholomew said, stunned at the beauty and intricacy of James's work.

"Glass scraps or not, that is absolutely stunning," Mrs. Tillman said.

James nodded. "I'm hoping someday to have a home to hang it in."

Beautiful, *lovely*, *extraordinary*, they all commented. Bartholomew was speechless by the gifts the others had made.

"Oh." James hopped up and returned with a box. He put it in the center of the table and withdrew small glass shapes. "For when you decorate your trees next year. To remember me—well, now so we'll all remember Leonard and the Christmas we shared."

"I'll keep this one out for Bella," Penelope said. "For when she's up to coming back."

"She's given us so much with the eggs and she's the one who invited us here."

"Wait!" Penelope said. "She wrote this little story yesterday and tucked it away wanting to share it later."

"Read it," Clemmie said. "There's a chance I could be dead by nightfall so let's not tempt fate."

Penelope opened the pages and cleared her throat.

"Once upon a time there was a woman who lived happily alone with nothing but borrowed books and enough good luck to last a lifetime. It was the kind of fortune that came in spurts and just when she needed it. Good fortune once allowed her to eat for a week off ice diamonds that had been laid in a great snowfall and solidified with days of windless, cold air and bright sun so far off that even though she could see it, the sun's heat couldn't touch the diamonds, not for a week. Alone, she enjoyed them but wished to share. If only she'd had someone beside her. The years went by and she fell in and out of other people's lives, not really minding when the time came to leave, always content and looking forward to the next good thing. But then something started to change.

"The woman saved a man who gave her spent hens and a place to sleep. And she met the beautiful maid and kindly butler. And the woman cared for a barn cat and the hens that gave just enough eggs for just enough people that others brought spent hens and those laid more. And her world could not have felt warmer or brighter. Something had opened her eyes, just a little. Maybe she wanted more in her life than just her.

"And then… A Mother Goose who made a home in a shoe for a baker, a candlestick maker, a kind doctoring engineer who gave all his money away, a gifted fiddler, and a tall, dark, handsome banker, and a cranky seamstress."

Penelope eyed Clemmie who broke into laughter, the rest following suit. "She saw me sewing that pillow. I knew she was spying on me."

Penelope continued. "And so when a great fire swallowed up their home, Mother Goose gathered them all in her arms and made a family in a palace meant just for them."

Mrs. Tillman looked up. "Bella's the one who gathered us, not me."

Bartholomew coughed, covering up the sensation of a sob forming in the back of his throat. What was happening to him?

Penelope continued. "Together when their world seemed darkest, blackened by the brightest fire and hottest flames, the baker, the candlestick maker, the fiddler, the needlewoman, the banker and the hen keeper, and the maid with child, Mother Goose made them all feel as though they were part of something big and wonderful even though their time together would only last a short bit. They were very rich indeed—full to bursting with the kind of riches that lasted a lifetime.

"They filled the kitchen with Christmas carols and joy, making a holiday that would outdo any ball or party they'd ever been to. Not that the hen keeper had ever been to a ball. But she knew their Christmas Eve celebration would be the grandest of gatherings and so she invited others, putting little notes in her eggs for sale. A bonfire, marshmallows galore, and a skating rink. The doctoring engineer's grand plan. He looked to the sky a hundred times a day, hoping the weather would come, that all those who arrived at the palace from one end of the city to the other would marvel at the sight of an ice rink, like he had so many years before. He wanted this gift for his friends, for families who lost their homes, for parents to see the glee on their children's faces if only for a few moments on Christmas Eve night. He wanted to share Christmas with the world. If only the wind would rush in cold and heavy, then settle, dropping diamond snow, the kind that made people want to stand out in it forever. If only, the doctoring engineer said so many times that week. *If only.*"

Penelope stopped.

Clemmie turned. "That's it? Ends right there? Like that? That's not an ending."

"If only?" Nathaniel took the paper.

Penelope sighed. "Bella had just started it and then we had more to do for the party, so for now, yes, *if only*, that's the end. For now, anyhow."

Bartholomew straightened at hearing those words. *If only. For now.*

He had never received something as touching as the seeds, or the ornament or a recipe, or listened to a story written about the people in his life. These *were* the people in his life. The sense of togetherness, of them having known each other for a lifetime rather than days, struck him.

"I'm sure she'll finish the story," Penelope said. "It's a lovely narration of us. Especially now."

"Well, I have nothing to give to you all, to help remember Leonard," Mrs. Tillman said.

"You give love," Penelope said.

"I *really* have nothing to give," Margaret added. "No skills other than dusting and following along to pick up behind people with enough of everything to drop spare diamond broaches without a care because I'll come along and scoop them up for them."

Bartholomew's chest felt as though someone was sitting on it. It was he who truly had nothing to give. Not in the way that was tangible, giftable. Bella had been right. Bankers don't make anything that lasts, that people actually can count on. Not even the banker himself.

Penelope was tucking the story back between the canisters near the window when she picked up a second sheet of paper. She held it up. "Leonard's plans for the rink."

"Such a shame," Mrs. Tillman said, dabbing her nose with her handkerchief.

"It figures the weather changed just when he passed," Nathaniel said. "He must be getting a good laugh out of that."

"I'm going to go ahead and just think it was Leonard himself who turned the weather. When he passed. Too big of a coincidence," Arnold said. "He dies, it starts snowing big fat flakes?"

"That was all he wanted, and look…" Penelope pulled the window curtain aside. "The most beautiful snow I've ever seen. I agree, Arnold."

If only, for now.

The words tumbled through Bartholomew's mind over and over. Between Leonard's death, Bella's ousting of him—all of them apparently, as she had yet to show up at the big house. He couldn't just sit there any longer. He needed to do something. Even something that was as ephemeral as paper money piled in a bank. He shot to standing and stalked toward Penelope. "That's it."

She drew back. "That's what?"

He drew a deep breath and exhaled deeply. "I'm finishing the rink. It's all I have to give."

And with that, he took Leonard's plans, put on his coat and hat and gloves and took to the cold.

Outside he grabbed a shovel on the way through the courtyard, clearing a path to the rink. He stopped when he got to the edge of the lane where it splintered off, winding through the trees to Bella's barn. He hesitated, thinking maybe the reason she hadn't joined them for Christmas supper was the snow had gotten too high. But he knew that wouldn't have kept her away. He would get this rink to the next step of completion, then go to her and make sure she at least came for dinner.

Arnold came up beside Bartholomew with a second shovel. "She's all right. Just needs time, I'm sure. Remember, of all of us she's always been the most... *not* one of us. I think she actually likes solitude."

Bartholomew nodded. He liked being one of them, but wanted Bella to be one of them as well. He and Arnold shoveled the rest of the way to the retaining wall that outlined the rink, or at least where it should have been as now it was blanketed in thick snow. He removed a glove with his teeth and pulled Leonard's drawings and notes from his pocket.

Nathaniel and James came along with shovels and the hose.

Bartholomew pointed. "There—Leonard noted that the north end is slightly sloped. And according to him the heavy snow is perfect for leveling it if we just..." He started shoveling snow to bring the sloped end up. He gestured toward the walls. "Be careful packing around the tree in the center. The burlap will help protect it. And pack the rest of the snow around the edges, tight as possible. That thick pack will keep water from leaking out before it freezes," he said and sighed. "I dunno. This sounds impossible. I mean I can imagine ice freezing here and there and in lumps and valleys but how on earth is it going to work so people can skate?"

Nathaniel gripped Bartholomew's shoulder. "It'll work. You're not the kind of guy to just jump in and do something impulsive, so if you took up the mantle for Leonard's rink then I know the effort will be worth it."

James pulled the thermometer down from the side of the garage. "Eighteen degrees, fellas."

Bartholomew felt a surge of excitement and held up the instruction paper. "Says here, below twenty degrees is ideal."

"And we got that. Leonard sent the weather."

Bartholomew attached the hose. "Plans call for a light spray." He turned the faucet on, unsure if anything would flow. But it did. The water came and he plugged half the opening with his thumb, creating a gentle mist. His thumb grew numb quickly.

Arnold nodded. "A little at a time. Just coat it and we'll let it freeze."

Nathaniel turned off the faucet when Bartholomew gave him the word. Arnold handed him a glove to warm up his thumb. And then they stood staring at the ice, checking the flows that they'd created at the base of the walls.

"I thought watching water boil was the first order of hell," Nathaniel said.

"Turns out watching water freeze is worse." Arnold clasped his hands and blew air onto them.

"This is gonna take a while," Nathaniel said.

Bartholomew nodded, looking over the instructions. "Got that right. After there's a quarter-inch or so we can add more water to fill in the holes, but not too much or they won't freeze fast enough. Layers are best."

"Looks like it's leaking. There on the east side." They grabbed shovels and brooms and tried to better pack the ice near the retaining walls.

"All right. Let's see if that keeps the water back long enough to freeze in the center," Nathaniel said. "I didn't realize how long this operation was going to take to do it right."

Bartholomew glanced at Leonard's plans then laughed.

"What?" Arnold shouldered up and looked at the paper. "PERSISTENCE."

The word was written in all capital letters.

Nathaniel sighed. "Persistence, patience, boredom, hope, impossibility. They all go together. I'm with Bartholomew. Not sure this will work."

Bartholomew looked up. "I think it will. I didn't before but… It has to."

"Pray for clouds," Arnold said.

"Hark! The herald angels sing." Nathaniel rubbed his hands together and sang.

"Clouds are Pittsburgh's specialty," Arnold said.

"Sure are." Bartholomew felt a little twinge of optimism. "Says to watch the back left corner, that the retaining wall wasn't flush as it should be and could allow leaks."

They checked and packed more heavy snow into the space. Then they crept around the rink, monitoring and adding and packing snow until they couldn't bend their fingers anymore and tucking them under their arms no longer warmed them up in the least.

Bartholomew nodded, satisfied. "Go on in. I'll do one more spray and then we'll stop watching water freeze and warm up our hands and have some bean sandwiches for dinner."

"It almost feels like Christmas," Arnold said over his shoulder as he and the others headed for the courtyard. "Jingle bells, jingle bells," the men sang their way into the house.

Bartholomew let the sentiment—*feels like Christmas*—sit with him. What did Christmas feel like for him? He wasn't even sure. Since his parents died, his Christmas days were spent with friends, eating enormous meals and watching them open gifts with their children. He'd never really minded not having any of that for himself, having to share in other people's holidays, but he could not say he'd associated a particularly warm feeling with Christmas day since he was a boy.

He added about an inch of water to the rink and shut off the hose, watching as the sun was setting behind the trees. Movement in that direction caught his eye. *Bella*. She blended in with the snow, only her black boots exposing her as she came through the snowy trees. She was wearing a cream-colored hat and a milky-hued sweater. As she got closer he saw that it was knitted with thick braids and buttoned down the front with leather-covered buttons. He remembered her giving the sable cape to cover Leonard.

Her long blonde hair hung down and her cheeks were pinked. There was so much he wanted to say to her, but he didn't want to anger her like she had been when she kicked him out. So he went to her, the two wordlessly staring at each other. He wanted to ask if she was all right, but already knew the answer. So he simply reached for her hand.

"Snowfall covered where you buried Mississippi," she said. "Can you show me later where she is?"

He nodded, his hand still extended to her. She acknowledged it with a glance and scowled, but then grabbed onto it and they walked toward the house.

When they got within sight of the back windows she wiggled her hand away from his and entered the home ahead of him. He shook out of his coat, hit by the scent of beans, coffee, and noodles with cheese. Casserole dishes on the top of the stove, cheese bubbling and hot, and crisp, golden brown where the edges met the pan.

"That smells delicious," Bartholomew said. "Where'd we get that?"

"Reverend Carlson brought it. Arranged for food for us. He'll do the service tomorrow," Mrs. Tillman said through watering eyes.

Bartholomew hugged her, wishing he could take away her pain, but knowing he couldn't.

They crammed around the table, shoulder to shoulder, while James went for more wood for the fireplace. Arnold shoveled coal into the stove. Margaret's belly was so large she had to sit back further than the rest. When she leaned in to spoon some casserole onto her plate she bumped the table, making the silverware shimmer and chime. Everyone started laughing and moved away from her to make more room.

She waved her napkin. "That won't do anything."

"It's like you have alligator arms," Bartholomew said.

They all looked at him.

Bartholomew bent his arms and wiggled his fingers, miming how an alligator might have to jerk its body to reach for the spoon with short arms. All gazes settled on him but no one seemed to get the joke.

Heat spilled through him, embarrassment. He jerked his body again, miming how an alligator would have trouble reaching and grasping something. "Alligator arms, get it?"

Clemmie leaned on the table and let her laughter unfold into the room, leading another round from everyone. "Bart's loosening up. Good to see," she said.

But Margaret's breath-stealing laughter soon turned to tears and she buried her face in her hands, shoulders quaking.

"I'm sorry." Bartholomew reached toward her. "I shouldn't have made the joke."

Bella popped up and scooted around the table, hugging her from behind, shushing her. Margaret wrapped her arms around Bella's, clasping on tight.

"It's not that," she said through tears. "That was funny."

"Margaret." Mrs. Tillman dashed toward the pregnant woman. Bella released her and went back to her seat. Margaret gently batted Mrs. Tillman away saying she was all right. Bartholomew got up to let Mrs. Tillman sit beside Margaret and took another seat. Penelope brought a fresh coffeepot to the table and put on a second one.

They passed the coffeepot around the table as they tried to comfort Margaret.

"Had three babies myself," Clemmie said, breaking the silence. "None were healthy. Yours is healthy. I can see it in your coloring."

"It's not fair, is it?" Mrs. Tillman said. "Some healthy, some not."

Margaret put a quivering hand to her mouth.

"You're going to be all right, Margaret," Mrs. Tillman said finally sitting down.

The silence around the room said that everyone knew Margaret was unmarried. Bartholomew knew plenty of women who eloped with pregnancies that were threatening to reveal their premarital activity. Or their parents would shuttle them off to special homes where people gave birth and reappeared slender and new and refreshed from a rest "abroad," or at a favorite aunt's "country home." Mostly, in his world, wealthy, powerful fathers of single, pregnant women forced the marriage on soft men who agreed to a life they didn't really want. But once a baby was involved everything changed.

"We can help Margaret raise the baby," Penelope said.

Everyone stared at her as though Penelope suggested they eat their arms for breakfast the next day. She shrugged. "Why not? We're a family. Sort of. Look at us."

"Look at us, yes…" Arnold said.

Bella glared at Arnold, making Bartholomew wonder if she was going to kick him out of the kitchen like she'd done to Bartholomew the night before.

"Not that I wouldn't want to. Operate as a family, I mean," Arnold said. "Margaret's lovely and I'm sure her child will be too. But…"

"But a child out of wedlock," Margaret said. "I know. I…"

Bartholomew couldn't imagine such an undertaking either in practical or societal terms. "It's simply never done."

"Though we'd like to do it," Nathaniel said. "Margaret's like my sister now."

Penelope finished a mouthful of casserole and leaned back in her chair, hands wrapped around the coffee mug. "Margaret and her baby need a family. Why can't it be us?"

"*Where* would we be a family?" Bartholomew said. "In eight days we'll be escorted out of here. None of us have anything. Mrs. Tillman's insurance man is bankrupt." Bartholomew couldn't stop himself from being the wet blanket on this idea.

Margaret nodded. "It's just not done that way."

"What about you and James?" Arnold asked. "He dotes on you like no man I've seen."

"I can't ask James to… no." She shook her head like the idea itself caused her physical pain.

The back door opened and James came in, arms laden with wood, looking around the side of the stack to keep from tripping as he entered.

He dumped the wood near the fireplace, threw a few logs on the flames and turned, wiping his hands together. It was then his eyes went wide, surveying the group, settling on Margaret. "What's wrong?"

She shot a hard look at the group. "Just talking about Leonard."

Bartholomew exhaled, glad that the conversation about Margaret and her baby was put to bed. He eyed Bella who also appeared relieved.

James accepted Margaret's response and poured himself some coffee. He lifted the mug. "Merry Christmas, everyone. Even in the sadness of Leonard's death and the…" He glanced at Bella and added, "…your hen… I am so happy to know you, and to spend today, the blessed day of Christ's birth, with you all. I feel rich right now, in this moment, knowing all of you."

"It's just the house, James," Clemmie said. "Feeling rich isn't being rich. Wish it could be."

And they began to bicker about the definition of rich and poor and only Bella was quieter than Bartholomew. He tried to engage with the others, but all he could do was imagine different ways to ask Bella to let him talk to her again and explain what he was feeling. He thought once more of her scarred arms and was met with the urge to protect her.

He knew the limitations of what he could offer her. In fact he was starting to think his hesitancy to really sort through putting the pieces of his life together was because once he managed that, including Bella in it would be harder than anything. She was rough around the edges, though beautiful, savvy and way more well-read than him, but he couldn't get past how he'd ever introduce her to the friends that inhabited his old world.

Friends. Were they really? Had he been a true ally to them? He wasn't sure how to measure such things anymore. For his entire life it had been the physical proximity of people occupying rarefied air that defined friendship. The mere presence of people who populated the universe as defined by wealth and education and achievements created mutually beneficial alliances. Society's markers of wealth built a resume that allowed entrée into places like the Duquesne Club, holiday dinners with industrialists, galas, and balls. But that qualification process didn't seem to work for Bartholomew anymore. The alternative? He still couldn't imagine.

CHAPTER 19
Bella

The day after Christmas, the little group living at Maple Grove, along with a few others including the Hansens, held a solemn service to commemorate the life and death of Leonard Hill. Reverend Carlson had arrived, mentioning that this was the first of three funerals for him that day. He hauled a dark-stained coffin in his wagon. It was simple but elegant with some fine molding along its edges—the perfect piece for Leonard who was elegant and simple himself.

Bella went with the men to the carriage house, carrying the tie and coat Margaret had fished out of the box of cast-off clothing in the attic. With the help of Bartholomew and Nathaniel, she threaded Leonard's arms through the coat sleeves, fixing the tie, remembering Leonard's face when he would give a small knowing smile, or a kind nod of the head while listening to someone speak.

With him dressed, she watched as the men lifted Leonard and moved him into the box. The sight of them working together, carrying Leonard, reminded Bella of the day they'd hauled the Christmas tree into the foyer with Leonard helping direct the process. Their gentleness with the live tree was mirrored in their gentleness carrying Leonard. These were thoughtful, tender men and Bella was so glad to know them.

With a path cleared through the snow and the coffin placed at the center of a stand of apple and maple trees near the ice rink, Reverend Carlson gave his sermon. With scripture serving as anchors, he considered life and death and the ways people like Leonard lived on in memories, in deeds, in all the ways that mattered.

Reverend Carlson talked about the ways holidays are never the same after a person dies, but the living should use the memory of the loss to celebrate Leonard. Yes, Christmas was about Jesus's birth, but Leonard, having died just after the midnight service, with all the love and joy that was present right then might be comforting for them in the future.

And so when the service was complete and Leonard's coffin was placed in the wagon with two other empty boxes, the little group watched Reverend Carlson drive away. Arm in arm, watching the wagon disappear around the driveway bend, they decided how they would view Leonard's passing. It was a chance to remember more deeply what Jesus's birth meant and to celebrate a life they could strive to emulate. They knew they would keep their vow to help those in need whenever they could.

The Hansens and others left and Bella helped Mrs. Tillman with her chores, helped Penelope reheat the beans and macaroni and cheese and made maple toast using leftover Camembert cheese that had come from France. "No eggs today," Bella said.

Mrs. Tillman put one arm around her. "It's all right. We all need a rest today, don't we? Even the hens."

They washed and dried the bean vats and bean crocks and made a pile of clean containers that people had dropped off for them since Leonard died. "Hope we can return these before we're booted out of here," Penelope said. "These are good crocks."

"Who brought them all?"

She shrugged. "I didn't see. But with Leonard's work in medicine during the war years and beyond, he made a lot of friends."

"Why'd he live at the boarding house then?"

"Think it was his illness. Just too much to be sick and keep up a house on his own."

Mrs. Tillman settled a dry crock on the pile. "Lungs were bad since the day he moved in. Never thought he'd live this long. With Thomas's death, Leonard really helped me out, let me grieve while he helped with the house. Took me years to admit how much I loved him because I figured it wouldn't last and it would hurt so much to really love him. So we just went along, loving each other quietly, not officially."

"A good lesson for us." Penelope dried the lid to a pot. "Seize the love!" She shook the hand towel over her head.

"He gave away everything he owned when he moved into the house. I think he just wanted someone to care for him like he took care of all those patients and soldiers. *Things* didn't matter to him," Mrs. Tillman said. "Sometimes people just get tired, and accepting care can be as generous as giving it. He let me care for him and that gave me purpose.

Think it took him five minutes to fall in love with me. Took me a little longer." She chuckled. "I was lucky to have two men to love me over my life."

Bella let Mrs. Tillman's words wash over her. "That must have been nice, to be loved like that."

Penelope and Mrs. Tillman stared at Bella, their silence startling her from her thoughts.

"What?" Bella asked.

"You have to be open to being loved," Mrs. Tillman said. "You have such a good heart, but it's like your eyes are bad."

"Bad eyes?"

"You really can't see it?" Penelope asked.

"See what?"

"The way Bart looks at you? Listens to every word you say? Follows you around making sure you're all right?"

"What? No. He's nice to me and all. But that isn't like you and Leonard. Bartholomew Baines—"

"Oh, it's *Bartholomew* now, is it?" Penelope scowled.

"That's what he wants to be called so… Fancy name for a fancy man."

"Oh, Bella," Mrs. Tillman said. "He's smitten and you have to feel it even if you won't see it."

"And he may have fancy education and once was rich, but he's here now just like the rest of us," Penelope said.

She shook her head. "He's with us temporarily—"

"We're all here temporarily," Penelope said.

"But as soon as Bartholomew can, he'll slip right back into his old life—he's in a whole other orbit from us, from me. This is just a visit for him. His proper home is in the heavens all shiny and starlit, and I'm an earthbound woman, dressed in clothes people give me, watching over hens too old to lay. How on earth could we—could he? No. He's just… No." And she walked away unwilling to entertain the idea that Penelope and Mrs. Tillman were right about Bartholomew Baines in the least.

Bella woke and treated her daily schedule as though the group at Maple Grove wasn't even there. Instead of hastily feeding her animals and dashing off to see her friends, she made oats and talked and read to the hens and collected their eggs, humming along in order to keep from choking on the sadness of Mississippi's death, that it was her own neglect that led to the coyote getting to her.

Then shooting the coyote. She hated that she'd done that as well, even though it was necessary. She'd gotten there at the right moment to give the other hens and Simon time to fly into the trees. The whole mess left her with a mass in her belly, weighing her down.

So she collected the eggs, surprised at the number they'd laid after the traumatizing coyote experience. When she slid open the barn door there was a basket with a couple slices of bread and a note. *"Penelope added cinnamon and raisins to the bread this morning. Hope you like it— Bartholomew."*

She gobbled up the bread, grateful that he'd brought her food, but didn't push his way in. She let the hens into the open air, knowing that she couldn't watch them every minute, reminding her why she didn't want to be close to people—a few hens and the cat was all she could manage worrying about. And once January 2nd arrived she would be done worrying about the group gathered at Maple Grove.

Her life would narrow down to nothing but her books and animals. The thought that she had nowhere to go sent acid into her belly, but she told herself not to fret over that. She would find somewhere for herself and the animals. If there was anything, she trusted it was that.

She dropped some eggs in the kitchen and headed to sell at the market. Mr. Hansen picked her up at their usual spot at the end of the driveway on Ellsworth Avenue. They were quiet, discussing how the funeral service had gone.

Mrs. Taylor had cleared the usual spot for Bella's eggs and the two made small talk as customers bought what they needed. People shouting startled Bella and she followed the sound of the ruckus only to find mothers fighting over flour and beans again. Bella's mind raced. She didn't want to see anyone go hungry, or as they were accusing the dry goods man, of him selling flour cut with poisonous ingredients. She looked back toward Mrs. Taylor's booth. She should just give away the eggs, let these mothers with children in arms and little pull wagons have the eggs for free. But their tattered clothing told the story—they would have nowhere to cook the eggs or anything to combine them with to stretch ingredients like the eggs had been known to do.

The shouting grew louder and women's faces grew redder, their eyes conveying a desperation Bella had never felt and never wanted to. Suddenly she knew exactly what to do.

She stomped over to the women and took two of them by their arms and screamed out, "Stop!"

A few snapped in her direction, staring.

"Just stop!" she shouted again.

More turned to stare.

"Please."

Bella tried to reason out what she could do for them that was tangible. It would take time to really do something. But she had access to Maple Grove for another week. She could at least gather some more ingredients and make them something wonderful.

"New Year's Eve. Come to 5720 Ellsworth Avenue. Seven at night. I'll make sure you and your families have something to eat."

The crowd stared at her. "What good is that? A week away?" one of the women said.

Bella shrugged. She understood the sentiment. "I've got to get some things together in order to feed you. I don't have anything right now, not enough." She dug into her pockets and held out every coin she had with her. The women swiped them out of her palm, still eyeing her suspiciously.

"That Maple Grove you're talking about?" A woman came up beside Bella. "The Westminster place? They're going to give food away? Just like that?"

Bella looked at the woman and saw she was dressed in clean clothing, not elegant or expensive, but her wool coat was in good shape, all the buttons there, no holes, her face was clean and she wore gloves and had a nice scarf and matching hat. She wasn't wealthy and could not be in the social circle with the Westminsters. A wind blew her coat open and Bella recognized her apron—the applique on the top of it shaped distinctly like the Heinz food company logo. A working girl. Certainly she wouldn't make trouble for Bella. Her biggest trouble would be following through with what she just promised these women.

Bella decided saying as little as possible was best. "Maple Grove, yes, it is."

"Are you the egg lady?" the woman in the apron asked. "The one whose eggs make more food than imaginable?"

"I am."

She held up a bag by its rope-tied top. "I was just looking for you. Spent hen in there. Do your magic."

The crowd of mothers drew closer around Bella and the woman with the Heinz apron disappeared into the crowd.

Bella loosened the neck of the bag and peered inside. A little white hen looked up at her. She reached inside and petted it. "Oh my, how lucky," she said and then finished her work with Mrs. Taylor before hitching a ride back with Mr. Hansen.

"Got myself into a jam, I think," Bella said to Mr. Hansen after showing him the new spent hen and deciding to call her Lucky.

"Strawberry or marmalade?"

She chuckled. "I just invited a bunch of women and their families to the Westminsters' for New Year's Eve."

He did a double-take. "You did what?"

She'd expected him to say it was a good idea and tell her it would all work out because what else do you say to a person who just invited people to a house that wasn't hers? Once the invite was given, no point in being dour, but here he was, quiet and grim. "Mr. Hansen? Help?"

He shook the reins. "Not sure what I can do other than bring some ham. But probably not enough… How many people did you invite?"

She visualized the mothers and how they were arguing with the dry goods man and she tried to count. "Well, with children and maybe husbands and… a bunch?"

He drew sharp air through his teeth. "Can't even say the number aloud? Must be a lot."

She sighed.

"So a bunch. All together or just the mothers?"

She grimaced. Would downplaying it do any good at this point? "Maybe I can get more beans from Ada. We've still got maple syrup for those."

"How many people, Bella?"

"Um, well, fifty. Maybe."

"All together or just the mothers you saw at the market?"

"Just the ones I saw."

He groaned. "You know that's just a fraction then."

She sighed. "So a hundred and fifty?"

He let out a long, high whistle. "That's no party, my dear Bella. That's a New Year's Eve ball you just promised to throw."

She looked at his profile as he focused on the road ahead. He was right and she wasn't sure how she was going to manage. But she would. She'd find a way. She hugged Lucky against her belly. "A ball. So it is," she said disbelieving that it was she, the one seeking to seal her world into a party of one, who had just decided to host a party of hundreds.

After introducing Lucky to Mabel, Matilda, and the coop, Bella unloaded the goods she bought at the market. She told everyone about Lucky, but searched for the words to tell the others what she'd done. A ball. *A ball!* She would have accused another person of having been drunk if they'd done such a thing, but she'd been stone sober.

"What are you mumbling about?" Margaret said from the settee. James was wrapping her ankles in chilled rags.

Bart was eating leftover maple toast. Mrs. Tillman was washing mugs and Penelope was kneading dough.

"Better late than never," Bella said, thinking that she should have invited the starving families to Christmas Eve but hadn't.

"For what?" James said.

"I did something that might feel shocking to you. But once you really think about it…"

"What?" Nathaniel said, inching closer to her.

She held out her hands. "Well, remembering our vow…today at the market I ran into the mothers who were hungry, fighting with the dry goods man again, desperate, just about to start rolling barrels of flour again and—"

"And what?" James asked.

"I invited them all here for New Year's Eve so we can feed them a meal and give them a beautiful night—a ball, Mr. Hansen said it was, but that's a little over the top. I'm thinking it's more of a party."

"You did what?" Bart choked on his toast.

Bella shouldn't have expected support from him so she ignored him.

James looked around the kitchen. "You mean another bonfire, outside?"

Bart's eyes lit up. He grinned, making Bella stare at him, surprised.

"The ice will be ready," he said. "It's perfect. Just like Leonard would have wanted."

James came around the other side of the settee. "Outside then. We have to remember what Mr. Buchanan laid down for us as conditions. This isn't our house, Bella. What did you do?"

Bella felt her throat start to tighten and the realization that she'd just opened someone else's home up to the world settled in. She put a hand over her mouth. What had she done?

Bart put his hand on her shoulder. "No, James. This is right. Bella is right. This is exactly the kind of thing we need to do to honor Leonard and that vow."

Bella's face warmed under the encouraging smile from Bart.

"But it's *not* right. It's not our house. And I could tell that you didn't even want to do the rink or Christmas Eve, Bart," James said.

"That was before. Before I understood."

Margaret nodded. "Think of it as giving the Westminster home a grand send-off. Wherever they are, they're probably going to dress up and bejewel their hair and have a fabulous New Year's Eve. It's not like they even gave us a note saying the home was being sold out from under us."

"It's not ours to be sold out from under us," James said. "I mean, this has been nice and all, but Margaret, you're going to have a baby soon and you're not even—I mean, shouldn't we be focused on finding places to live and jobs instead of—" He glared at Bella.

"How many people?" Mrs. Tillman asked.

Bella swallowed hard. "Well, maybe a hundred and fifty."

Bart choked and covered his mouth. She patted him between the shoulder blades. "I know it's a lot."

Bart rubbed his grizzled chin. She observed him. Something had changed. She had to admit that. Not just that he wasn't perfectly groomed and dressed, but there was a softness to him now. She didn't have to believe he cared about her specifically, but she could work with him if he was willing to help with the party.

"All that food showed up for Christmas Eve," Margaret said. "And I believe the right things will happen again. Jesus is about every day, not just one night. We can make a beautiful ball and even if there's nothing but magic eggs and magic beans it will be something more than those families have been eating."

James poked at the fire with the iron, shaking his head. "Bart, you have to agree with me. Christmas Eve was one thing, but this?"

"Don't do that, James." Margaret's voice came thin, worried. "What if we leave here and that's *me* next year? Starving, alone with a baby, begging for flour from some vendor unwilling to even sell a product that isn't half cut with gypsum? What if that's me? Wouldn't you want someone like Bella to help someone like me?"

James's shoulders tensed and he stabbed at the wood harder, sparks flying onto the rug. He stamped them out, cursing like Bella had never heard him.

Bart straightened. "James, this time, I agree with Margaret, with Bella. I can't believe I'm saying this." He wore a shocked expression as though his very own thoughts weren't his own. "It's not like me at all. But yes. I don't know how we'll make food for a ball or... I have no idea, but I'm going to finish that skating rink and we'll build a fire and we're going to pretend as though we are the richest people ever to grace Maple Grove."

Mrs. Tillman dabbed her eyes and let out a little sob. "I love that, Bart. I just love that."

And so they made it their business to ready the house and each other for the most wonderful New Year's ball in the world.

175

The days leading up to the party, Bella made sure she didn't neglect her animals. She kept them safe and made sure Lucky was acclimating to Simon and her new home. Bart, Arnold, and Nathaniel helped care for the animals when Bella asked for help.

They all took shifts adding water to the rink and when Bella went to check the latest frozen layer, she saw ice glistening all the way to the top of the seven-inch retaining walls. "Yahoo!" She couldn't hold back. She lifted her hands over her head and danced around the perimeter.

Bart came loping out of the carriage house with the broom. "Is that your jig? You're doing your jig. That means—"

"Yes! It's my *ice rink is ready* jig, just like I promised!" She grinned and shimmied and shook.

"Well, I'm taking a spin." He buckled on skates and whipped around the rink, swerving this way and that, narrowly skirting the tree in the center, laughing like a person without a care in the world.

"Put on that pair, Bella," he said pointing to the bench.

She latched them on. "A little long."

"They'll do. Come on in. The ice is nice." And he cackled and laughed as he skated backward and forward, circling with the most blissful laugh Bella had ever heard, like a carefree stranger had slipped into Bart's handsome body.

When Bella tried to enter the rink she wobbled and fell on her bottom. "Just remembered I don't know how to skate very well."

Bart flew up to her and reached for her hands, clamped on, and pulled her to standing without even stopping. "I've got you," he said.

He skated backward and pulled her forward. Before long she'd gained her balance and found herself moving with long strides and laughing with him as they circled the rink, holding hands, Bart slowing enough to keep her from falling when she got shaky.

On one of the straightaways she looked up at him, the glee on his face intoxicating. She was so happy for him, that he'd achieved this thing that was so inconsequential, yet not. "We did it! *You* did it, Bart! You finished Leonard's rink."

He reached around her and scooped her up, tossing her around the back of his body and catching her in his arms again, cradling her as he circled the rink. The wind whipping through her hair, she fully trusted him not to drop her. Such an odd limbo. She closed her eyes and everything went quiet in her weightlessness. The wind brushed across her face and she thought the only thing she could compare it to was the hammocked bit of time between sleep and wake when her stories came to her clear and lovely. Those moments where she created fantasy worlds she hoped to write one day—that was where she was in Bart's arms, on that ice.

She opened her eyes. Bart looked down at her, smiling, and then dropped one arm, softly setting her down so that her skates caught the ice exactly right. They slowed to a stop and he pulled her into him, sweeping loose hairs off her face.

"Bella," he said.

The sound of her name on his lips, the *way* he said it with raw longing emanating from deep inside him, from the place she imagined yearning started because she felt it too, sent excited shivers turning through her. He skimmed his lips over hers and she let out a little moan, melting into him, clutching him, her fingers playing with the hair at the nape of his neck. This was the attraction she'd read about countless times in books. She pulled him tighter. This was what it felt like to lose herself in sensations that could only be explored through wordless touch. She cataloged every one of them to call up later. He pulled back with a satisfied smile then kissed her harder.

The back door slammed and she leapt away from Bart, almost falling again. He caught her around the waist with one arm and got her balanced.

Bella turned away and shuffled to the edge of the ice, having suddenly lost her ability to skate with long strides. Maybe she had been caught between sleep and wake.

"Whoopee!" James said coming toward them. "The rink is ready!"

Bart pushed a fist in the air. "It's sublime, James, my friend. Like magic. Try it."

Bella froze at Bart's use of the word *magic*, then looked up from unbuckling her skate. Their eyes met and her cheeks reddened, still submerged in what she'd just felt in his arms.

James tossed Bart a bundle of rags. "Here are the rags you wanted."

Bella glanced at Bart who seemed as shaken as she.

"Yeah, yeah. The rags," Bart said. "Bella, you brush the ice and we'll follow behind, smoothing it, and then we'll let it set, maybe spray again, but it will be ready for the party."

"You mean the ball," Bella said, her feet finally free of the blades.

"Well, if it's really going to be a ball, you'll need a gown, Bella Darling," Bart said. "You can't attend a ball in run-of-the-mill clothing. And I'm willing to bet the attic of this home is stuffed full of beaded and sequined gowns that ladies wear to balls."

Bella eyed James for his reaction to that suggestion.

"I've come around to the idea, Bella. And I'm sorry for being so short when you first told us. I know we're all careful stewards, but I just panicked at the thought and… We want to remain careful guests so we can leave with a clean conscience, and maybe I can still swing a job in another home. I'm going to need it if—"

He paused.

"If what?" Bella asked as she swept the ice.

"Well, a job. A fella needs work and I've only done one thing my whole life so… I need to provide…"

"Provide? You mean?" Bella said, hoping he was referring to asking Margaret to be his wife. She couldn't imagine him not doing it, even with the baby being someone else's. He clearly adored her.

"Nothing, Bella. Let's just get this done."

And so they did.

CHAPTER 20
Bartholomew

Bartholomew had been hopeful and excited about the ball, but still had moments of uncertainty. How would this event be anything even close to a joyous ball when they had very few resources? Yes, they could borrow clothing from the attic and they had some foodstuffs left over but that was it.

His unexpressed questions started to get answered the very next day. And with every answer, his view of people, random strangers, helped him further understand why so many held bankers in such extreme disregard.

As they were in the kitchen inventorying what they could make for the ball, it started. An avalanche of things began arriving as though his concerns had summoned the food gods. Packing cart after packing cart rolled up to the back door. Bart was confused but rather than turn the packages away, he ignored his hesitation and signed James's name to three of the deliveries that came at once.

Mrs. Tillman, Penelope, Margaret, and Bartholomew dug into the crates. He couldn't believe what he was seeing. "The world doesn't just send food and alcohol willy-nilly," he said through what could have been called drunken laughter as he sorted through the gifts.

He looked at one note. "Sauerkraut and horseradish from Heinz." It indicated that present was a New Year's gift. "Good people."

James poked his head into the group. "Yeah, the Heinzes always attend the Westminsters' New Year's ball and always send something. But this is... wow."

Bartholomew studied James. Then alarm set in. "You think the Heinzes think the Westminsters are throwing the ball? That they don't know they're romping around Europe or wherever they are now and that the house is foreclosed on?"

James looked at the note again. "I'm sure it's just that his secretaries sent something without checking… Heinz can't think there's a ball."

Bartholomew nodded. "You're right." He continued to look through what had arrived. "Kielbasa from Mr. Novak's meat shop."

"And he sent potatoes and plums for plum dumplings," Penelope said, showing him the recipe that came with the delivery.

"Wait. So the man sent it specifically for this party?"

"No, that wouldn't make sense," Penelope said.

"Take a look at *this* note." James held out a paper. "Mr. Buchanan sent a side of beef."

They tore into the package. "It's enormous." Penelope thumped it with her fist. "And a ham." She shook her head. "I cannot wait to get my hands on this stuff. I have recipes for horseradish spread on beef, a horseradish rub."

"And there—a barrel of flour for pastries, and look there! Already made pastries from Fait Maison, cheeses, wines, and champagne from every vendor in town."

Bartholomew took it all in.

"The rich get richer," James said.

"Certainly appears that way," Bartholomew said.

"Well, I'm ready to get busy making food," Penelope said. "So check outside for any more deliveries and I'll organize it all and get busy."

Bartholomew watered the rink one last time, just a little to keep it smooth and ready. Then he headed into the attic to locate a suit. Being tall and lean, it wasn't hard to find something that looked decent, though certainly not bespoke. Trying on another man's clothes felt as strange as anything that he'd experienced in the past two weeks. Being clad in borrowed clothing called up a little of the dread that had gone missing for most of the day.

The only time he'd worn something not made just for him was when he shot up six inches in half a year and he had to wear his father's tuxedo to a summer soiree. Nathaniel was accustomed to dressing nicely, trading tuxes and suits depending on what a particular musical event called for, so it didn't seem strange to him to page through racks of clothes finding something that was just right.

Arnold needed a little assistance getting into something as he spent his life in work clothes. "I've got to get into that greenhouse. I found some herbs to use in Penelope's horseradish rub, spreads, and dips." And James still had formal wear in his closet as being butler at Maple Grove required various levels of formality on a regular basis.

Laughter from the other end of the attic drew Bartholomew's attention. Margaret was standing in front of a mirror. "Come here, Bart." She waved him toward her. "Look at this monstrosity."

She was draped in a glittering gown that skimmed over her belly.

"You don't even look like you're with child in that," Bartholomew said.

"I look like someone beaded the side of Bella's barn," she said holding her hair up.

"You look beautiful," Bartholomew said.

Margaret turned and planted a kiss on his cheek. "Thank you, Bart. You are the most polite man. I don't want to miss the party so I'm going to wear this thing that Mrs. Westminster wears when she's gone puffy. And I'm going to enjoy it! Because I've never been a co-hostess of a ball before. And I'm quite sure I never will be again." Her voice cracked.

"Nathaniel's friends are coming to play music with him," Penelope said from behind a rack of clothing. "They're all laid off and available. How lucky is that?"

She burst out from between old coats, arms thrown wide. She looked elegant and natural in the formal gown. It was gold and red and squeezed her chest then fell straight, catching her curves in just the right way.

He drew back. "Oh my goodness. That's gorgeous. You're gorgeous." He'd never been in the position to see women trying on gowns and marveled at their comradery. There was a closeness with these women, like sisters, and the goodness of it brought tears to his eyes.

"You're balm for my soul, Bart Baines," Penelope said. She stepped back through the coats. "I've got to get back to the kitchen."

"Wait," a third voice came as Margaret and Penelope came back into view, dressed in their normal clothing. "I can't find anything. They're all too big or too daring."

Bella.

Margaret eyed Bartholomew and rubbed her belly. "Bart's here. He'll help."

He raised his hand. "Oh no, I just give the final praise."

"Don't undersell yourself. You can and you will help her," Penelope said as she took Margaret by the elbow and led her toward the stairs that went to the kitchen. "We've got work to do and as soon as you're done, we'll need you."

Bartholomew sighed.

"I heard that sigh all the way back here. You don't have to help," Bella said.

"No, no. I want to."

"With the snow you're going to need to pack the rink and smooth it out before much more falls."

He looked out the dormer window, watching tiny pinprick flakes drop fast. "That snow will be perfect for another layer and for packing the sides. But I'm happy to help you decide on a gown."

"Oh, all right. But stay back and I'll come out when I've got a dress on."

He sat on a trunk waiting, tapping his fingers. She came out in a navy-blue gown with a fitted waist that flared in a bell shape, reminding him of something old-fashioned like his mother wore when he was young. The gown had a dull sheen and was littered with odd-shaped appliques all over her chest. The sleeves came down just below her elbows. She covered one arm with a hand and then the other. He could see she was trying to cover her scars, that she was uncomfortable.

She stopped as soon as she saw him. Her shoulders drooped. "You look like you just ate a plate of lemons. I knew this one was no good the minute I popped it on. I was hoping that the easy clasps in front would make it worth wearing."

"Trading elegance and attractiveness for ease. That's not the kind of thinking that gets a woman her prince."

She popped a fist on one hip. "What makes you think I'm waiting for a prince?"

"All those books you read."

"Hmm. I see your point."

"But I didn't say you were waiting for a prince. I see you as more of a chooser than a chosen one."

She lifted her arms and turned this way and that, looking at her figure in different angles. "That little nuance is much appreciated." She stood in front of the mirror and yanked on the sleeves.

"No," he said.

She looked over her shoulder.

"I mean no to that dress," he explained.

"I suppose wealth doesn't always bestow taste, does it?" she said.

"It's not near beautiful enough for you."

"Bart. That's so... thank you."

"Just telling the truth. Presenting the facts."

She went back to the racks, fussing where he couldn't see her. "I'm going to need some gloves if I choose this one." She sauntered out from behind the gowns, taking purposeful, long steps with her chin in the air. "And what does the gentleman think of this?" She spun around, arms out.

"No."

She looked wounded.

"You *like* that?" he asked.

She pranced to the mirror and studied herself. "I, uh." She lifted the skirt and dropped it, the burnt-orange taffeta making loud whooshing noises when the material moved. "*No.* I don't. I feel like someone's grandmother in this."

"You just didn't want to agree with me," he said.

"That's not it."

She disappeared again.

He loved spending this time with her doing something that far exceeded their familiarity with each other. Yet it didn't feel intrusive, at least it didn't to him. "Then what?"

She stuck her head around a rack of coats. "Don't really know what but can you dig through that trunk by the window? Margaret said there were gloves in there. Ball gown gloves, she called them. I'm sure you've seen your share of women wearing them."

He definitely had. "What happened to your arms?"

She froze, staring at him, but not responding.

He inhaled deeply. Uncomfortable silence sat between them. He wished he could take the question back.

She ducked behind the racks. "You know. Playing where I shouldn't have been. Learned the hard way that hot water is as dangerous as fire."

He was surprised at her tone, as though she was describing someone else's injuries. "You sound so blasé."

She peeked back around the rack. "They told me I was two years old. I don't remember a thing other than a vague sense of a doctor and women helping me and…" She started to breathe heavy.

"I'm sorry. I don't want you to be upset."

Silence.

He sighed. "Really. I'm sorry. I shouldn't have said anything."

"It's not you. It's a reaction deep inside me that when I think too hard about it, I feel all woozy, like the… it must have been horrible for my parents and the people helping and…"

"It's all right. We don't have to talk about it."

She whipped through the racks, the hangers squeaking as she shoved gowns to the side. "Oh, jeepers. Nothing. Maybe I'll just help with cooking, baking, and serving. Stick to my own wardrobe."

"There has to be something back there almost as beautiful as you."

He dug through the glove trunk. She rustled gowns, hidden from sight.

"I take it back. You are a blend of delicate and steely," he said. "So I can't imagine there's a dress back there that can highlight your grace and strength at the same time. But there has to be something you'll like well enough. At least that."

She poked her head through the middle of the coat rack. "Did you just read that from a book?"

"You don't think I can present honest and beautiful thoughts without plucking the words out of another man's mouth? Out of a book?"

"Or a woman's. What you said there sounds like something Jane Austen might have written."

"Hmm. How about that?"

He pulled four sets of gloves from the trunk as the sound of clothes shifting and the tops of hangers clicked again, sounding in between

Bella's frustrated sighs and groans. Finally she reacted in a way that could only be characterized as liking what she saw.

"Put *that* one on. Whichever one made you respond like that."

"I'm putting it on."

"Good. I knew there must be something."

"Ohh. Yes. I think this is it."

"Well, come on, we've got Croatian plum dumplings to make and ice rinks to water and smooth."

"No."

"No, what?"

"I am looking in the mirror back here and I think I absolutely love this dress."

"Well, let me see."

"No, because if you don't like it then you'll ruin it for me, and I want this one to be the one, so you'll just have to wait and see. And be sure your face lights up like the sun when you see me in it."

He laid back on the trunk near the mirror and stared at the ceiling. "I like that. If you love it, it must be just right."

When she came back out clad in her ordinary clothing, in her stocking feet, she bumped him over and sat on the trunk beside him. She started to put her boots on.

He wanted to run his fingers along her shapely ankles but wouldn't dare for a million reasons.

"Shoes," he said.

"Yes, these are shoes, Bart."

"We're back to Bart?"

"I can't decide."

"Well, stand up. This label on the trunk says *shoes*. You can't wear those clodhoppers with your fancy dress."

She stood. "James told me men don't notice shoes."

Bartholomew narrowed his gaze on her. "Well, I suppose you can hide the boots under the hem, but then when you dance…"

She pulled a face and her cheeks burned. "Dance. I don't know about that. This isn't my debutante ball. I'm just going for the kielbasa and champagne. Maybe another spin around the ice."

He held his hand out, thunderstruck. Bella was like no other woman he'd met or even dreamed of. "A woman after my own heart." And he hadn't even known what his heart wanted until she showed up.

Bella took his hand and he twirled her into him. She was as graceful as a woman who'd attended dance classes her whole life. She smelled like pear soap. She looked up at him, her eyes, blue like a deep ocean in the sun. She had a piece of thread at the corner of her mouth. He brushed it away. She pulled back and put her hand to her mouth.

"A thread. From the dress. Green. You chose green?"

"Velvet." She smiled and looked away. "Where are those gloves?"

He showed her four sets. "But it sounds like you need green velvet not this material."

He dug through the trunk again looking for the right ones while she rolled up her sleeves. He tried not to appear shocked at the marbled scarring he could now see distinctly. She struggled to get the first one on. "Guess I'm not used to fine materials that aren't all stretched out."

"Let me help. There's a trick to it."

She raised her eyebrows.

"I had a fiancée once. She told me all about it."

"Had or have?"

"Long gone."

Bella watched as he gently rolled the arm part of the glove down to the hand part. "Slide your fingertips in." He wiggled the material so each one met the slot, then smoothed and pressed between each finger before he unfurled the first glove halfway up her arm. She winced and he stopped, pulling his hands back.

Their eyes met.

"It's all right," she said. "Doesn't hurt. Not at this point. It tickled."

He smiled, relieved, and smoothed his hands up her arm, the velvet curving around her elbow. He did the same for the other and her shyness struck him as unusual for her, so after the second one was on he backed away, wiping his hands on his pants.

"Shoes," he said, opening the trunk he'd been sitting on. "Four pairs of green velvet shoes in this trunk."

She helped dig them out and set them beside each other.

He closed the lid. "Sit there, madame. I'm here to serve."

He held the shoe and she wiggled her foot into it.

"Too big."

Next pair.

"Way too small for the left." She circled her foot. "Right's sort of all right. The right could work."

Next pair.

"Both are way too small."

They eyed the final set.

She crossed her fingers and held them up. "Maybe one of the sisters has weird sized feet like me?"

He drew a deep breath and ran a finger over the arch of her foot.

She threw her head back with a laugh. "Don't make me wait anymore. If I can't find matching shoes, I can't go to this fancy ball. Unlike Cinderella, Cinder Bella doesn't have a fairy godmother." She giggled again.

He winked at her. "You're right. You're the fairy godmother," he said. He moved closer and put her foot on his knee. "All right, Bella, this is it. The right one from that other pair worked. We just need a left." He shimmied the left shoe on. She wiggled her foot, but didn't say anything. He adjusted it again. Her eyes lit up. She gestured for the right shoe from the other pair. He slid it on, stood and took her hands to help her stand. She circled the trunk then met his gaze.

"*They work.*"

He shoved his fist in the air. "Yes. You're set for the ball."

She pointed one foot then the other, looking pleased at the sight. "I do feel like Cinderella with all this beautiful fuss," she said. "Cinder Bella goes to the New Year's Eve ball," she whispered under her breath.

"Not Cinderella or Cinder Bella. Not at all. The queens of great lands must fear you ever showing up in their worlds, for nothing they could wear or do could ever compete with how you look, with who you are."

She tilted her head and put her hand against his cheek, the velvet soft on his skin.

"That's so nice of you," she said.

"Nice?"

She pulled her hand away.

"I don't mean it to be nice," Bartholomew said. His voice cracked and in doing so he was moved to tell her what he was feeling. He couldn't stop himself.

She looked at him confused and sat on the trunk, taking the shoes off. She pulled one foot up and shoved it into her regular boot.

He dropped to his knees and gripped hers, glad that her skirt was down so he wasn't making contact with stockinged skin. "You are so amazing," he said.

She looked like she was going to say something but then didn't. She just shook her head.

"You've been through so much and yet you smile and make your life work and I know you like to be alone, but can't you give me a chance to—"

She pushed his hands away and relaced her boot, tying it as though angry.

"Did I say something to upset you?"

She shook her head.

He stood and paced while she tied her other boot. "I'm just going to say everything and get it all out."

She looked worried. "Get what out?"

"You see." He paced again. "It's that when I'm with you and when I see you and when I learn more about you, it all leads to me thinking about you nonstop. Making the ice? I thought of you laughing in the snow the first day we met. Shoring up the wall? I thought of you tending to your animals. Eating bean sandwiches three days in a row? I think of you and how I'd love for you to make us maple syrup and I'd eat beans every day for the rest of my life if you were with me."

She glanced up at him with a scowl.

"Okay, I'll make the syrup."

"Hmm."

He stopped pacing.

She sighed. "This is really strange," she said.

"That's your response?" He spread his arms. "You don't have anything to convey that might be parallel to the feelings I just expressed? That you think of me, too, that way? At all?"

"When eating bean sandwiches, you're hoping I'd say?"

"Not specifically beans. But in *any* instance?" His face flooded with heat, he grabbed at his neck. "Strange? That's all you have to say?"

"Well. Things are awkward now—"

"Awkward? That's not good news. For me, I mean." He rubbed his eyes with both hands. When he pulled them away he got back down on his knees and took her hands. "Look. I love you, Bella. That's what I'm saying. I love you. I know it's crazy and I can't believe I'm saying it. But it's true. It's been building and now I just have to let it out so I am. Letting it out. There it is." He swung his hand to emphasize.

She grimaced.

"What?"

"That's insane. You don't know me."

He felt as though she'd jabbed him with a hot poker right through the chest. "You said that doesn't matter. When I said your hens and cat can't possibly like me, you said they loved me and said it didn't matter that they didn't know me. And now I see that can happen. Your hens came out of the tree for me when they were afraid. So you were right. And now I see. I feel it. I love you and I may not know you the way you are meaning, but I know who you are."

She stood, pulled him to standing, and gripped his shoulders. For a moment he thought she might get up on her toes and plant a kiss on him, but she pushed him back and stepped around him.

He turned and sat against the trunk. "You said the animals felt my goodness. Heck. You trusted me to whirl around the ice rink on skates, holding you, your eyes shut, that smile you had. You trusted me to do that and you can't trust how I'm saying I feel."

She hesitated and looked away. "The skating was different."

"How is it different?"

"That was just a couple of moments. The future? You're a banker, a man with upward aspirations. My aspirations are flat, maybe a small house with book-lined rooms, but I don't have upward aspirations. Not like railroads and banks and…"

"I *love* you."

"No."

"You can't just say no. You feel the same. I can see it. I feel it. It's not just me."

She shook her head. "Bart. You're intelligent and business savvy—well, maybe not *that* as evidenced by your bank collapse, but… We're too different and you simply losing everything you own doesn't change what's different about us deep down. Our differences are beyond the obvious and you know it. You've had a lifetime of all the things that make people full of grace and exude a lifestyle that I can only read about in books."

He approached her. "No. It's only on the surface that we're different. We're not different down deep. It's the opposite of that."

"You can't even tell me a favorite line from one book."

"Once upon a time there was a beautiful woman who loved books and her hens and a cat. And she met a man who didn't understand anything other than how he felt about her. How he loved her."

She pressed her fingers against his lips. "Right now you think you love me because I've told you stories are important and we're living this little group fairy tale in a home that isn't ours, with packages of food arriving by the half-ton, but that's not how things work. I know that more than anyone. Much as I love to invent stories to forget and to lose myself in books, I know the reality of my life and there's no way you, a Harvard man, a banker, can live like this forever."

He took her hand from his lips and gently rolled down the ball gloves, caressing her as he did. "We don't have to live in borrowed homes and wear borrowed clothes forever. This fairy tale two weeks is amazing. And I realize it's not how things will be next week. But we can leave here together. It doesn't have to end just because—" He removed the last of the second glove.

"No." She latched onto his hand. He caressed the back of her fingers with his thumb.

Couldn't she see that her actions didn't match her words? She clearly didn't want to let him go.

"You can't fully understand what it feels like to have nothing because whatever you've lost, you'll get back soon. And though you've lost things—"

"And my reputation."

"Yes, that. You are still completely utterly different than me in terms of experience and expectations for society life and education."

She sighed and withdrew her hand from his, making him feel as though she'd extracted his beating heart.

"It can't be," she said. "The eggs went to the wrong person."

"That? That's what you're worried about? Really? Those egg notes? I am so much more than that, than my lack of literary interest. Can't you see? I'm not a reader. You really want that to be how you choose someone to love?"

"Love isn't a choice. Those notes were invitations. And you accepted the invitation but didn't like the theme of the party once you arrived."

He pushed his hands into his pockets trying to contain his panic that she may not feel the same as he did. "So you don't want me? Not at all?"

"It's not that."

"Then what?"

"The river between us is too wide and deep to jump over to be together. There's no bridge, there's no way."

"You don't love me? You don't feel this?" He took her hand and pressed it against his chest. "What I feel?"

Her gaze flicked away from him then back. He saw the sharp intake of her breath.

She pulled her hand away and tucked one inside the other, like the action was holding her together. "Like I said, this is awkward. We have to spend our last two nights enmeshed with this strangeness and…"

He couldn't breathe. His heart pounded and he wanted to scoop her up and hold her until she had no choice but to love him right back. But that wasn't what he really wanted, how he wanted her to love him loud and clear, like he was loving her right that moment. "Fine. I've got a rink to prepare." He strode away.

"I'm sorry, Bart, I just don't think this can be anything other than what it's been."

"Fine," he said and started into the stairwell, his pounding feet winding down to the kitchen where he grabbed his coat and sprinted out the door.

He turned on the hose and sprayed a light coating of water onto the fresh snow-covered rink. It froze quickly with a dull, rough finish. So he brushed the ice then wiped it down until it gleamed. Fingers raw and red, but unwilling to go back into the house, he went to the carriage house, needing to expel nervous energy.

Entering the carriage house reminded him of Leonard. So he stalked over to the blacksmith shop. He couldn't imagine ending the two weeks, having fallen in love just to have it be something else, like the light mist of hose water freezing into ice. But he couldn't force Bella to love him back.

In the blacksmith shop he paced, his mind reeling. Broken colored glass on the worktable reflected sunlight so bright it brought clarity to him in an instant. That was it. He'd never been in love before. He'd never loved anyone like he did her. It explained the absolute unsteadiness that came over him at the thought of her not loving him, too.

It made him think of his parents, his love for them, how much they'd loved him, adored him until the day they died. He felt that for Bella and so much more. The exciting fluttering kind of love that knocked him silly when she touched him, but also something else, an undercurrent below the excitement, something that latched to his soul and told him Bella was the person he was meant to marry. She was the woman he would love until the day he died.

How could he feel that for her yet she feel nothing for him? He understood what she was saying about living in two different worlds. He understood that his business was not something Bella was interested in. But she could grow to love it. She didn't have to become a socialite. But he was sure she could make a good home. If only she loved him. If only.

He bent over the worktable, running his fingers over the glass pieces. The green and blue and clear and red pieces were like cast-off jewels. James had made something so beautiful from the broken shards.

Bartholomew picked one up and looked at the dark green glass. And with nervous energy coursing through him he grabbed the sandpaper and started to work the edges of the pieces, sanding away the roughness, wishing he could sand away the rough edges that kept him and Bella apart.

He couldn't do it. He couldn't just go on with life as though nothing had changed. Not just the obvious changes that came with going from wealthy to poor, but that he'd experienced the kind of change deep in a person that makes it impossible to go backward, to not even want to look back. Even if someone stopped by and dropped ten bags of cash and gold into his lap, he wouldn't take it if he couldn't live differently than he had been.

He moved from glass piece to glass piece, wracking his brain for not only how he could recognize that he felt differently but how he might be able to actually live differently.

A knock on the doorjamb of the shop startled Bartholomew.

"Hey, there." James inched forward. "It's dark. You missed dinner and—"

"Help me with something. Please." Bartholomew held up his sanded and polished glass pieces in his palms.

James cocked his head as though this was a dire request.

"Just show me one thing and then I won't bother you."

"There's lots to do for the ball and—"

"I know. Just this one thing. Please."

James nodded and approached Bartholomew with a wide, knowing smile.

CHAPTER 21
Bella

After the incident in the attic with Bart, Bella split her time between her animals and helping prepare for the gala. When she was back at the barn, fire lit and settled in to read before bed, she was surprised to hear a knock at the door. She slid it open expecting to see someone. But no one was there.

Footprints led to the door and back to the path. The sound of rustling made her look down. A cage stood right outside the door. She lifted it up. A rooster. She set the cage down inside and got on her knees to open it. She picked him up and nuzzled him, her fingers brushing past a note tied around his neck. She pulled the string over his head and read the note. "Something to help protect your hens. Arnold traded with a caretaker from another estate. He says to keep it in the cage for a while so the hens can decide if they like him, if they like his smell—Bartholomew."

She giggled and did just that. The hens circled the cage checking out every angle and then plopped down right beside it. Simon joined them, purring and rubbing the top of his head against the bars. "Guess he's all right with all of you, then, isn't he?"

And she went off to bed knowing the next day would be long and full of excitement. Instead of drifting off to sleep reading, she thought of Bart instead. She thought of his little story starting with once upon a time. What if she believed his story? What if she admitted what she felt about him? His enthusiastic proclamation had taken her by surprise. She saw his sincerity—no, she felt it to her core. And that energy sparked what she'd been denying since Bart rescued her hens from the tree. Seeing him subvert his discomfort with animals for her made her shudder with… love. She'd recognized it as love immediately. But then she'd counseled herself wisely to let those feelings only into the fringes of her being.

Her argument in the Maple Grove attic was exactly right. She encased her heart and soul in a thin eggshell, keeping both safe. She'd made it through life alone, she'd made it through life loving only the things she could count on, in situations she could control. And that had kept her safe and content. She could depend on that.

And yet, she fell asleep replaying how it felt when Bart touched her ankles and shimmied the shoes onto her feet. How it felt when he brushed her fingers with his thumb, and rolled the gloves up past her elbows, how his heartbeat felt against her palm, how his lips felt brushing across hers when they kissed. And, how she had indeed trusted him to hold her while skating. And just on that cusp between awake and sleep where she made up the stories she would write someday, her mind conjured an image of Bart holding her close—this time, her heart beating right against his.

Bella wakened with a start on New Year's Eve day. No lingering between sleep and awake, no long stretches or languid yawns. There was far too much to be done. Hopping out of bed quickly meant she could spend extra moments with the hens, the rooster, and Simon. She monitored the rooster whom she named Hamilton, but decided to call, Ham, while he interacted with the hens.

They seemed to happily take him into their flock, but Bella cleaned the cage so she could put him back inside it when night came, before she got dressed for the ball. She smiled as she walked the property with Ham and the hens, thinking of Bart arranging for the rooster with Arnold.

It was as sweet a gift as she could have fathomed. And it was from Bart. Another intriguing unfolding of him, something unexpected, when she'd thought she'd decided exactly who he was. Even with her lack of family and friends, she knew better than to think a person was the sum total of what you saw in little bursts and blips. But now, little by little, she wondered if Bart truly was a better person than she'd ever imagined.

When the animals were fed, the coop was clean, and they were free to roam for the day, she fully emerged into preparation for the ball. In the kitchen at the Westminsters' she made egg and sausage casseroles to get everyone ready for the day. They were on their second cups of coffee when they began to really understand the enormity of the event that Bella had created.

The notion of a New Year's ball at the Westminsters', that Bella had invited struggling families to join the festivities, had spread far and wide. Not only had Ada Pritt stopped by with canned pickles, she reported there were scores of people planning to attend, that people were grateful and excited to come.

Knock after knock at the door interrupted the food preparation. The musicians who would play with Nathaniel arrived to rehearse, tuxedos in hand to change into later. Out-of-work maids, friends of Margaret's, bakers who'd lost jobs, cooks who'd been set aside when restaurants went under, all showed up to help ready for the party, wanting to be part of something both extravagant and generous. So many people came to help that the Maple Grove crew almost had nothing to do.

A few hours before the ball was to begin, Bella got the animals into the barn and Ham in his cage. She gathered her fresh underthings and headed back to the house where she would dress with Margaret, Clemmie, Penelope, and Mrs. Tillman. They bathed in lavender and rosemary waters, styled each others' hair and carefully buttoned one another into the exquisite gowns they'd selected from the attic. Bella slipped into the emerald-green, velvet shoes and couldn't help remembering Bart's gentle touch on her ankles and feet.

"Why are you shaking your head like that?" Margaret asked.

"Hmm?"

"You are so beautiful," Margaret said.

Bella caressed her smoothed-back hair, the low bun, then pressed her hand to her chest, just below her neck. The compliment stunned her, the feel of naked skin, exposed above her breasts, shocked her as well.

Margaret pulled Bella's hand away and handed her the velvet gloves. "Don't cover up. You're perfection. The way the sweetheart neckline cuts you, the off the shoulder sleeves... your waist!"

Bella pulled on the gloves then brushed her hands over her waist and belly, liking how the corset built into the dress nipped in all the perfect places then dropped into a column with a small bustle at the back. "These Westminster women have some beautiful dresses, that's for sure. I feel like the bustle is chasing me around every time I move," she giggled and wiggled back and forth, "but... the gown *is* exquisite."

Margaret laughed, too. "Well, the Westminster daughters never looked as stunning as you in that."

Bella straightened at the thought.

"That's it," Margaret said. "Shoulders back, and Bart will..." Margaret rubbed her belly and seemed to flinch.

Bella waved her gloved hand through the air, surprised to hear Margaret mention Bart's name. "You're all right?" Bella looked at Margaret's stomach. "The baby?"

Margaret nodded and stepped closer. "You're not going to ignore what's happening, are you?"

Bella looked at Margaret directly. "You know I'll help you when the baby arrives. But tonight. You are beautiful and you should enjoy the food and dancing and—"

Margaret looked confused. "No, Bella. That's not what I meant."

"You ladies all dressed?" James's voice came with a knock on the bedroom door.

"We are," Margaret said. She bent into Bella's ear. "I was talking about you and Bart."

James, Arnold, Nathaniel, and Bart entered the room, stopping Bella from responding to Margaret. The men were dressed in black tails with stand-up and wing-tipped collars. The lapels of their vests made them appear as though they'd lived among the class of ball-goers their whole lives. Each had combed hair and groomed beards.

Finally Bella looked at Bart. His clean-shaven face looked dewy and handsome. But it wasn't his handsomeness that knocked her over, it was how he was looking at her. He mouthed her name and drew a sharp breath before looking away then back, shaking his head a little, as though disbelieving. "You are so beautiful," he said.

She saw her beauty in his reaction. She felt it. She warmed all over as it was confirmed. She'd picked the right dress.

James held up a small bundle wrapped in golden tissue paper. "For you, Margaret."

She unwrapped the gift while he held it in his palms. She bent in and gasped. "A... James? What is this?"

He lifted the object up and the tissue paper fluttered to the floor. He bent down to get the paper but didn't get back up. On one knee he held up a ring to Margaret. "Made it myself. And if you'll take me for your husband, I will take you for my wife and we'll start this little family."

"You would do that for me? Even though..."

"You haven't been able to tell that I'm fully madly in love with you and it doesn't matter that..." He paused and swallowed hard.

She covered her mouth.

"I will love and honor you for the rest of our lives."

She latched her arms around his neck and he stood, the two clinging to each other.

Bella started to tear up, thinking she was witnessing one of her books come to life.

The couple separated far enough from each other for him to slip the ring onto her finger. "First class window glass, shattered during a storm and remade into something that signifies how we can make a life together, even if things haven't unfolded as we might have wanted." Margaret nodded and fell into his arms again.

Bart cleared his throat. "I've got something, well, a few somethings for the other ladies." He drew a deep breath and released it. "The other day I took a risk and bared my heart..." He looked at Bella.

She couldn't speak. She glanced at everyone else, felt her eyes widen and heat creep up her neck. What was he doing?

"And when things didn't just go as I planned, I went outside and laid another inch of ice on the rink and then wandered into the carriage house then to the blacksmith shop, just needing to occupy my body since my... since the rest of me was just too antsy, unsure, un-everything, I guess. Lost. I had to do something to occupy my hands even if I couldn't occupy my heart." His voice cracked. "And I remembered what Clemmie said about the tree—that even though it was beautiful without a single ornament, that women like, they *deserve* a little sparkle and color."

Bella's emotions swirled inside her, a blend of pleasure that Bart was thinking of others, and anticipation and curiosity. What had he done?

He lifted the packages toward James. "And James was kind enough to help me. As you all know, we have limited time left here and I have zero funds to buy a symbol of what I've felt living here with all of you. In my need to keep moving, I found myself sanding and polishing glass shards in the shop. I needed something permanent to express my thanks and my hope that somehow we can all stay connected even though we… Well." His voice cracked, making Bella hold her breath.

"So, James and Arnold and Nathaniel helped me take those glass pieces and make something for Penelope, Mrs. Tillman, Clemmie, and Bella." He looked directly at Bella. "For Bella."

The whispery way he said her name made her knees weak. He walked toward her with a bundle wrapped in the same gold tissue that Margaret's ring had been in.

Arnold gave wrapped pieces to Clemmie and Mrs. Tillman and Nathaniel gave Penelope one, too. Hair pins with red balls on each end to match her dress. Clemmie and Mrs. Tillman opened bracelets glistening with blue glass shapes to complement their gowns.

"Open it." Bart held the last package in his palms.

And even though she knew everyone in the room was watching, Bella's perspective narrowed to the width of the package in his hands as they quaked, rustling the paper. She smiled up at him and he winked, making her giggle. She untied the ribbon and opened the sides of wrapping, revealing five glass pieces soldered and joined at their tops, creating a spray of "jewels."

She looked at him, then back at the necklace. "Oh, Bart. It's the most beautiful thing I've ever seen. And it matches my gown."

"To my eye, this bottle glass is every bit the emeralds that a Westminster might wear with a green, velvet gown. When you wear this, the old broken pieces become as precious as…" He shook his head. "…as any gem in a queen's tiara."

She ran her finger over the glass faces. "But how did you get the chain to connect it all?"

"I dug through my trunk for the first time in ages and I had my father's watch in there and I took the chain off of it. Had enough length for your necklace and Mrs. Tillman's and Clemmie's bracelets. James really is a craftsman with this glass. It was him, really. I just had the idea."

"Oh no. I made the ring," James said. "But the rest was all Bart. Once he got started and just let the ideas come, well, it was like an entire universe came into being right in front of us."

Bart latched the necklace around Bella's neck, his fingers brushing against her skin nearly making her faint. If only this could be a real dream coming true. She couldn't have written a better story if she'd set out to do it. She showed off the necklace to their little group, feeling Bart's gaze on her as she moved from person to person, accepting the praise for the necklace on Bart's behalf.

"Leonard would have loved this," Mrs. Tillman said.

They all agreed.

Bart wiped his eyes at the mention of Leonard, making Bella feel more connected to him than ever.

The ringing doorbell interrupted the silence that came with thinking of their lost friend.

"It has begun," Mrs. Tillman said.

"I've got to get to the skating rink," Bart said. "I imagine there will be lots of brushing the ice if this ball is as big as we expect."

"Wait, Bart." Bella took his elbow. "Thank you." She touched the glass that skimmed along her collarbone. "It's the most beautiful thing I've ever seen."

"You are the most beautiful woman I've ever seen."

Bella almost melted into him, wanting to tell him she did feel the same. Maybe she could take a chance with him.

Nathaniel nudged Bart away. "You lovebirds can take this up later."

They trailed downstairs, going over the plan. Several musicians would play near the rink for the skaters and the rest would be in the parlor for dancing. Arnold would assist at the rink. Penelope would oversee the food, and James and Margaret would man the front door. Nathaniel took his place with the orchestra, while Mrs. Tillman and Clemmie assisted Penelope, directing last-minute preparations, and Bella helped greet guests.

Some people streamed into the home, others went around back, heading right to the rink and bonfire. Laughter and happy chatter followed, ballooning into the air with this magnificent gathering where no one seemed to feel despair or worry, or even irritation.

In addition to the guests, jugglers, magicians, clowns and puppeteers showed up, all adding to the enchanted evening. The chefs and maids who came to help make the ball happen took turns with Penelope and others so they could all enjoy the food and revelry. After the last new guest had trickled into the foyer, Bella went outside to see the families skating, their heads thrown back in laughter. It was like nothing she'd ever seen before.

"Utter joy," Bart observed.

"Yes, yes," she said. "It happened. It really came to be."

"I couldn't have imagined that building this rink would ever be worth it," Bart said. "When Leonard brought the idea up it sounded ridiculous. So much work for something that would disappear with the weather, possibly leaving rotted grass. What a waste of time and energy, I thought."

She looked up at him, the awe on his face as he watched the skaters making her smile.

"Thank you for the stunning necklace and the rooster. I just can't thank you enough for thinking of me."

He was about to respond when a gregarious voice overshot the murmurs of the crowd. "Bartholomew Baines—there you are," a man said, approaching with his hand extended.

"Mr. Heinz?" Bart said with a chuckle. "What on earth brings you here?"

"A ball. I was told there was a ball being thrown for the best people in town. Leading citizens and the people who make the world run, those who I'd argue *are* the leading citizens."

"I have to agree," Bart said.

Bella suddenly felt self-conscious. She knew Mr. Heinz's name, knew every single product he made, even knew what his workers' aprons looked like as she remembered seeing the woman at the market the other day.

"Listen." Mr. Heinz bent in to Bart, but spoke loud enough for Bella to hear. "I wish I would've thought of this myself. I take great pride and effort in making my factories clean, and I go so far as to offer uniform washing for the women who work at the factory so they don't have to wash their clothes at home and… well, you've inspired me even further, Mr. Baines. And I know you've fallen on hard times. And this ball for the masses. What you've done—"

"We—" Bart gestured toward Bella. "What we've done. This is Bella Darling. She's at the heart of it all."

Mr. Heinz eyed her. "Bella Darling. I've heard about you. Word's gotten around about all of you here. You've certainly surrounded yourself with the best people with big hearts and the understanding that money isn't everything. I'm sure the Westminsters are proud to be associated with all of you. Have to admit I'm a little surprised that Archibald Westminster had this kind of transformation, that he's now hosting a grand ball for people he didn't normally..."

Bella studied Mr. Heinz, wondering if he was sincere. His warmth seemed to indicate he was.

"Anyway," he said. "One of my line girls, Miss Plant, saw Bella here at the market and let me know what your plan was. So I sent some supplies along this week. I trust you got them."

Bella went on her toes. "Oh yes, Mr. Heinz. The horseradish has made wonderful beef rub and toast and... I remember the woman."

"Miss Plant," he said. "When she got to work that morning, she was distracted and seemed worried. But turns out she was just trying to figure out how we could help. And I'm so glad we did." He surveyed the space. "This is truly a wonder. You should be proud. All of you."

"Thank you," Bart said, extending his hand.

Mr. Heinz shook his hand and leaned closer to Bart. "When I heard what you did for that family during the bank panic, that you took it on the chin for them, that you gave the widow and her children every dime you had left in the bank? That right?"

Bart nodded.

"And then your friends abandoned you—unable to see that there would always be more money for them? But that widow? She and her children would suffer more, untold amounts if you hadn't helped her like you did."

"Thank you, sir," Bart said.

Bella couldn't believe what she was hearing. Bart gave everything away? Even with just lantern light around the rink she could see him blushing.

"I should have reached out to you," Mr. Heinz said. "I was worried, because even though you did the right thing, I couldn't help thinking you should have kept a little bit back for yourself. It's easier to help others if you have some means yourself. But then you went missing. I got busy with pushing food safety legislation and had some equipment breakdowns and marketing ideas gone bad and I just forgot until Miss Plant explained how Bella here and you all created this amazing celebration. You are a brave soul, Bartholomew Baines. What foresight to engage the Westminsters. What creativity."

Bella and Bart eyed each other. She wasn't going to reveal that the Westminsters weren't involved and certainly weren't aware.

"I'm not brave at all. Not like Bella."

"Sharing the path of life with other brave souls is important." He gave Bella a nod. "But is it true that you really have nothing to your name?" Mr. Heinz said. "Nothing?"

Bartholomew looked up to the sky. Bella held her breath wondering if this would have him falling into another stretch of despair or disappointment, dropping him back into a Scroogy mood.

He shook his head. "Not true at all. I've got these wonderful friends—Penelope the baker, Arnold the herbologist and candlestick maker, James the jewelry maker, Nathaniel the fiddler, Margaret the mother, Leonard, God rest his soul, the doctoring engineer, Clemmie the straight shooter—sort of a lighthouse seeing the truth about things, Mrs. Tillman who organizes us all."

Bart glanced at Bella who was left speechless as her heart expanded so big that it stopped her breath.

"And Bella with the magic eggs." He kept his eyes on her.

She tingled all over.

"Oh, those eggs. I've heard," Mr. Heinz said, making Bella pay attention to him again. "As a man in foods, I'm more than intrigued."

"Thank you," Bella said, feeling the warmth of regard from such a successful man, a man who'd heard of her.

"So I have plenty saved or to count as mine, riches I mean," Bart said. "The tangible things I own now fit inside one trunk, one briefcase, and one satchel. And until the other day I'd ignored them for quite some time."

Mr. Heinz took his shoulder and shook it. "Sounds like you have more than most men. And better than having more is that you have exactly what is needed to make it in the world, to make the journey count. No one can wipe out your education, and paired with kindness and a view of society beyond fancy luncheons at the club and a different ball every night in the holiday season… I know you'll be just fine."

"Thank you," he said.

Mr. Heinz gave Bella a nod and backed away. "Thank you for being generous, Miss Darling."

"Thank you," she said.

He pointed at Bart. "Come fit me in some skates. The wife is waving at me like a lunatic from the other side of the rink and if I don't give her a round or two on the ice she'll freeze me out later."

And so Bart took Mr. Heinz to the bench where he could sit, and buckled on the blades. Bella was left standing there, staring after them completely stunned.

Bart hadn't just stupidly lost his money or not hidden it well enough to escape his own downfall. He'd given it away to a widow and her children. He'd given it *all* away.

She watched him help Mr. Heinz and a few kids. Could Bart possibly understand more about living without than she'd thought? Was it possible that the two of them could love each other in a way that brought happiness? Was it as impossible as she once thought it could be? She swept one hand over her low bun. Could she accept a better life without fear of losing those she'd come to love?

CHAPTER 22
Bartholomew

By the time midnight struck, Bartholomew had buckled and latched a hundred children and adults into ice skates just by himself. A blast of fireworks and hand-held sparklers caused the skaters to halt, faces upturned, watching as shimmery colors peaked near the stars and showered down through the treetops. Mr. Buchanan and his wife had donated those, trying to tightrope-walk between saying that they didn't completely approve of the ball, but that they weren't going to stop the celebration either. Certainly the roast and ham they sent for the soiree said what they truly believed.

As firework colors mixed with falling snow, the display put a lid on 1893 and opened its arms to 1894, and Bart was again reminded of Leonard and the impact he had on him in just a short time. When the final shots of every type of firework at once drizzled their last bit of silver and blue light, cheers went up from the rink, from around the bonfire, from the partiers who'd trailed out of the house to watch the grand exhibition. Champagne was passed, hugs given to loved ones and strangers, and the last of the food was consumed with gusto by people who ate like kings nightly to those who would never eat like that again. They were all one for that night and it was magic, a pure enchanted world.

Bartholomew felt a hand on his back and he turned to see Bella looking up at him. They stood like that for a moment before he swept her into his arms and spun her.

"I've never felt such joy in my life, not ever," Bella said, her lips brushing past his ear, causing fireworks to shimmer over his skin.

She squeezed him tighter, giving him hope. Maybe she'd come to see him differently.

He set her down.

"This happiness has swallowed me up and I'm overflowing with it. I feel like…" She shook her head.

He knew she couldn't measure the wonder she was feeling, that she was amazed at how more and more of it just kept coming like an artesian well supplied water at a constant rate.

"I want this to go on forever."

"It can." He took her hands. "Trust me. I don't know how, but I know it can."

She squeezed his hands. "Why didn't you keep some money for yourself? I thought that's what bankers did, save themselves so they could… Like Mr. Heinz said, maybe it's better to keep some for yourself so you can help others. I've even said that myself—that I feel most unhappy when I have nothing to give when someone needs it."

Bart paused. He wasn't sure the truth would be enough to convince Bella of anything she hadn't already believed about him. "Because it was the right thing to do. Simple at that point. I'd made wrong decisions before that and the Franks family was suffering because of it. So when I had the chance to at least help her rebuild from her losses, in a small way, I helped. I trusted my friends could remake their lives. I know they still can, whether they do or not. But Mrs. Franks? She would have been one of the women you saw fighting over poison flour at the market. I just knew what I had to do."

"Oh, Bart."

"So, while I have no idea what I'm going to do when we leave here, I want you to know that I will make a life again and if you will trust me, come with me, I know I can't fail."

She looked shocked and didn't speak.

He kissed the back of each of her gloved hands. "We can't fail. You are the mirror that reflects back what is true about me instead of what I want to see. And if you will marry me—"

She gasped.

"Yes. If you will marry me. I will be the richest man to ever walk the earth. And I will make you happy."

"But—"

He held up a finger. "No. We'll build contentment, but don't worry. I promise we'll pepper it all with tonight's brand of immense thrill. I learned what you meant about contentment, the small things like when you said you loved reading in bed all day on New Year's Day. I understand now." He pushed his hand through his hair. "You read stories about other people. You want to tell stories about other people. But this is our story." He nodded. "Ours."

"But it's only been two weeks. Barely—"

He gripped her arms. "Who cares? What do you *feel?* You move through the world feeling your way, keeping distance, but giving so much to others. What are you feeling for me right now?"

She looked like she might fall over. He nearly let go of her, afraid he was being too harsh, but then she grabbed onto his arms, looking right at him. "I'd have to say, but I can't be sure, because I've never felt like this… I've loved lots of animals and even people I've met along the way for a minute or two, but—" She exhaled deeply. "I love you. I'm in love."

"But you've never *been* loved," he said in a whisper, a realization settling in. "You've never been loved and I've never loved anyone."

Her mouth dropped open.

"We fill each other's missing parts," he said.

Her eyes brightened then she looked away like she was considering it.

"You," he said, "who believes in the power of stories and happy endings and magic. *Wonder.* You get hens to lay eggs that no one can explain their quality or quantity. You put notes in eggs that bring people together." She glanced at him then away again. "You who believes in luck and magic and loving people deeply even though you step away before they can love you back…"

She met his gaze again, this time holding it.

"Will you let me love you like you deserve?"

She put her hands flat against her waist, shoring herself up. He wasn't sure if she was readying to run or fall into his arms.

Please, please, let me love you.

"That's it exactly," she said.

He could barely hear her over the crowd. He leaned down.

"We fill each other's missing parts." Her warm breath against his ear sent shivers through him as he embraced her tight.

He put his hand around the back of her neck, wanting to pull her in for a kiss but she turned his head so she could whisper into his ear again.

"I thought there was no way for us, that our lives would set us too far apart to suit one another, to truly be what I wanted in life. You are right. Deep inside where I couldn't see, we actually fit."

"Perfectly," he said.

She nodded.

They looked into each other's eyes and he kissed her, knowing everything right then was exactly as it should be.

Most of the guests left, but each and every one stopped to thank Bart and Arnold for helping them skate.

They searched out Penelope and Mrs. Tillman and Nathaniel. And they found their way to Bella, smothering her in kisses and hugs, wishing her the happiest new year.

The band stayed, playing long into the deep night hours, thrilled to stretch their fingers and lungs after a long time off.

And Bart and Bella found their way into the parlor, slow dancing, moving from formal dance positions to intimate clutches where his breath matched hers.

Exhausted, but unwilling to go to sleep, they were shocked into full wakefulness when Mrs. Tillman burst into the parlor.

Her cheeks were wet and her lips quivered, looking exactly like she had the night Leonard died. Bartholomew's mind filed through who was at risk for the same end… But it was only when he cycled through the list twice that he realized. "Margaret. The baby," he whispered.

Mrs. Tillman nodded and fell into Bartholomew's arms, sobbing.

CHAPTER 23
Bella

Bella's insides twisted. *Margaret was in danger!* Mrs. Tillman cried so hard against Bart's chest that her words were incomprehensible.

The musicians must have realized something was wrong and their playing trailed off to screeches and sour notes then nothing.

"The baby," Bartholomew said.

"A girl, a girl," Mrs. Tillman finally spit out.

"What happened?" Bart shook her. When she still couldn't confirm more than that a baby girl had been born, Bella darted toward the doorway.

As she reached the threshold to the foyer, James flew down the steps, rushing toward the parlor, latching onto Bella's hand and pulling her with him back into the room. Tears streamed down his face. Chills dumped through Bella's body, spilling from the top of her head. *No!* That would be too much. Not another death.

James bent over, hands on thighs, catching his breath.

Bella couldn't speak.

He covered his face with his hands and wiped away his tears before lifting his hands to the heavens. "A boy."

Bella drew back.

They looked at Mrs. Tillman who stopped crying, practically choking. "But I saw…" she said. "I saw *her.*"

"Yes," James said.

"She let out a scream like a bearcat," Mrs. Tillman said.

"The baby's alive?" Bella asked.

"Yes, yes, red-faced and screaming," James said.

"But then…" Bart said, eyes narrowed. "What do you mean *a boy*?"

James choked on a laugh and then threw his hands in the air again. "Twins. Margaret just gave birth to twins."

And the band struck up a waltz tune called "After the Ball."

Bella grasped Bart in a tight hug. "Oh my, twins!"

Mrs. Tillman caught her breath, fanning her face with one hand. "I'm sorry I frightened everyone, I was just so happy and when Margaret said she was naming her daughter Lena for Leonard, I was just overcome so I bolted down here and I couldn't get my words out right."

Bart hugged her. "We forgive you, Mrs. Tillman."

Her face grew brighter again. "But twins! A girl and a boy born on New Year's Day. What luck."

"What good luck," Bella said. "Oh my, this calls for coffee, doesn't it?"

"At least coffee," James said, leading the way to the kitchen. He waved the band members to come along. "We might as well drink up the champagne. We've got thirty-two hours before we're all kicked out of here. Might as well make the most of it."

And Bella grabbed Bart's hand and the whole gang gathered in the kitchen to wait for more word on Margaret and her New Year's babies.

The first of January, 1894, blasted into being with fireworks, dancing, embraces, passionate kisses, and the birth of twins. Then it turned soft and cozy as snow piled up outside the kitchen window and all but the original Maple Grove crew had left.

The group, minus James and Margaret, removed the decorations from the Christmas tree named Margarite and returned her to her rightful spot on the property. Seeing her magnificence, stripped of anything glittery and gold, made Bella grateful the tree hadn't had to die just to make them happy for two weeks.

Back in the kitchen, Bart fell asleep on the settee, but Bella's mind wouldn't settle enough to allow for slumber. She pulled on high boots and trudged to her barn, appreciating quiet moments saying goodbye to the place that had warmed her, sheltered her, provided the contentment she'd always dreamed of. She piled the borrowed books she'd need to drop off to the woman heading up the Carnegie Library committee for giving.

Bella organized the pots and tools that allowed her to complete her daily chores. She explained to her animals that they'd be moving on. Her voice cracked when she realized she had no plan to tell them in terms of where they'd be going.

Her throat tightened and for a moment she panicked. In the enchanted celebration, Bart's declarations of love and new babies, she'd allowed herself to ignore the dire straits in front of her. None of that other stuff that was so thrilling and wonderful would yield a place to stay once they left at noon the next day.

She collapsed onto the settee and gripped the arm, forcing breath into her lungs. The hens gathered around her feet, Ham, the rooster, nuzzling her too. Simon leapt into her lap and rubbed his head against her belly. All of this reminded her of Bart when the animals had perched on every part of him as if to say hello. Now, Bella realized they had also been saying, "*Don't go.*" Stay long enough to love our Bella.

The thought startled her. Like the story characters that leapt into her mind most mornings, that thought did the same. Her panic subsided. She wasn't alone. And she realized that although she had no plan, she had Bart.

"I have Bart," she said aloud.

"Yes."

She startled and turned to see Bart had entered the barn.

She stood but stopped herself from rushing to him. Then she let herself go. She leapt into his arms. He held her tight, the sense of trust coursing from his arms right into her. She knew he would protect her and love her. They would protect each other. That was absolutely what she wanted, what she could believe in. And she bridged the gap from trusting only herself to believing that Bart would stand with her, no matter what life brought. She'd never been so relieved.

Bart helped her carry a load of books to the house so they could more easily be moved out when the time came. The tools and pots would be needed the next day for a final animal feeding and cleanup of the barn.

When they entered the kitchen James was reporting on the babies. "Lena and Leonard," James said bright and cheery. "They're pink and chubby and quiet. They came out screaming like madmen and now, nuzzled into Margaret, it's like they are the picture of calm and peace."

"All we can wish for," Mrs. Tillman said. "Leonard would be so honored by using his name. Twice."

"We'll think of him always," James said.

Penelope prepared some broth and bread while Bella and Mrs. Tillman scrubbed pots and set everything back where it belonged. With each item replaced, Bella felt a sadness grow.

She'd been so busy cleaning and organizing that when Bart disappeared for a while she assumed he must be napping after a practically sleepless night. She wasn't sure how any of them were still awake. And that again gave her a moment's panic.

Bella would be all right. Bart would help her protect the animals. But what about Margaret and her newborns? She couldn't imagine her and James taking to the weather with no place to go. Suddenly, all the revelry seemed shortsighted. They should have focused on finding places to live, jobs to do. Someone should have thought harder about the fact that Margaret's baby might have been born any day.

Bella and Mrs. Tillman were a good team, getting much of the kitchenware put where it belonged. And Bella had to admit that when exhaustion finally forced her to the settee to sleep, that she was grateful she could no longer keep her eyes open, that she no longer had to worry where they would all end up.

Bella woke, realizing she wasn't in her barn but in the keeping room part of the Maple Grove kitchen. She grabbed the back of the couch and pulled herself up, squinting at the scene before her. With scratchy eyes and dry throat it took a moment for her register what she was seeing.

At the kitchen table, Bart, Nathaniel, Arnold, Clemmie, Mrs. Tillman, Penelope, and…

Bella rubbed her eyes. Henry Heinz and Mr. Buchanan, the banker? The group was fully engrossed in something at the center of the table.

Bella rose and shuffled toward them, craning to get a look at what was drawing all the attention.

Notebooks were scattered, and Bart and Mr. Heinz had pencils in hand, excitedly adding words and drawings to blank and already covered pages of journals.

"Ah, there's Bella," Mr. Heinz said.

"Awake and ready to go," Mr. Buchanan said.

"Go?" She shook her head. "Not until tomorrow."

"Not to leave, but to help us figure this out."

"While you were Rip Van Winkling over there," Clemmie said, "we were figuring out how to save us."

They all smiled at her.

"So sit. Come see," Bart said.

And so she did.

Mr. Heinz leaned in. "Well, it all started with Bart here digging through his trunk for a gift for the new babies that I hear were born just last night. Beautifully named for your friend, Leonard."

Bella nodded, then glanced at Bart and was reassured by a sweet smile. She suddenly felt warmed by every expression he gave her, as though each glance or touch held a thousand secrets only the two of them would understand.

He leaned on his forearms, keeping eye contact with Bella. "I found my old pocketknife. Every boy should have one. So that is for little Leonard. I'm still on the hunt for something for Lena because unfortunately I don't have much in the way of a girl's gift. But the real treasure was that I took just one second to open my father's notebooks. And soon a few moments turned into hours as I read what he'd written—his notes, his dreams and losses and wins and his business plans for how he built his trapping business. Well, I started to think. And I know I never considered how to create something—like dear Bella pointed out to me the third time we spoke. It just never occurred to me that I could.

"My father's notes about building a business that is inspiring and fulfilling, that doesn't scrimp on materials, that doesn't take advantage of nature or the people he hired… It was like I was meeting a man I never even saw before. It wasn't that my father didn't mention these principles to me, but I was young when he died and there was money for my education and seed money to start my bank. I was more enamored with what I could buy than what I could build."

Bella sat back. "Sounds right."

"Absolutely was."

"But what are you talking about doing?" Bella asked. "Starting a trapping business?"

"Not at all. That wouldn't feed our souls or use any of our gifts and talents," Bart said, eyeing Mr. Heinz and Mr. Buchanan. "We're joining forces with these two men."

Bella felt her head lose its blood. Was he really suggesting they should ask these two men to invest in a bank or... "What do you mean?"

"Bart came to us with his plan, scratched into notebooks first written by his father. That right there made me take a hard look," Mr. Heinz said. "Family business is my life's blood. But then his idea itself. It was perfect."

"What idea?"

Mr. Buchanan leaned in now. "First, I own this house. And I'm willing to offer it at a low price, rent to own probably."

"To Bart?"

"For your business."

Bella pointed to herself.

"Not just yours." Bart reached across the table and squeezed Bella's hand. "An inn. Ours. All of ours." He scanned the room.

With the mention of an inn, the men started gushing with every detail they could think of. "Pittsburgh is growing in leaps and bounds and people want to and need to stay in areas with less smoke. Shadyside is perfect. Maple Grove Inn."

"I'm still not grasping all of this. An inn?"

"This is so much larger than that, Bella," Bart said. "Yet smaller and intimate and personal. What I learned over the past few weeks was that people and community matter to me more than anything. This group... each of us has a different skill or interest."

Mr. Heinz leaned in. "Arnold will develop the land for food to feed the guests at the inn. But that food will also be a test garden for my company. Penelope will work with Miss Plant to experiment and record the food items that are enhanced or overpowered by Heinz condiments and foods."

"Heinz will underwrite the meals served here for our guests—" Bart said.

"Wait… Here?" Bella's sleepy mind was finally catching up. "Our guests?" Bella asked, turning to Mr. Buchanan. "You really mean you aren't kicking us out?"

The banker shook his head. "The opposite. James and Margaret will meet, greet, and tend to the needs of guests. When she's feeling up to it again, Margaret will hire the inn staff. This will be an inn of the highest order of luxury—but most of all, of family. When guests stay here, it will be like staying with family."

Bella looked at Bart. "What about you? I mean it's your idea but…"

"Bart is charged with making sure the brand stays true to its mission."

"Brand?"

"Well, this is only one inn. Why wouldn't we recreate it all over the city, over the region? Bart will lead that endeavor," Mr. Heinz said.

She glanced at Bart, excited that he seemed to have found something he felt was important. "Bart creating a set of inns. Not a bank?"

"Nothing like it," Bart said.

Bella was starting to grow excited at the thought.

"Mrs. Tillman will oversee day-to-day operations, working with a manager at each inn."

"And me?" Clemmie leaned in. "Oh, I just bankrolled inns two and three—City Center and Allegheny City."

"Bankrolled?" Bella asked.

Clemmie hauled a suitcase onto the tabletop and popped it open. It was stuffed full of cash and gold.

Bella fell forward with a laugh. "What is that?"

"Money, Bella. Lots of it," Clemmie said.

"But… That's yours?"

"All mine. My husband Iggy's too, but he's… you know…" She shut her eyes and dropped her chin to indicate death.

"Then what were you doing at the boarding house?" Bella said.

"Turns out Bart and I have a lot in common. I was rich in money but short on friends. No loved ones to name. So it just seemed natural. Go where the people were, and if I didn't like anyone, then I could leave. No harm done."

"Oh, my God," Bella said.

"Turns out Clemmie was smart enough to not put her money in a bank," Bart said.

"Turns out I like you people," Clemmie said. "I've chosen you as family. So when I saw old Bart pouring over those books and we talked, I let the cat out of the bag… or the cash out of the suitcase. And then we fetched these two fancy hatters and… I'd say we just created one of the greatest business ideas ever imagined. A series of family-style inns where every guest feels pampered and loved even when away from home. Good food, good conversation, good bed, recreation, ice-skating, bike riding in the summer."

Bella couldn't believe her ears. "What about me? How do I fit?"

"What do you want to do, Bella?" Bart asked with a wink.

"I don't know. No one's ever asked me that. Aside from raising my hens and… a library!"

"Hens in a library?" Clemmie joked.

"Raise hens, yes. But I'd like to have a library. A small one here in Shadyside. Part of the Maple Grove property."

They all agreed.

"But…" Mr. Heinz leaned in, his face appearing dire instead of excited. "Not to make demands, especially when I hear you are the impetus for inspiring so much of the giving and learning that brought us all together… but would you be willing to house the Heinz collection of recipes and courses for employees in your library? It's everything we try to do to make the workplace clean and healthy. It's our philosophy on work, and well, how commerce can work together with purpose. My wife is elbow deep in plans to create community spaces for those in need and I think you and she would work perfectly together."

Bella gasped. "Could some of the gardens be used to teach? Mothers who might need jobs? Could they work at the inns? Would your wife support that?"

Mr. Heinz paused then leaned in. "I think Sarah would love that idea."

And though she was trying to hold back, Bella burst into tears, completely shocked.

Bart came around the table and hugged her, finally kissing the top of her head. "What do you say?"

"Yes, yes. I would absolutely love that."

Bart pulled out his handkerchief. "Commerce with purpose," he said. "I think that defines what we could be exactly."

"My lawyers will draw up the papers tomorrow," Mr. Buchanan said.

"But until then," Mr. Heinz interrupted, "would you all mind signing the plans we've just written out?"

They looked at him, unsure of what that would accomplish. "For posterity. For the library." He beamed at Bella.

"For the library," they all toasted.

And as the evening burned on and Mr. Buchanan and Mr. Heinz left for their homes, the weight of what they'd all just done settled in.

Bella's insides swirled with excitement, but laid over it was that simple contentment she loved so much. She was pleased to know what could happen when a person combined purpose with commerce.

They spent the rest of the night scratching ideas into notebooks, remembering how it was they had come to have created such an endeavor, remembering the night of the fire.

"To starting again," Mrs. Tillman added.

Bart looked at her. "Yes. Yes, Mrs. Tillman. That's what I didn't know that night. If not for all that had gone wrong for me, if I hadn't had to start again, I would never have known anything important. I would never have known you, Bella, any of you."

"I'm happy for your losses, then," Bella said, and he kissed her hard, making the others whoop.

Penelope pulled the crushed box out from under the sink. "Remember this, from your house, Mrs. Tillman?"

She pulled it onto her lap.

"Want us to open it?" Bart asked.

"We could wedge it open, I bet," Arnold said.

Mrs. Tillman ran her finger over the crushed metal. "I think I'll let it sit for a bit. I kind of like the idea of not knowing what's in it…"

And as each person trailed off to sleep that night, Bart and Bella walked back to the barn to get the animals ready for sleep.

Traipsing through the snow, the two of them laughed as they fought the high banks. Bella let him lift her and carry her over the threshold of the barn.

"I love you, Bart Baines."

"And I love you, soon-to-be Bella Baines."

They sat on the settee in front of the fire, blankets covering their legs. Simon leapt onto Bart's lap, purring as they watched the flames dance in every shade of red.

"Once upon a time, there was a small house with floor-to-ceiling bookshelves in every room," Bart said.

Bella's mouth fell open.

"Don't look so shocked," he said. "I've learned the importance of a good story. I told you that."

She tucked into his shoulder and he put his arm around her, pulling her tight. "Shelves in every room including the kitchen," he said.

Bella giggled. "Who needs to cook?"

"Not this pair. They lived on the property of a wonderful inn called Maple Grove…"

Bella snuggled closer and thought of Fanny Fern as a writer and woman. Bella finally knew with all her being—she too could be independent and a happily married woman.

And the two fell asleep on the settee, wrapped in each other's arms, wrapped in the same dreams, the unexpected life that was unfolding in front of them. Bella was once more content. But more than that. In the moments between sleep and awake, heart-bursting joy found its place in her life.

But this time it was all real. It was everything she could have imagined and more.

AUTHOR'S NOTE

Cinder Bella was inspired by historic details that sparked plot points and character development. Some of these tidbits included vintage holiday recipes (advertisements and articles in antique magazines), recipes from friends and modern websites (Maple Toast—thank you, Denise Weaver!), the idea that people might send notes in eggs for sale (antique articles found at mrsdaffodildigresses.wordpress.com), quotes from *The Moonstone*, by Wilkie Collins (1868, public domain), the ice skating rink (antique Christmas magazine), the impact that the Panic of 1893 had around the world, and famous Pittsburghers like Henry Heinz.

All historic elements used in the story are fictionalized including any real people I stumbled upon while picking through historical documents. Henry Heinz appears at the end of the novel and his interactions with characters illustrate his progressive attitude toward business. At a time when industrialists rarely considered the health and well-being of their employees, Heinz's philosophy, roughly said, was something like *"In order for employees to do their best work for the company, the company needed to do their best for them."* Heinz also was on the forefront of food safety and factory cleanliness (helping to push the Pure Food and Drug Act into being), seeing these endeavors as beneficial to business and the people who made his business work. He, his wife Sarah, and their children worked to create opportunities for people of every social class, helping them live healthier, richer lives.

Also by Kathleen Shoop

Historical Fiction:
The Letter Series:
The Last Letter—Book One
The Road Home—Book Two
The Kitchen Mistress—Book Three
The Thief's Heart—Book Four
The River Jewel—A prequel

The Donora Story Collection:
After the Fog—Book One
The Strongman and the Mermaid—Book Two
The Magician—Book Three

Romance:
Endless Love Series:
Home Again—Book One
Return to Love—Book Two
Tending Her Heart—Book Three

Women's Fiction:
Love and Other Subjects

Bridal Shop Series:
Puff of Silk—Book One

Holiday:
The Christmas Coat
The Tin Whistle

Made in the USA
Coppell, TX
07 November 2021

65345411R00134